All In

BRANTLEY WALKER: *Off the Books, 1*

By Nicole Edwards

Alluring Indulgence

Kaleb

Zane

Travis

Holidays with the Walker Brothers

Ethan

Braydon

Sawyer

Brendon

The Walkers Of Coyote Ridge

Curtis

Jared

Hard to Hold

Hard to Handle

Beau

Rex

A Coyote Ridge Christmas

Mack

Kaden & Keegan

Brantley Walker: Off the Books

Mission: All In

Mission: Without a Trace

Austin Arrows

Rush

Kaufman

Club Destiny

Conviction

Temptation

Addicted

Seduction

Infatuation

Captivated

Devotion

Perception

Entrusted

Adored

Distraction

DEAD HEAT RANCH
Boots Optional
Betting on Grace
Overnight Love

DEVIL'S BEND
Chasing Dreams
Vanishing Dreams

MISPLACED HALOS
Protected in Darkness
Salvation in Darkness
Bound in Darkness

OFFICE INTRIGUE
Office Intrigue
Intrigued Out of the Office
Their Rebellious Submissive
Their Famous Dominant
Their Ruthless Sadist
Their Naughty Student
Their Fairy Princess

PIER 70
Reckless
Fearless
Speechless
Harmless
Clueless

SNIPER 1 SECURITY
Wait for Morning
Never Say Never
Tomorrow's Too Late

SOUTHERN BOY MAFIA/DEVIL'S PLAYGROUND
Beautifully Brutal
Without Regret
Beautifully Loyal
Without Restraint

STANDALONE NOVELS
Unhinged Trilogy
A Million Tiny Pieces
Inked on Paper
Bad Reputation
Bad Business

NAUGHTY HOLIDAY EDITIONS
2015
2016

All In

BRANTLEY WALKER: OFF THE BOOKS, 1

NICOLE EDWARDS

Published by Nicole Edwards Limited
PO Box 1086, Pflugerville, Texas 78691

All In
Brantley Walker: Off the Books, 1
Nicole Edwards

This is a work of fiction. Names, characters, businesses, places, events and incidents either are the products of the author's imagination or used in a fictitious manner. Any resemblance to actual persons, living or dead, business establishments, events, or locals is entirely coincidental.

COVER DETAILS:

Image: © Petr Joura (90933000) | 123rf.com
Design: © Nicole Edwards Limited

INTERIOR DETAILS:

Formatting: Nicole Edwards Limited
Editing: Blue Otter Editing | BlueOtterEditing.com

ISBN:
Ebook 9781644180266 | Paperback 9781644180273 | Audio 9781644180280

SUBJECTS:
BISAC: FICTION / Romance / Gay
BISAC: FICTION / Romance / General

Dedication

To the men and women who fight for our freedom.

Prologue

June 2019, Location Classified

"ABORT! ABORT!"

The words were shouted through his earpiece, but Brantley Walker was having a difficult time hearing them. Probably had everything to do with this godforsaken ringing in his ears.

To top it off, he couldn't see a damn thing. What was left of the dilapidated concrete building was filled with dust, dirt, and debris, which not only affected his eyesight but was permeating his lungs, making it damn near impossible to breathe.

"Phantom One, get your ass outta there! Now!"

Coughing in an effort to expel the dust from his chest cavity, Brantley shook off the initial shock and pain, taking stock of his surroundings.

"Phantom One! Do you read?"

Did he? Brantley wasn't sure.

"Phantom One? Goddammit, Phantom One? Comm check."

Before he could force a few words to assure his team he was still in one piece, sounds came from above. Instinct and training caused him to go completely still, only his eyes moving to scan the space.

The main floor—now above him—of the single-story house had given way, sending him careening into what appeared to be some sort of concrete bunker beneath the structure that had supposedly housed the hostage they'd been sent in to retrieve. Intel had placed the thirty-year-old nuclear physicist here. Right fucking here, which was the only reason Brantley and his SEAL team had slipped silently into the building, intending to be in and out in under a minute.

Bad news: the fucking scientist wasn't here. Worse news: the tangos were moving in.

"Phantom Two, I don't have eyes on Phantom One. Repeat, I don't have eyes on."

"Roger that, Phantom Six. Fall back. We'll get eyes on him."

Would they? Brantley had an eerie feeling no one was going to see much of him once this was over.

How long had it been, anyway? A minute? Ten? Not that it mattered. The mission was a goat-fuck of epic proportions. The extraction team was likely gone, his own team scattered about. The most he could hope was Phantom Team was nearby, keeping a close eye on the exterior.

And here Brantley was, in the middle of it all, surrounded by broken slabs of concrete, rebar, and dirt, all piled high in the space, offering absolutely no protection should one of those damn tangos appear above his head.

The bad guys had been expecting them, the proof in the explosion that had triggered soon after Brantley had entered the premises. The explosion that had rocked the floor right out from under him, sending Brantley deep into the earth with the aforementioned concrete, rebar, and dirt. Not all of which had been beneath him after the descent into this fucking hole.

Speaking of bad guys…

The voice was growing louder from above, the language one he didn't recognize. Not surprising considering the hotbed they'd dropped into. God only knew which terrorist group was leading the charge in this shithole. Probably not the one they'd suspected considering everything they'd believed up to this point was proving to be bullshit.

"Phantom One. Sit tight. We're making our way to your location."

Unable to speak without revealing himself to the fucker stalking him, Brantley kept his trap shut, clamping his molars together as he attempted to heave the concrete slab off his fucking leg. Damn thing had trapped him in place, no doubt shattering his leg on impact. The pain threatened to blind him. He forced his heart rate to slow, honing the skills drilled into him by the US military. He would get out of this if he kept a level head.

It took tremendous effort, but Brantley managed to shift the concrete slab enough to allow him to drag his leg free. Once he did, he slid backward into the darkened corner, the spike in his adrenaline making him light-headed. Aside from the debris, there was no protection or cover, but at least this way the fuckers would have to come into view to take him out.

The only thing he could do right now was sit and wait.

A grunt escaped before he could swallow it down. His leg was broken, no doubt about it. But unless he wanted to add more injuries—like a bullet to the skull—he had to swallow the pain. Not easy to do as he dragged himself deeper into the space, over the piles of rubble that had come down with him. As he shifted, one of the sharp ends of some rusted rebar stabbed into his thigh, dragging through his flesh before he could stop it.

Son of a fucking bitch.

A blaze of fire ripped through him as he manhandled his left leg, unhooking his flesh from the rusty metal. Gritting his teeth, he fought the darkness that threatened to take him under. No way could he pass out now. Not if he wanted to live through this clusterfuck.

The only sounds he heard were his ragged breaths and the voice growing louder as it came closer. Without looking, he knew someone was above him, staring down into the rubble. It wouldn't take much for the asshole to find him.

A flashlight clicked on.

Mother. Fucker.

That beam of yellow light swung through the room, passing over his injured leg more than once before his terrorist visitor hopped down onto the pile of concrete. There was no stealth to the guy's movements, telling Brantley he wasn't worried that he'd be found by the enemy. Then again, at this moment, Brantley was the enemy, the intruder, the guy who didn't belong.

Brantley gripped his Sig firmly in his hand, ignoring the blinding pain that was threatening to darken his vision.

The beam of light grew brighter, cutting through the dust lingering in the stifling air. Lifting his hand, supporting it with his left arm, Brantley leveled his sight on the tango. Best-case scenario had him taking the bastard out, which he could do in his sleep. The only problem with that, the shot would most definitely alert his terrorist buddies, and at that point, Brantley'd be a sitting duck.

"Fall back! Phantom Team, fall back!"

The words were in his ear, but they sounded as though they'd been blasted through a bullhorn. A semaphore flag would've been less of an announcement of his presence.

The tango started shouting something over his shoulder, the beam of light landing on Brantley's wounded leg again. He held his breath, not moving a muscle, praying like fuck the dickhead would suddenly go blind. Otherwise, there would be nothing more he could do.

More shouting. Despite his inability to translate, Brantley wasn't an idiot. Fucker was calling out to his buddies, inviting them over for the party.

The fact that no one came—bad guys or good—should've been a sign, but Brantley's brain was fuzzy, his body one big throbbing heartbeat. Blood coated his BDUs, oozing from the open wounds. No doubt, if he looked close enough, he'd probably see his femur poking out of his skin. The thought made him woozy, which was saying something considering he didn't have a weak stomach.

"Phantom One." This time the voice was soft, almost reverent, which was telling. Things weren't looking good from their vantage point, either. "We're comin' for you, buddy. We're comin'. Hang tight."

All In

The terrorist in front of him started kicking rocks aside, moving closer. Brantley couldn't see the weapon in his hand, but he didn't need to. Asshole was no doubt armed with whatever assault weapon they'd managed to get their hands on. At this point, it wouldn't surprise him if it was a fucking rocket launcher.

More yelling, more urgency. Based on his frantic shouts, the guy wanted backup, but they still weren't coming. Seconds ticked by while Brantley maintained his position, pretending he was invisible but knowing this asshole had found him. Only reason the fucker didn't shoot him full of holes was because he was more valuable alive than dead. Which meant, any minute now, he would be dragged out of here, thrown in a fucking hole, where they'd ensure the shattered femur was the least of his worries. It was a risk he took whenever they went out on a mission, so he was at peace with it.

But Brantley wasn't ready to give up yet. The longer he could hold this bastard off, the better chance his team would get here.

The beam of light moved, lowered, which meant the guy had made it down to Brantley's level. It began a slow creep up his leg, his torso. The tango's face came into view, his dark eyes following the yellow glow. Right before it could blind him, Brantley pulled the trigger, nailing the bastard between the eyes. He took a deep breath, gritted his teeth as the reverberation sent agony rippling through his leg.

A deafening silence followed the gunshot, the ringing in his ears right on its heels. There were no pounding footsteps, no voices calling out his location. For a brief moment, Brantley thought the stars had aligned, that the bad guys had taken a dinner break, retreating.

"Phantom Team," Brantley rasped, his words scratching along his throat, sending his diaphragm into spasms. "Need help."

"Sit tight, B," came the response.

"Not goin' anywhere," he said softly.

"B, we're comin'."

No, they weren't. He could hear it in that tormented voice. Something was keeping his team from coming for him. Either they were pinned down or—

That was when he heard it. The familiar whistling sound alerted him to a big fucking problem. The only thing he had time to do was scramble in his brain for a prayer that might get to the big guy's ears before—

The blast shook what was left of the house overhead as well as the ground beneath him. Another was right behind it, closer, bringing the building down on top of him. The third was just icing on the fucking cake.

Sometime later—hours, days, who knew—his team would do as they promised. They would eventually find him, dig him out of the rubble, evac his battered and broken body, deliver him to the nearest medical facility, where he would cling to life for weeks. Numerous surgeries would be performed to repair the extensive damage to his leg, drain the fluid off his brain, and ultimately keep him alive. Months of agonizing therapy would follow, during which Brantley would finally learn how to use his leg again.

Nine months after that clusterfuck of a mission, his superiors would add insult to injury, releasing Brantley from his duty as a United States Navy SEAL.

Good news: he was alive.

Bad news: every-fucking-thing else.

Chapter One

Thirteen months later, July 2020

"SUN, SAND, AND SURF. WHAT MORE CAN you ask for?"

Brantley Walker glanced over at his sister, frowned. "Heat, dirt, and salt. Damn sure don't see the appeal."

"Says the man who's spent most of his adult years in Afghanistan."

More like all over southern Asia, but he didn't bother to correct her. "Exactly."

"Good news, there's water," Bryn tacked on.

"*Salt*water. Not exactly refreshing."

"The eternal pessimist, you are, Brantley. You know that?"

"I prefer realist," he countered, ambling along the water crashing gently against the shore. He did his best to ignore the throbbing in his left thigh and paid attention to his gait. It had taken endless months of therapy, but the limp was finally gone. Mostly. Only when he was exhausted did it make an appearance.

"You wanna take a break?" Bryn asked, her tone chock full of sympathy. "We can sit and watch the sunrise?"

Evidently he wasn't as good at hiding it as he'd thought.

Brantley glared over at her, the words coming out a bit harder than he'd intended. "No, I don't wanna take a break."

"Okay. Be a stubborn ass, see if I care."

"Sorry," he muttered.

"Then tell me this," Bryn prompted as though the break in their conversation hadn't happened, "where would you rather be?"

"Anywhere but here," he grumbled.

"Liar. One more. That's all you've got. One more day, one more night where you're subjected to the ultimate in torture techniques."

And by torture techniques, Brantley knew Bryn was referring to the Walkers' yearly retreat to the beaches of Galveston. And, fine, maybe he hadn't attended these annual get-togethers for a good portion of his adult life. In his defense, before now, he'd usually been otherwise engaged. Being a SEAL in the United States Navy wasn't conducive to a whole lot of family time, no matter how well-planned.

Of course, that was no longer a problem for him. Due to that unfortunate event—namely the ill-fated op that went sideways, resulting in his medical retirement from the Navy—Brantley had found himself with quite a bit of time on his hands. Hence the reason he was walking the Texas shoreline at the ass crack of dawn with the youngest of his three sisters while the rest of the Walker clan were still snoozing in the beachside house.

"Six and a half days too long," he said, grimacing when he stepped on a broken shell.

This was Frank and Iris Walker's annual vacation, the time set aside when they would all get together for one week out of the year. Why they chose mid-July to make the trip to the overcrowded, not to mention, ridiculously hot beach on Galveston Island, he would never know. Yet they'd been doing it for as long as he could remember and years before that. According to Mom, they'd started this tradition when Sadie was two. In an effort to create memories, they'd toted his oldest sister and every kid who came along after down here once a year.

They called it fun. Brantley compared it to Hell Week. One mom, one dad, seven kids. All cooped up for a week except for those brief few hours they would traipse down to the water, sit in the sand, and let the brutal sun beat down on them. He remembered a lot of aloe and pain relievers involved, not to mention yelling. So much fucking yelling. Didn't matter that it came from the younger set, one of his brothers or sisters always attempting to have the last word.

And fine, maybe Bryn was right. He was a pessimist.

Granted, the family had grown up, expanded in the past decade. What had once been a trip for nine had nearly doubled. To accommodate and keep everyone under the same roof, his parents had traded in their tiny two-bedroom condo for a six-bedroom house right on the beach. Even then it was cramped, filled to capacity with Mom and Dad, three brothers, three sisters, one future sister-in-law (potentially), two brothers-in-law, plus two nieces and a nephew. Pretty soon, the folks would need to invest in a hotel just to house them all.

"How's school?" he asked, hoping to keep his sister from harping on him for his inability to relax.

"Good." Bryn smiled brightly. "Only five semesters away from graduation."

"The eternal optimist," he quipped.

"I know, right? Sometimes I think I'm adopted. There's no other way to explain how I ended up in this family."

"You're tellin' me. What I don't get is what prompted you to want to go back to school now."

"Are you sayin' I'm old, little brother?"

He pretended to think on that. "Thirty-six isn't exactly young, sis."

Bryn huffed a laugh. "Careful what you say, kid. You're not all that far behind."

No, he wasn't, but age was just a number as far as Brantley was concerned. At thirty-five, fresh out of a seventeen-year stint in the Navy, Brantley felt as though he was starting over. A kid, right out of high school, without a clue what he was going to do with the rest of his life. Only, he was equipped with knowledge most people couldn't fathom, a skill set that wouldn't do much for him as a civilian but could likely make him a good living if he wanted to go the mercenary route. Plus a leg that ached when it rained and recurring headaches that ranged from irritating to debilitating.

At least his family had stopped asking him if he was all right.

"Why a teacher?" he inquired, wanting to keep them talking about her.

"Molding young minds," she said simply, flashing another bright smile. "Imagine if there'd been some decent teachers around when you were in school. Maybe you wouldn't be such a dummy."

Brantley stopped, pinned her with a look. "A dummy? Really, sis?"

Bryn's blue eyes flashed with amusement. "Yeah. Dummy. What're you gonna do about it?"

Before he could grab her and toss her into the water, Bryn took off at a run. Brantley chuckled, then pursued, his bare feet sinking in the wet sand as he jogged behind her. Didn't take long before he swept her off her feet and charged into the water, dumping her unceremoniously before he dove into the next wave. When he came up, Bryn was sputtering, tossing her hair out of her face, the long dark strands plastered to her head.

"I'm gonna kick your ass for that, Brantley Walker!"

"How many times have I heard that one?" he countered, wandering over and escorting her back to the beach, arm in arm.

"You just wait. When you least expect it"—she clapped her hands together, jerking on his arm—"bam! I'm gonna take you out."

As usual, Bryn was laughing. Otherwise he would've been apologizing. Brantley couldn't count how many times he'd said he was sorry over the years. To all of his sisters. Didn't matter that Sadie, Tori, and Bryn were the oldest of the seven, there was no doubt they'd been harassed plenty by their younger brothers. Sometimes more than they deserved.

Redirecting them back to the house, Brantley threw an arm around Bryn's shoulders, tugged her against his side, and planted a kiss on her head. "Now, if you don't mind, I'd like to get some coffee in me."

"Fine. But you're not goin' back to bed."

Nearly twelve hours later, the blazing Texas sun having finally taken a hiatus, Brantley was sitting on the third-floor deck, staring out over the water, wishing like hell he'd ignored Bryn's order and caught a few hours of sleep. After an eventful day spent entirely down by the water, he had that rode-hard, put-up-wet feeling. Good thing he only had a few feet to wander before he could be facedown in a bed.

He had his nephew and nieces to thank for the endless hours near the water, and his brothers for the overindulgence tonight. It had been Trey's idea, the fucker. His oldest brother had thought it would be wise to crack open a bottle of Jameson and play Who's the idiot, a game they'd made up, where they recalled each other's most asinine feats to date.

For whatever reason, they'd all ganged up on Brantley, proving with one story after another that he was the reigning champ of idiocy. Better yet, it wasn't over. Trey was currently choking on a laugh as he attempted to retell their favorite story of them all.

"What was that guy's name?" Trey clanked the ice in his glass, eyes bouncing to each of them.

"Danny," Griffin offered. "Danny Musket."

Brantley groaned. Never failed they'd bring this one up.

Trey snapped his fingers and pointed at Griff. "Yes! Danny Musket. What a loser. I was on duty at the time—"

"Off duty," Brantley corrected. "And mall security doesn't exactly make you a cop."

"Yeah, well, Danny didn't know that."

No, he hadn't. And Brantley remembered the look on the guy's face when Trey's mug had appeared in the driver's-side window. Might as well have been the chief of police for as panicked as Danny got.

"Anyway," Trey continued. "That night, I was headin' home. Stopped in at E-Zs for a cup of coffee—"

"Pork rinds and Dr. Pepper," Brantley corrected.

"—when what did I stumble upon?" Trey chuckled, clearly enjoying the memory. "There I was, minding my own business, strolling through the parking lot—"

"Checking out the beer delivery guy," Brantley offered because it was the truth.

"—when something caught my attention. Rocking." Another rumbling laugh. "That shitty old Ford of Danny's was rocking on its axles."

"It was a Toyota," Brantley said with a huff. "And it was only a couple of years old."

"Whatever. My story, my details."

Brantley smiled, couldn't help it. That was Trey for you.

"Didn't Danny work there part-time?" Cal inquired.

"Yep," Trey answered. "And he was on his break. Just gettin' some action, he said."

"He did not say that," Brantley huffed.

"Right up until you put an end to their fun," Griffin noted.

Trey smirked. "What are big brothers for?"

Brantley rolled his eyes, didn't bother looking at Trey. "Regardless of how you tell it, the crime certainly didn't fit the punishment."

That got his brothers laughing.

"Maybe not, but it was fun as shit," Trey countered. "Dragged both of you morons outta that truck, had you assume the position."

"Because he hadn't been assumin' it before you got there?" Griffin snorted.

"Not helpin'," Brantley said with a glare.

"Tell 'em what happened next," Trey insisted with a smirk.

Brantley exhaled, knowing this would never end if he didn't tie up the story in a neat little bow. "You dragged us out, frisked us both, then told Danny you'd bring him up on charges of seducing a minor if he put his hands on me again."

"Damn straight I did. And the look on that kid's face," Trey guffawed. "Priceless."

Never mind the fact that they'd both been seventeen, Danny had honestly believed he was in trouble. Then again, the guy hadn't been the brightest bulb. But he'd been hot as fuck, the only thing that had really mattered to seventeen-year-old Brantley.

To add to the humiliation, Trey had snapped a picture of Danny with his wild red hair and haphazardly buttoned shirt using his prized Nokia camera phone, printed it out, then spent the next two months pinning that picture up in various places in the house just to piss Brantley off. Not that he would remind Trey of that part.

His brothers were good at that. Pissing him off. But Brantley had gotten in a few good ones over the years. Too bad he was too drunk to remember them now.

"Whatever happened to that one guy you dated?" Griffin asked, lifting his glass and pointing at Brantley. "Marvin? Martin? What the fuck was his name?"

"Markus," Cal supplied. "The doctor."

"He wasn't a doctor," Trey corrected. "He was a medical examiner."

"A medical degree, Trey," Brantley grumbled. "Makes him a doctor."

"He worked on dead people." Trey's smile was slow. "But I suppose he put the degree to good use? You two play doctor and patient?"

Oh, they most definitely had, but rather than share the details, he rattled off a "Fuck. Off."

"Didn't last long, that one," Cal recalled. "Then again, none of them did."

"I have to say, though, you do know how to nail the hot ones," Trey added.

"Hey, I tried to pass that one guy off to you, but you were too good for him," Brantley reminded him.

"Dude was an insurance salesman," Trey said, his tone making it sound like the guy had been a convicted felon.

"You didn't have to marry him," Cal teased.

"Whatever. This is not about me," Trey stated. "This is about you, little brother. When are you gonna settle down?"

Brantley shook his head, resting it against the headrest and staring up at the sky. The last thing he intended to do was discuss his personal business. Privacy was something to be coveted in the Walker family. Not only did he have nosy brothers and sisters, there were dozens of cousins, many of them having grown up in Coyote Ridge with Brantley. Everyone knew everyone's business, no matter how hard they tried to keep it on the DL.

"He likes playin' the field," Cal said, his smile still firmly in place.

"No time to date," he grumbled, realizing they weren't going to drop it. "What about you?" He glanced at Cal. "When're you gonna tie the knot?"

"One of these days," his youngest brother said with a wide grin.

Whether it was the cheery admission or the blush that brightened Cal's face, the words captured everyone's attention, taking the heat off Brantley. Finally.

Trey sat up straight, narrowed his eyes. "Seriously?"

Cal's face was beaming. "Yeah. Seriously. I was thinkin' about askin' her while we're here."

"You're runnin' outta time," Trey supplied.

"Holy shit, man." Griffin slapped Cal on the back. "Congrats."

"Don't congratulate him yet," Brantley interrupted. "She hasn't said yes. Maybe I should sit April down, make sure she knows what she's gettin' herself into."

Cal laughed. "Like she'd believe a word you said."

Brantley smiled, maintaining eye contact with Cal, ensuring his brother saw he was happy for him. Although they did enjoy dogging one another whenever the situation warranted, they were a tight bunch. And that meant they celebrated the highs and mourned the lows. Together.

"Well, on that note, I think I'm gonna hit the hay," Trey announced, getting to his feet. "See y'all bright and early."

"You might be early, but you damn sure ain't bright," Griffin quipped, dragging himself to his feet.

"What he said," Brantley agreed as his brothers filed past him, offering fist bumps on their way.

"You headin' in?" Cal asked, standing tall and stretching.

"Yeah. In a minute."

"Cool. See you in the mornin'."

"Yep. You will."

Finally alone for the first time since he woke that morning, Brantley stared out into the night, beyond the pitch-black water to the flashing lights in the distance. The lapping of the waves down below lulled him toward sleep. His ass was numb, his mouth dry, and he knew he needed to locate that soft mattress if he was hoping for any chance of avoiding a massive hangover in the morning. He wasn't exactly eager to make the three-hour drive back to Coyote Ridge, but he damn sure didn't need a pounding head to accompany him.

He debated on going inside but thought better of it. He wasn't willing to take a header over the rail if and when he stumbled. And with his luck as of late…

Brantley found himself smiling, recalling all the stories his brothers had told tonight, all the idiot things he'd done. The one thing he hadn't done was settle down, but that seemed to be in the cards for his brothers and sisters, not him. First Sadie, then Tori, now Cal. Wouldn't be long before the rest of them were getting hitched. If all went well for Cal, one day soon, Brantley'd be donning another tuxedo, this time standing up for one of his brothers who pledged to spend the rest of his days with one person.

"And they call me the idiot," he chuckled.

Chapter Two

AFTER A WEEK AT THE BEACH AND another doing his damnedest to keep a low profile, Brantley's luck with avoiding his extended family had finally come to an abrupt end. Noticeable by the fact his cousin Travis was standing in his kitchen watching him as though he was a caged animal about to break through the bars keeping him contained. And here Brantley was thinking he was hiding his restlessness rather well.

"Four months," Travis stated. "You've been here four months. Think maybe it's time to furnish this place?"

Brantley flashed a smile while he waited for the coffee to finish brewing. "What's wrong with my place?"

"Well, for one … where the fuck's the couch?"

That was Travis Walker for you. Brantley's cousin was always looking out for them. All of them. And if Brantley didn't know better, he would've thought he'd become Travis's personal pet project in recent months. Not that the guy had time to do much of anything else with all those rug rats, a wife, and a husband to tend to. Couldn't forget the six brothers Travis ran roughshod over, or the demolition company he'd built, or the fetish resort Travis had, with help from his brothers, turned into some destination hot spot over the years. Guy should've been too busy to sleep much less take up extracurricular activities.

Yet here Travis was, harping on Brantley for his lack of decorative abilities.

"Don't need a couch," he countered, passing over a cup of coffee, then taking one for himself.

"I beg to disagree." Travis picked up the mug before taking a leisurely stroll through the open space.

If he were being honest, Brantley was just content to have a place to lay his head. He hadn't been too terribly concerned with the condition of the house or the amount of furniture he could stuff into it. Having spent the better part of his life in the military, it was taking some time to adjust to this unexpected, and not entirely wanted, civilian life. He figured that meant he deserved props for buying, rather than renting, and impressing a permanent footprint in the small town of Coyote Ridge. Who the fuck cared if he had a couch or a dining room table? Or anything else, for that matter.

"Did you stop by at the ass crack of early just to give me shit?" he asked Travis.

"Yep." It was simply put, and Travis had no shame, evidently.

"Liar."

The smirk he got in return said it all. Travis was clearly up to something. The question was what.

"Tell me you at least have a bed."

"And a television," Brantley boasted.

Travis's gaze swung to the living room. "You SEAL boys have nifty invisible gadgets these days?"

Chuckling, Brantley pushed off the counter, strolled toward his cousin. "It's in the bedroom. Only time I've got to watch it."

His cousin grunted. "Beds are meant for sleepin' or fuckin'. Who the hell has time to watch TV in the bedroom?"

"The single guy, Travis."

That got him a grin.

He didn't bother telling Travis sleep didn't come easily these days. In the same regard, he was happy to say it wasn't nearly as bad as he'd thought it would be. Having been in the Teams for the past decade, it hadn't been easy processing the fact that he'd been forced out. A medical discharge, they called it. Thanks to his femur being snapped like a twig and the subsequent issues that had arisen from the building falling on him and damn near crushing his skull, Brantley was no longer fit for duty. Rather than ride a desk for the rest of his days, he'd begrudgingly taken the discharge, walking away from the Navy, the Teams, his other family.

It was taking time to adjust, to pretend that the real hell on earth wasn't right here in his hometown of Coyote Ridge, Texas.

Oh, it was a great little town, mind you. Chock full of nosy people who were curious as to what he was going to do with the rest of his life. Those who didn't care for the details merely kept their eye on him, as though waiting for him to lose his shit. There were times he wasn't sure they wouldn't bear witness to it.

"How's the rehab on the leg goin'?" Travis asked.

"Almost done."

"Heard you were runnin' again."

Brantley nodded, took a sip from his coffee, stared out the back door. Yeah, he'd taken up his running routine again. Figured it was his duty to follow through considering it was one of the many things he'd pledged to get back to once he healed. Those endless months of recovery had been hell, hearing the doctors tell him he might not ever walk again… Brantley was too hardheaded for that shit. And he'd set out to prove to them he was as fit now as he'd been when he enlisted seventeen years ago. Still some aches and pains, but none the worse for wear.

"Your sisters been by here yet?" Travis inquired, drawing Brantley out of his thoughts.

"Yep. Gave it their stamp of approval," he lied. Of course, Sadie, Tori, and Bryn had stopped by more than once, as had Brantley's brothers. And sure, Trey, Griffin, and Cal might've given him shit about his lack of a dining table, but they hadn't harped on him about it. Much.

Travis snorted. "Maybe I'll call 'em. See what they really think?"

Brantley figured the guy had already done that. More than once.

"You like it here?"

"It's growin' on me," he admitted.

Initially, Brantley thought he'd go batshit crazy being pinned down to US soil. Truth was, it wasn't quite so bad. Or rather, it was getting easier to accept with every passing day. He was beginning to see the merits of sitting on his ass every day, trying to find something else to do with his life. What that something else might be, he didn't know yet. However, he knew what he wouldn't be doing, and he suspected that was the reason Travis was here. To follow up on the proposal he'd made right after Brantley returned home back in March.

Taking a sip from his mug, Brantley decided to wait Travis out, knowing the man would get around to the point eventually.

Thankfully, he didn't have to wait long.

"So, you give any thought to my offer?"

Brantley set his mug down, thrust his hands in the pockets of his BDUs. "I have."

Travis pinned him with a curious stare, one dark brow slowly lifting, that steel blue gaze assessing him.

Grinning, Brantley broke the eye contact. "As generous as it is, Trav, I can't do it. Right now … shit." He looked at his cousin again. "I haven't figured out what I wanna do, but I figure when the time's right, I'll know where I fit in."

Travis's slow nod reflected his acceptance. "I had a feelin' you'd say that. But I had to make the offer."

"I know. And I appreciate it. Really."

"I assume it's not about the money," Travis noted.

"It'll never be about the money."

"Figured." Travis gulped what was left of his coffee, set the cup on the kitchen island. "Like I said, had to try."

"Understood."

"If you change your mind…"

Brantley nodded. "I won't, but thanks again."

"Fine. Now for the second reason I'm here."

Surprised, though he wasn't sure why, Brantley met Travis's gaze, held it.

"Sunday nights we meet up at my folks' place for dinner. My momma insisted I invite you."

Brantley chuckled. "I apprec—"

"Uh-uh," Travis interrupted. "This one's nonnegotiable. You show up for dinner or my momma'll sic someone on you. My brothers'll be there, wives, kids. Kaden and Keegan have found permanent seating at the table. Once in a while, Jared'll stop in."

"And if I wanna visit my own folks for Sunday dinner?" he asked, grinning.

"Feel free. But don't think Iris won't get a call just to make sure you're spendin' it with family."

Another laugh escaped him. Brantley was all too familiar with Lorrie Walker, Travis's mother. And he loved his aunt, he really did, which was the only reason he found himself nodding in agreement.

"Fine. I'll head that way tomorrow night."

"Six sharp. Don't be late."

He wasn't making any promises, but he nodded anyway.

"And we're talkin' about hittin' Moonshiners tonight if you're up for it."

Although he had been back for four months, it was true Brantley had been keeping a low profile. He'd managed to grab lunch with his sisters and shared a couple of beers with his brothers during that time, and yes, the trip to the beach, but the whole social scene wasn't high on his priority list.

Then again, not much was at the moment.

"No pressure," Travis tacked on. "Just show up if you wanna hang out."

"Thanks."

Travis nodded. "I'll get outta your hair."

Brantley followed him toward the door, coming up short when Travis turned back.

"It's good to have you back, man. I hope you know that."

Surprised by the sincerity in Travis's voice, he found himself nodding again. "Thanks."

"I just hope with time, you'll improve your coffee-makin' abilities. That's the weakest shit I've ever had."

Brantley barked a laugh, stared as Travis continued to the door.

Before it closed behind him, Travis peered back over his shoulder. "Buy yourself a goddamn couch, Brantley."

"I'll consider it."

And he did. For about three seconds, then he tossed it aside, just as he'd done with everything on his to-do list lately. The only time he worked on his house was when the quiet became too much.

Which, these days, seemed to be all the damn time.

A beer tonight, dinner tomorrow.

Brantley took a drink of his weak-ass coffee, smiled. If this was weak, Travis must've been used to drinking motor oil.

Staring out the back door, he noticed the sun was just coming over the horizon. Sure, he'd been up for a couple of hours now, but that was par for the course. His day started long before everyone else's. Probably would've made sense if he was doing anything with the fifteen acres of land he'd planted his ass on. Like plowing the earth, harvesting something.

That was something else he'd considered. For about a minute.

Nope. Farming, like working for his cousin, was not on his bucket list.

Not yet, anyway.

And if he was lucky … not ever.

Later that night, Brantley found himself sitting at a table in IHOP with nearly a dozen of his cousins and a couple of guys he'd been briefly introduced to.

His cousin Sawyer's idea, of course.

After a round of beers had been downed at Moonshiners, someone had mentioned pancakes, which had gotten Sawyer, another of Brantley's cousins, riled up until, eventually, they piled out of the small bar and made the thirty-minute trek to the neighboring city. They'd gotten comfortable at the table a good hour and a half ago, and based on the slumberous gazes, they'd all gotten their fill, yet no one was moving to leave.

And though he'd participated in the conversation, the topic had shifted to kids, leaving Brantley on the periphery. At the moment, Travis and Kaleb were relaying stories of their school-age kids and the interesting details Mason and Kate would relay when they came home.

Brantley remembered those school days. Oddly enough, he'd been sandwiched between two sets of Walker twins. Braydon and Brendon—his uncle Curtis's set—had been in the same grade as him while Leif and Lance—his uncle David's set—a grade below. But all of his classes had been dotted with one or more cousins. That was what happened when you came from a big family and lived in a small town. And while he'd been surrounded by cousins, his closest friends hadn't been related.

"Oh. My. God."

All heads at the table turned, including Brantley's.

Standing just a few feet away was none other than his best friend from back in the day, as though Brantley had conjured her with his thoughts.

With a smile, he was instantly on his feet. "What the hell're you doin' here?" he asked by way of greeting.

JJ went up on her toes, threw her arms around his neck, and hugged him tight. "I could ask you the same thing."

Someone cleared their throat, dragging a chuckle from him as he stepped back and turned to give the group his attention.

"Y'all, this is Jessie James, a.k.a. JJ." He glanced at his longtime friend. "I'm sure you know a lot of these guys." He pointed as he called out names. "Travis and his husband, Gage. Sawyer, Kaleb, Braydon, and Brendon. That there's Ethan. Beside him his husband, Beau. That's Zane, then CJ, Jaxson, Kaden, and Keegan."

Not that an introduction was necessary because everyone knew everyone in Coyote Ridge. It was the way of small towns. And JJ had gone to the same schools as they all had, growing up with them the same as Brantley. Only difference, JJ had stuck around while Brantley'd opted to see the world on Uncle Sam's dime.

Brantley's eyes paused on the last guy at the table. "Last but not least, that's Reese Tavoularis, no relation."

And thank fuck for that, he thought. He didn't know Reese, but he'd gone to school with Reese's brother, Z. According to their brief conversation, Reese had started high school the year after Brantley graduated. However, he was all grown up now.

Reese tipped his head in greeting, then his eyes cut back to Brantley's momentarily. They held for what felt like a lifetime but was no more than a couple of seconds.

Had this been any other man, Brantley would've considered his options for later. Unfortunately, Reese was straight as a fucking arrow, which meant there were no options. Nor would there be a later.

"All in one place," JJ teased. "I'm assumin' they've got law enforcement on the lookout."

"Hey, I resemble that remark," Zane called from the back, earning himself a direct greeting from JJ.

"You're one to talk," Sawyer noted. "You're the one named after an outlaw."

JJ grinned. "That outlaw's got nothin' on me," she noted, turning her attention back to Brantley and giving him a good once-over.

And just like that, everyone seemed to be finished, ready to head home for the night. After some pats on the back, promises to check with him later, the rest of them filed out of the restaurant, leaving the two of them standing in the nearly empty restaurant.

"You meetin' someone?" he inquired, taking in her attire, which included a pair of painted-on jeans and a black, sleeveless silk shirt that showed off her toned arms and a hint of cleavage. Clearly she'd gotten dressed up for someone's benefit tonight.

"Actually, I just finished."

Brantley glanced around, looking for whoever she'd come with.

"It's IHOP, Brantley. The guy brought me here for our first date." She flashed a bright white grin, showing off that crooked incisor that gave her mouth some character. "And last, might I add."

A waitress chose that moment to come over, snagging the check from the table.

"Any chance we could sit at a smaller table?" Brantley asked.

"Of course. Take your pick. Can I get you something?"

"Two coffees," JJ told her, then led the way to a booth. "I heard you were back," she said as she sat across from him. "Been plannin' to drop in, force you to see me."

"You wouldn't have to force me, JJ."

"No?" Her perfectly plucked brows lifted as she leaned forward, her light green eyes skeptical. "Then why the fuck haven't you called me yet?"

Brantley had expected no less from the girl he'd come to love like family.

"Sorry," she said, patting his hand. "Had to get that out there. Now that it is, we'll pretend I didn't say it."

Grinning, he gave her hand a squeeze. "How're your parents doin'?"

"Good. My mom's retiring next year. Dad's excited. They want to travel the world."

"Do they?"

"Yep. Figure it's time they got out of here." Her smile fell. "Too many memories, you know?"

Yeah. Brantley knew. He knew all too well.

Nine years ago, Jessie's brother had taken his own life. Jeremy had overdosed on pills. Jessie's dad had found him two days later when Jeremy hadn't shown up for lunch when he'd promised he would. Not more than a year before that, Jeremy had been diagnosed with bipolar disorder, which hadn't surprised his family. Not the way it had Brantley. He hadn't suspected Jeremy was depressed, but looking back, he wasn't sure how he'd missed it. Sometimes he wondered if that was the reason Jeremy had ended things with him so abruptly right after he'd enlisted. One minute they'd been talking about doing the long-distance thing, the next, Jeremy had insisted it wouldn't work and that they both needed to move on with their lives.

Truth was, Jeremy James was the only man Brantley had ever thought he'd loved, the one he'd actually imagined himself spending his life with. Of course, knowing now what he didn't know then, Brantley recognized it as lust, not love. But he tried not to think about it, not wanting to diminish the memories.

The waitress delivered their coffee, passing over tiny tubs of cream before disappearing once again.

"So, what're you up to these days?" JJ inquired.

"Little to nothing," he admitted.

"Well, why the hell not? I figured you for the kind who'd blaze a trail after he left the military in his dust."

Brantley offered a shrug, then found his coffee cup interesting.

"As much as I want to coddle you, B, you know I won't do it," she said softly.

That pulled a grin from him. "I know. And I appreciate it."

Her gaze swept over his face before she smiled brightly. "So. You still into dudes?"

He laughed, couldn't help it. "Yeah. I'd say that's probably the only thing that hasn't changed about me."

She seemed to consider this. "Figures. Hottest guy in town's gay."

JJ had always given him shit about it. One time, she'd even made him promise that if he ever switched teams, he'd let her know so she could throw her hat in the ring. Of course, she was kidding, though she had copped to having a crush on him when they'd been in high school. He'd known and pretended he hadn't. It was easier that way and it had worked in his favor because that high school crush of hers had turned into a lifetime friendship, one they'd maintained even while he'd been gone. As for why he hadn't reached out to her since he'd been back … Brantley didn't have an answer for that.

"Okay. So." JJ took a sip of coffee, set the cup down. "Now that you're back and you're officially out of hiding, I think it's time we got you acclimated to bein' here."

Leaning back, he studied her. "And just how do you propose we do that?"

Her gaze dropped to his chest. "For one, you're not in the military anymore, sailor. It's time you stopped dressing like it."

Brantley peered down at the black T-shirt he wore. As far as he was concerned, it went fine with the black BDUs and the combat boots. "What's wrong with my attire?"

"Put it this way," she said softly. "Add a ski mask and this place is gonna clear out."

Cocking an eyebrow, he waited for her to continue because he could see her determination.

"Tomorrow, we're goin' shoppin'," JJ declared, knocking back the rest of her coffee and blinding him with a smile.

"Are we?"

"We are. Pick me up at ten. We'll make a day of it."

Interesting how, for the first time, Brantley didn't even consider declining the offer.

Although shopping … right up there at the top of his things to avoid at all costs list.

Right below: eating glass.

Chapter Three

AFTER SPENDING THE MAJORITY OF THE NEXT day with JJ, eating glass now sounded preferable to shopping.

Every single thing Brantley had selected, JJ had shot down. Good thing he was a SEAL. Otherwise, she might've managed to persuade him to shift from his comfortable cotton T-shirts to those fancy button-downs she said made him look hotter than hot. Her exact words. In the end, he'd told her his goal was to be comfortable, not hot. She'd told him his reasoning sucked but had finally given up. And fine, as a concession, Brantley had bought a few pairs of Wranglers, some boots, a belt. He'd declined the fancy buckle. Not his thing.

And yes, he'd bought a hat. Two, actually. One straw, one felt. They were seasonal, after all.

But when JJ wasn't looking, he'd tossed in a couple of trucker caps. While every cowboy needed a Stetson or two, Brantley was more of a cap kinda guy.

Thankfully, the rest of the day hadn't been horrible.

Once he'd finally convinced JJ that he had no desire to buy anything else, he had treated her to lunch. Then she'd treated him to an hour at the gun range. Before they left, JJ had introduced him to the range owner and Brantley had gotten himself on the schedule for the next few weeks. He tried to tell himself it was to maintain his skills, but he knew better. It was the best way for him to blow off steam. Shooting things was always a stress reliever.

Evidently, Reese Tavoularis had thought the same thing, because they'd run into the man on the way out. The conversation they'd shared had been brief, but that too short encounter had solidified a couple of things for him. One, JJ was wrong about the hottest guy in town being gay. As far as Brantley was concerned, Reese far surpassed Brantley in the looks department. And he was pretty sure, after that brief chat, JJ was on board with his way of thinking. As for the second thing, there was no doubt JJ would get farther with Reese than Brantley would.

Very unfortunate.

Now, as he and JJ headed back to Coyote Ridge, Brantley peered over at her. "Mind if I ask what you're doin' these days? In regard to employment?"

"I'm in between jobs," she said, not looking over at him.

He'd noticed she had avoided his questions most of the day. Only those specific to work, of course, which had piqued his curiosity. Never had JJ been the secretive type. Or one to avoid anything.

"What were you doin' before?"

She shrugged, then pushed her sunglasses farther up on her nose. "This and that."

Brantley sighed. "You know I've been trained in interrogation, right?"

"Trained to withstand interrogation," she countered.

"Doesn't change my question, JJ."

"It's not important," she said easily. Too easily.

"Then what's the big deal? Why won't you tell me?"

Her attention shifted his way, but Brantley kept his eyes on the road.

"I've been helpin' out a friend from time to time."

Waiting, he dared a look her way, realized she was staring at him.

He quirked an eyebrow, urging her to continue.

"Dante."

Ah. Explained why she didn't want to tell him. Dante Greenwood wasn't high on Brantley's list. The bastard had dragged JJ through hell and back when they were younger. Guy had strung her along, then used her for his own gains, and finally dumped JJ without so much as a backward glance. Or so the story went. Never mind the fact that Dante had cheated on her for the better part of their relationship and raised his hand to her once, a move Brantley had warned Dante was the equivalent of a death warrant.

Brantley breathed in slowly, exhaled.

"I knew you'd be mad," she said softly.

Mad wouldn't begin to describe what he was. Dante Greenwood was a selfish prick, and if Brantley never saw the guy or heard his name mentioned again, it would be too soon.

"And what's Dante doin' these days?" he asked with a calm he didn't feel.

"He's workin' for a security firm. They help big companies shore up their cybersecurity."

"And that's where you come in," he mused, realizing where this was going.

"Yes. I've been hired a time or two to hack a company's system, to identify its weaknesses."

He considered that. JJ was a big girl; she could take care of herself. Didn't mean Brantley didn't want to wrap her up and keep her safe. From the government, who would most definitely not approve of what she was doing. From Dante, who would most definitely take advantage of her at the first opportunity. From—

"He's not the same guy you remember," JJ noted.

"No? He have a personality overhaul?"

JJ gave a lengthy sigh that said she'd expected that much from him. "No, Brantley. He grew up. Just like the rest of us."

Brantley sighed.

"I know you won't believe me," JJ added, "but he's changed."

He cut his eyes to her. "How so?"

"Well, for one, his dad's the governor of the state of Texas."

A laugh escaped him, but there was no humor in it. "Fantastic. Our own governor's one who condones hittin' women."

"Dante didn't hit me," she declared hotly. Her tone cooled when she added, "I know you'll never believe that, either, but it's true. What happened that night … it was unfortunate, but he didn't intentionally hit me."

"But he did hit you?"

"We were arguing, and I got rough with him."

"No excuse," he snarled.

Another sigh from JJ, then, "He's changed, B. You have to trust me on this."

Thankfully, they were pulling up to her house because Brantley was well and done with this conversation.

"You wanna come in? Grab a beer?"

"No. I've got things to do."

It was obvious she didn't believe him, but at least she didn't argue.

"I'll see you around then?"

He nodded and managed to look her way. "Yeah."

A slow nod was all she offered before JJ was out of the truck. Brantley waited until she'd made it inside her house before he drove off, managing to keep his foot from the floor. Barely.

Several hours later, Brantley was sitting at the small desk he'd stashed in one of the extra bedrooms, his laptop in front of him, an open beer beside it.

Bored out of his mind, Brantley had been skimming his Instagram feed, then followed up by checking on some old friends on Facebook. When he'd come across a familiar name, he had smiled and shot off a message before he could think better of it.

On the screen was the response: Holy shit. Are you back?

I'm back.

Well, hot damn. Where're you staying? Your folks' place?

I'm back for good, Cyrus. Got a place of my own.

The response wasn't immediate, and Brantley could practically see Cyrus letting that information sink in.

He smiled, ready to type something when Cyrus's message came back: And to what do I owe this honor?

The cursor flashed, waiting for him to type something in. For a second, Brantley considered ending the chat session, pretending he hadn't reached out in a rare moment of weakness.

Another message came in: Want to talk about it?

That got a smile from Brantley, his fingers sliding over the keyboard.

Last thing I want to do is talk, Cyrus.

The reply was instant: Of course you don't. Assume that's an invitation.

They both knew it was. That was the way things worked between them. They'd have no contact for months, sometimes years, then Brantley would come back to town, look Cyrus up, and they'd get together. No, they didn't do much talking, but they didn't need to. Their mouths were usually busy with other things.

It's an invitation, yes, he typed, then snatched his beer, took a long pull, his eyes never leaving the screen.

Give me an hour. I'll head over.

The door'll be unlocked, he informed his friend.

I'll need an address.

Smiling, he typed in the address, shot it over. Brantley didn't bother with anything more. He simply closed the laptop lid, leaned back, and downed half of his beer.

Inviting Cyrus Jernigan over was a mistake. He was man enough to admit that, but sometimes mistakes were necessary. The best thing about Cyrus? He knew what Brantley wanted and he didn't mind the fact that this encounter would lead exactly nowhere. That was the best part about it. Sex for the sake of sex. Fucking to blow off steam. They'd engaged on more than one occasion and never had Cyrus called him up for a date. Or vice versa. It had been working for them for the better part of a decade now, Cyrus making himself available whenever Brantley was in town. Why they hadn't hooked up since he'd put down roots a few months ago, he didn't know.

Okay, that was a lie. He knew. Hell, he knew exactly why he hadn't established a single relationship since his return. It was because he didn't know how to insert himself into people's lives. He'd spent so much time keeping his distance because it had been necessary, he'd lost touch with the part of him that knew how this worked.

He smiled to himself. And here he was kicking up old friendships left and right.

Looking forward to Cyrus's arrival, Brantley got to his feet, then headed for his bedroom, tugging his shirt off as he walked. In the bedroom, he tossed it onto the chair before making his way to his bed. He set down his beer, shucked the rest of his clothes, leaving them in a pile where they fell. Once he was naked, Brantley clicked off the lamp, picked up the remote, then flopped onto the mattress, propping himself up with pillows.

He didn't bother looking at the clock as he surfed the channels. Cyrus would show. The man was punctual. One of his many qualities.

Brantley thought about the last time he'd summoned Cyrus. It had been during a short leave he'd taken nearly two years ago. While he hadn't seen Cyrus in a few years before that, he'd hit him up via text message. After a few minutes of strategic questions meant to gauge Cyrus's current relationship status, Brantley had learned his old friend was single and, yes, on board with the idea of mindless sex. Better than with a stranger, Cyrus had mused. Brantley agreed. Needless to say, they'd engaged in quite a bit of it during that week he'd been home.

At some point, Brantley must've drifted off, because he woke to the sound of footsteps in the hallway. He'd known he would wake when Cyrus arrived. A keen sense of hearing had kept him alive all these years.

His bedroom door opened. The glow from the hall light silhouetted his friend. Even in the dark, he got a decent look at Cyrus, but his eyes weren't necessary. Time hadn't changed Cyrus in the least. He still looked as good as he had back in high school, when they'd been nothing more than friends. At six two, Cyrus was two inches shorter than Brantley and a good thirty pounds or so lighter. Where Brantley had packed on muscle since high school, Cyrus had remained long and lean and, yes, still a bit lanky.

Cyrus closed them in the room, the television offering enough light to see Cyrus was removing his T-shirt, his boots. His jeans followed before he joined Brantley on the bed, looming over him as a smile pulled at his handsome features.

Brantley returned the smile as he reached up, curled his hand around Cyrus's neck, dragging him closer.

"You smell good," he muttered.

Those were the only words spoken.

The kiss that ensued lacked the passion of two lovers drawn together by emotion, but there was plenty of heat fueling it. Brantley's hands weren't gentle as he roamed them over Cyrus's body, urging that eager mouth lower. Cyrus obliged him, his lips blazing a trail over Brantley's chest, gliding lower until finally the wet heat was right where Brantley wanted it.

He inhaled sharply, closing his eyes as the sensations pummeled him. It was then he saw an image in his mind, one that shocked him as much as it turned him on. Instead of Cyrus blowing him so exquisitely, Brantley imagined Reese Tavoularis was bent over him, the sweet suction of his mouth pulling ragged moans from his throat. He knew it was Cyrus who laved his dick, bringing him to the brink before easing off, but he couldn't help imagining the sexy, dark-haired man he'd encountered twice in as many days.

Gripping Cyrus's dark shaggy hair, Brantley held him in place, urging him to continue. Following his lead, Cyrus tormented him, bringing him to the edge, backing off. He did it several times, evidently trying to see how far Brantley would go before he broke. He wouldn't. They both knew that, but it never stopped Cyrus from making the effort.

His cock was throbbing, eager to slide deep inside the man when he finally pulled Cyrus up, fusing their lips once more. Brantley rolled them, taking the lead, giving as good as he got before he retrieved a condom from the nightstand, rolled it on. While he lubed himself, Cyrus flipped over onto his stomach.

Still no words were spoken as they went through the motions, chasing that elusive release.

Knowing what it would take to get Cyrus off, Brantley put forth the effort to entice, nipping his shoulder, his earlobe. And when he drove his cock deep inside Cyrus, he got a rough growl in response. It spurred him on. Rearing his hips back, he drove in deep, hard. Grunts and groans followed as Brantley fucked him. It was a give-and-take, a desperate attempt to ease the tension even though it would return moments after. This wouldn't sate Brantley, but it would suffice. It had to.

"Fuck me," Cyrus bit out. "Goddamn you, Brantley. Fuck me."

Using his knees, he forced Cyrus's legs wide, dug his fingers into his hips, and yanked him back at the same time he thrust forward. Pleasure shot up his spine, the kind that came with mindless sex. He didn't stop, but Cyrus knew he wouldn't. Brantley's stamina rivaled most, and he would go until he was satisfied, no matter how temporary the feeling.

Once more, Reese Tavoularis's face appeared in his mind, and for a brief moment, he let the fantasy consume him. It wasn't easy considering the significant differences between Reese and Cyrus. Where Cyrus was stick thin, Reese was muscled and an inch or so taller than Brantley. But it was hot to imagine, if only because he knew it would never come to be.

Cyrus cried out, his body jerking, a signal that he was coming.

Brantley impaled the man again and again, gritting his teeth until he couldn't hold back any longer. He came with a final drive of his hips, and when his cock was spent, he pulled out, flopping onto his back.

"Good to see you too, man," Cyrus said softly.

Smiling to himself, Brantley reached over, patted Cyrus's thigh. "Always."

It was all he could do to clean himself up before they both succumbed to sleep.

Brantley was up before the sun, slipping out of his bedroom and into the kitchen. He started a pot of coffee, then hit the guest bathroom for a quick rinse in the shower. Once he was finished, he grabbed a pair of shorts out of the dryer, dragged them on, along with his Nikes, then headed out the door.

Like usual, he spent the first hour of his day pounding the pavement. Running was something he did to clear his head. It had the added benefit of keeping him in shape, but he rarely gave that a second thought. Or rather, he hadn't before recently. Now that he was a civilian, he was more cognizant of the things that had come naturally while he'd been in the military. These days he had to put forth the effort of maintaining the simple things—like keeping his edge as well as his physique—or they would fall by the wayside.

Once he was back at the house, he found Cyrus sitting on a barstool, a cup of coffee in front of him.

"Mornin'," he greeted absently, heading for the refrigerator for a bottle of water.

"Anyone ever tell you mornin' starts when the sun comes up?" Cyrus grumbled.

Brantley smiled against the lip of the bottle, watching his friend drag a hand through his shaggy dark hair. He looked tired, but Cyrus generally did. It wasn't necessarily the best look for him, but it did little to detract from the guy's classic good looks. And it was true, Cyrus was a damn fine-looking man. Probably one of the main reasons Brantley invited him into his bed. Of course, the fact he was pretty damn skilled with his mouth was a bonus.

Ignoring the way his cock stirred at the idea of those lips wrapped around him, Brantley turned his attention to making breakfast. He pulled out eggs, a bell pepper, some ham. While Cyrus attempted to wake up fully, Brantley prepared the omelets, then passed one over to his friend.

As the fork went into Cyrus's mouth, Brantley voiced the one and only question on his mind. "Did you know JJ's workin' for Dante?"

Dark brown eyes lifted to his face as Cyrus chewed slowly. The man had a shitty poker face, always had.

"Any reason you didn't tell me?" he prompted, seeing the truth in Cyrus's cautious gaze.

"Because I knew you'd lose your shit," he muttered before taking another bite.

"Lose my shit?" He huffed, then conceded. "Fine. I'm not happy about it. That fucker hit her, man."

"They both say it was an accident. Why don't you believe that?"

Truth was, Brantley couldn't explain it. Someone had once tried to convince him he was actually jealous of Dante's previous relationship with JJ. That was the one thing he knew wasn't true. As far as their friendship, Brantley knew JJ had never trusted Dante the way she trusted him. As for anything intimate, that was a moot point. From the time he was old enough to acknowledge any sort of physical attraction, he'd known he was different than most. Even before he understood what being gay or straight really was, Brantley had accepted that he was attracted to the same sex.

Not that he'd felt the need to make that public, but he hadn't hidden it, either. He'd lived by the don't ask, don't tell rule as well as the equally important don't shit where you sleep. Meaning he'd never engaged in any sort of relationship with those he worked with. Still believed it was a bad idea.

"Look," Cyrus said, sounding as though he felt the need to apologize, "I didn't think it was a big deal. I know for a fact they're not dating—"

"How do you know this?"

"'Cause she told me. And yes, I asked. Damn it, Brantley. She's my friend, too. The thought of Dante hittin' her pisses me off, too. And I trust she's tellin' the truth. It was an accident. Not to mention, in the past. JJ's only involved with him when a job comes up."

Finishing off his omelet, Brantley nodded. He set his plate in the sink, downed the rest of his coffee, then tossed his empty water bottle in the recycle bin.

"I'm gonna hit the shower," he told Cyrus.

"And I'm gonna hit the road."

Cyrus came around the island, stopping directly in front of him. After gently setting his plate in the sink, Cyrus reached for him, pulling him forward until their lips met. The kiss wasn't a romantic or sweet gesture. It was a promise of what was to come.

"Don't be a stranger," Cyrus whispered then pulled back.

"I won't. Maybe you can stop by for a beer next week."

The slow smile said Cyrus knew what else would accompany that beer and he was completely on board.

Brantley patted Cyrus's cheek. "See ya."

"I hope so."

At five fifty-five that night, Brantley was pulling up in front of his uncle Curtis's house, mindful of the six-on-the-dot timeline Travis had referred to when he'd extended the invitation to Sunday dinner.

Why Brantley hadn't made an excuse, or even stopped by his folks' place for an alibi as to why he didn't make it, he wasn't sure. Oddly, after their Friday night IHOP encounter, he was looking forward to spending some time with his cousins and their families, seeing where everyone was at in their lives. It was one thing to hear about all the kiddos they'd mass-produced, another to witness them firsthand.

And witness he did.

From the moment he stepped into the house, he was surrounded. Mostly by the knee-high set, led by none other than Travis's daughter Kate, who appeared, much like her father, to be the self-appointed leader of the pack.

"Uncle Brantley!" she cheered, running toward him.

Surprised that she would even know his name, he smiled and managed to catch her when she launched herself into his arms as though that was where she belonged.

"Hey, kiddo," he greeted with a smile.

"Daddy-O told me to come say hi."

He knew from the stories his cousins shared that Daddy-O was how Travis's kids referred to him since they had two fathers. As for Gage, he had the honor of being called Daddy.

"Are you hungry? I'm hungry. We're havin' pig butt."

He chuckled. "Is that right?"

She nodded enthusiastically. "It's what Uncle Zane said."

"Then it must be true," he agreed. "Maybe you could introduce me to your friends," he suggested, peering down at a few more of his cousins' offspring, all wide-eyed and staring up at him.

"They're not my friends, silly. They're family." Kate shifted in his arms, apparently confident he would not drop her, then started pointing and rattling off names. "That's Kade. She's Avery. Matty, Kellan, Barrett. He's Mason." She glanced at Brantley. "He's the only one who's older than me."

"Is that right?"

"Yup." Her attention went to the kids again. "He's Rhett and that's Gabriel."

Yeah, there was no way Brantley was keeping those names straight.

"Kate, why don't you bring Uncle Brantley into the kitchen," Kylie said with a smile.

"Momma wants you in the kitchen," she whispered. "Daddy-O promised not to put you in the spot."

He chuckled, assuming she meant on the spot. "We shouldn't keep your momma waiting, right?"

Setting Kate on her feet, he let her take his hand, with Mason stepping in to take the other. Together, they led him into the kitchen, where his aunt was moving around the space with the ease of a woman half her age.

"Aunt Lorrie?"

Lorrie stopped what she was doing and spun around to face him. Her eyes widened in surprise, and the next thing he knew, the woman was rushing over and throwing her arms around him as though she was welcoming him home after a long trip.

Caught off-guard by her surprise, he managed to wrap an arm around her, pat her shoulder. When he caught Travis stepping into the room, he shot the man a glare. So much for Lorrie being the one to invite him over. Clearly she hadn't been privy to the invitation he was extended.

The smirk Travis shot his way said, It worked, didn't it?

"I am so glad you're here," Lorrie said as she stepped away. Her soft hand went to his cheek, cupping it gently. "You look tired."

Curtis appeared, offering his hand. "He's not tired, darlin'. Just hungry. Ain't that right, boy?"

"Yes, sir," he said, shaking the proffered hand.

"Glad you could make it."

"Thanks for havin' me."

And just like that, he was pulled into the fold, treated as though he was one of the pack.

Chapter Four

ON MONDAY MORNING, BRANTLEY WOKE BEFORE DAWN, but rather than hop out of bed, he remained where he was, staring up at the slowly spinning ceiling fan. It was becoming more familiar to him. Growing on him, even. The house, the solitude, being back home. Four months ago, he hadn't been sure he would be able to sit still. Now look at him. Relaxing in bed.

His thoughts drifted back to dinner with his aunt and uncle last night, to the conversation and laughter, the stories that had been told. It had been good to catch up with Curtis's family and to get secondhand updates on the goings on with the rest of the Walker clan. How anyone could keep it all straight, he would never know. Yet Lorrie seemed to have a finger on the pulse of every family member they had in Coyote Ridge, including all forty of Frank Sr. and Mary Elizabeth's grandchildren. Yep, that was thirty-nine cousins he had on his father's side alone. All but three were in the immediate area, most right there in Coyote Ridge.

Brantley knew he would have to put forth the effort to reach out to the others as well, catch up. Probably take some time, but hey, that seemed to be all he had at the moment. Enough he should be spending more of it with his parents, his brothers and sisters. Yes, he decided, he would put forth the effort to stop by there, share a meal. Maybe he could extend an invitation for them to come over. Or not. His lack of seating probably wouldn't bode well for a family get-together.

His brain shifted away from family and narrowed on the man who'd arrived at Curtis and Lorrie's last night, appearing in time for dessert because he'd been otherwise engaged for dinner. Reese Tavoularis had arrived without fanfare, settling right in as though he was part of the family. Based on the kids' reaction to the man, he spent quite a bit of time in their presence, every single one of them affectionately referring to him as Uncle Reese.

What it was about him that captivated Brantley, he wasn't sure. However he did know one thing: the guy was damn easy on the eyes. And that voice. He had listened to Reese talk easily to whoever lobbed a question his way, fitting in as though it was natural. He wondered if Reese's parents were in the area. Perhaps they'd moved out of Coyote Ridge at some point. If so, why had Reese stuck around?

With a grunt, Brantley shoved those wayward thoughts away and dragged his ass out of bed. Last thing he needed to do was feed his weird fascination with Reese Tavoularis.

Although he had nothing on his Monday agenda, he knew he had to do something to keep himself busy.

First off: exercise.

After he'd ticked his daily run off his to-do list, Brantley spent the better part of the day fucking around at the house, passing time with nothing to do aside from surf the internet. At some point, he'd stumbled upon JJ's Facebook profile, skimming it to see what she'd been up to for the past few years. Based on the overabundance of selfies, JJ spent most of her time alone. That or she wanted people to believe that was the case.

It was through her profile that he'd located Dante Greenwood's, not surprised to find that the two of them were "friends." From there, he'd gone down a rabbit hole, digging for dirt and coming up with nothing. Since Cyrus had told him Dante's old man was now the governor of Texas, it didn't surprise him he hadn't turned over some juicy gossip.

Of course, he'd had his reasons for skimming any and all information he could find on the man JJ claimed to be working for. Namely, a weird obsession with the guy because of his past dealings with Brantley's best friend. He tried to claim it was because he had JJ's best interest at heart, but Brantley knew better. He needed to address Dante, otherwise he feared his relationship with JJ was going to suffer and that was the last damn thing Brantley needed at the moment.

Because Dante's father was the governor of Texas, there'd been plenty of information to sort through, most of it painting the Greenwoods in the most positive light. Politics.

Of course, at some point, he'd felt guilty for digging into the guy's personal life for no other reason than he'd been bothered by JJ's reaction to his questions. His guilt had led him to text JJ. When she didn't respond, he'd called her. Three times, only to realize she wasn't taking his calls. Initially he'd been pissed so he bombarded her with texts until finally she replied. Her one and only reply was short and sweet: I want to quit you.

It was enough to make him laugh and to understand that JJ needed some space. Did it bother him? Sure. But he got her.

So, rather than drive to her house and risk irritating her, he made a couple of calls and got Dante's number. The text he sent to the man was also short and sweet: This is Brantley. Let's meet at the diner. Want to talk.

Expecting his request to be met with resistance, Brantley was surprised when he got a response within ten minutes: How's six?

I'll be there, he sent back.

And he was.

Brantley strolled into the diner at six o'clock on the dot. Now that he thought about it, six seemed to be when the dinner bell rang in Coyote Ridge. With a quick glance at the tables, he noticed Dante was waiting for him at a booth along the far wall.

"I'm meetin' someone," he informed the waitress who came to greet him.

She flashed a smile, then redirected her course while Brantley made his way past tables full of Coyote Ridge residents, a couple offering a wave for a familiar face.

When he took a seat, he could feel the tension coming off Dante. Clearly he knew why he was there, yet he'd come anyway. Had to respect that a little.

"I heard you were back," Dante said, reaching for the iced tea he'd obviously ordered when he arrived.

"Yep." Brantley flipped his gaze to the waitress who appeared. "Sweet tea for me. Plus a burger, well done. Keep the pickles. Two orders of fries."

Her smile brightened as she glanced at Dante.

"I'll have the same. Only one order of fries."

"Sure thing," she said kindly before sauntering to the back.

Although he'd had all day to gather his thoughts, decide what to say to Dante, now that he was in front of the guy, he was having a hard time swallowing the anger that he'd always harbored for the man. It took effort to keep from clenching his fist on the table or sending that fucker flying into Dante's face.

"I know how you feel about me," Dante said softly, clearly picking up on the tension. "I know you'll never believe it was an accident, Brantley. I swear to God it was. Never would I hit JJ. Hell, I wouldn't put my hands on any woman in anger."

So they were going to get right down to it. "Then tell me why you did it."

He still remembered the black eye JJ had sported thanks to a fight she'd had with Dante. Sure, it was more than a decade ago, but he'd never been able to wrap his head around it.

"Like I told you then, JJ was pissed at me," Dante said, his tone smooth and even.

"You cheated on her, you asshole."

The man nodded slowly. "I did. And I can't tell you how much I regret that, but it is what it is." He took a sip of his tea. "Anyway. She was pissed and hurt. Rightfully so. When she came at me, I didn't try to stop her. I let her whale on me because I deserved it. But she hit me one too many times and her right hook … that's some serious shit."

"So you hit her back?"

"No." Dante sat up straight. "God, no. I went to stop her, to restrain her in an effort to save myself. My elbow hit her in the eye. An accident. I was mortified when it happened. Still am, Brantley. Thirteen years later and I still think about that shit."

It was the exact same story they'd both given him through the years. At some point, probably in the deepest, darkest recesses of his brain, Brantley had believed them. Otherwise, Dante would've been sporting a permanent limp. But he couldn't explain the anger he still harbored, hence the reason he'd wanted a sit-down. He needed to work past this, especially since he was acclimating to this civilian world and being that Dante lived in the same small town, it was imperative they get beyond this.

Dante leaned forward, his voice lowered. "Do you honestly think she'd ever agree to work for me if I'd beaten on her? You know JJ, maybe better than I do. She's not that girl."

No, she wasn't.

The waitress appeared, delivering his tea, pouring more into Dante's glass from a pitcher she carried. Brantley promptly thanked her, then turned his attention back to Dante.

"She said you've got her hacking companies."

He smiled, visibly relaxing. "Not as illicit as you make it sound, but yes. She's helping me with cybersecurity. She uses her skills to reveal a company's vulnerabilities. From there, I've got a team who'll go in and shore them up for the client. She's good at what she does."

"You pay her well?"

"Of course. Better than well. Yet she still turns down the jobs from time to time."

"You know why?"

Dante frowned. "No. That's JJ for you, though. She's a commitment-phobe."

Yes, she was. Always had been. He figured that was the very reason JJ wasn't married with kids at this point.

"Is that why you asked me here, Brantley? To get the lowdown on JJ?"

"No. If I want the lowdown, I'll ask her."

"So what am I here for?"

"To clear the air," he admitted.

That revelation seemed to surprise Dante. Considering the guy hadn't walked up to death's door and knocked, he wouldn't understand. But Brantley knew it was critical that he tie up all those loose ends. It was the only way he'd be able to move forward.

And that was his ultimate goal.

"Well, I'm glad you reached out."

Brantley wasn't sure he'd go that far, but he knew it was a necessary step.

"I did it for JJ," he told Dante. "She's pissed at me for hating you. I'm makin' amends."

Dante smiled. "Whatever it takes."

"How's your sister?" he inquired, because that was what folks in a small town did. They checked in, got the scoop on how the family was doing, offered to help if someone was in need.

"She's good. Cori's going to UT."

"Wow." It wasn't that he was surprised that Dante's little sister was at the University of Texas, but that she was in college period. Sometimes he forgot the age difference between the two. Unlike Brantley's folks, who'd popped kids out one after the other, Dante's parents had waited eleven years before they had a second. And while they didn't admit it, speculation was Corinne had been a welcomed accident.

"Yep, going for a marketing degree. Happy as far as I can tell."

"And your folks?"

Dante's smirk was mischievous. "You heard my old man's the governor, right?"

"Yeah. I heard."

"Weirdest shit, I tell you. I mean, I always knew Dad was a politician, but governor? He surprised us all when he said he was gonna run. More so when he was elected. Now he's into his second term."

"And your mom? She happy bein' Texas's first lady?"

"She's makin' it work. I don't think it's exactly where she saw herself, but they're happy together. She spends a lot of time with Cori."

"You'll tell 'em I said hello."

"Of course. They've asked about you a few times over the years."

At one point in his life, Dante had been his closest friend. Back before JJ had taken up the spot. And truth be told, that black eye was the reason he'd cut ties with the man. It was good to catch up.

"Maybe we could grab a beer sometime," Dante offered. "If you're stickin' around."

He felt the tug of the lure, knew Dante was fishing. "I'm stickin' around. Bought a place and everything."

"I heard. Lotta land."

"Fifteen acres."

And just like that, they'd somehow made their way back to more even ground. After all these years.

Of course, that didn't change the fact that Brantley still harbored animosity for the guy. He was just now willing to give Dante the benefit of the doubt.

Didn't mean he was going to welcome the guy into his life with open arms. Trust was earned, and as far as Brantley was concerned, Dante had a long way to go before he earned Brantley's.

∽℮℮⁀

All In

REESE TAVOULARIS PROPPED HIS BOOTED FEET ON his desk, leaned back in his chair, and waited for Jaxson Briggs to finish his rant. The man had stepped into the small Walker Demolition office nearly a half hour ago, fit to be tied. It was the only reason Reese hadn't pushed him off until later, reminded him that it was closing time.

Not that Reese had pressing plans. In fact, the only thing waiting for him was a salad at the diner, maybe some television before he crashed for the night.

"I'm tellin' you, that asshole did it on purpose," Jaxson grumbled. "Waited until she was datin' somebody, then swooped back in. Fucker."

As usual, Jaxson was up in arms about some woman he'd been dating for all of a minute. Like Reese, Jaxson was single with no prospects for a happily ever after. Maybe that was why Jaxson stopped in so often to bitch and moan about the last woman who'd wronged him. They were kindred spirits in a way. Two single guys immersed in a world full of men who'd settled down and tried happily ever after on for size.

"That's the way it works," he replied, filling in the pauses where he was meant to. "I'm sure there'll be another right around the corner. You met her on the job, right?"

Jaxson's smirk was slow and wicked. "Yup."

The guy was rather proud of his job as a handyman, a jack of all trades, so to speak. Never had Reese thought it would've been a good way to pick up women, but it seemed to work for Jaxson.

Glancing at his watch, Reese let his feet drop to the floor.

"Is it that time already?" Jaxson asked, his gaze darting to the clock on the wall.

"It is. Another day down."

Jaxson nodded, slapped his hat on his head. "You got plans tonight?"

"Me and my remote," he said easily, grabbing his cell phone and truck keys. "Same as every night."

"Wanna grab a beer?"

"Nah. Gonna grab some food, turn in early."

"Cool. Maybe this weekend." Same thing Jaxson said every time he made the offer.

Reese replied with his own canned response. "Sounds like a plan."

After locking up the office, Reese shot a wave to Jaxson, then hopped in the Walker Demolition dually and headed toward town. It would've been easy enough to swing through a fast-food joint on the outskirts of town, take it back to the house, and eat in front of the television, but Reese was making an effort to not be pathetic. He'd gotten himself into a rut as of late, and the only way to get out of it was to change the way he did things.

Which was how he found himself at the diner, not at all surprised to find it was crowded. Didn't seem to matter the day or the time, Coyote Ridge's one and only sit-down restaurant was a popular place. Even on a Monday night.

When he stepped inside, he was greeted by the cheerful din of conversation as well as the radiant smile of the hostess/waitress, who happened to be strolling toward him. Rachel Talbott, the daughter of the restaurant's owners, Charles and Myrna, precariously balanced a tray with four glasses and three salad bowls, making it look easy.

"Hey, handsome. How many?"

"Just one."

"Again?"

Reese grinned. "I like the company."

"Keep this up, people'll start talkin'," she teased, motioning in the opposite direction. "Right this way."

Rachel showed him to an empty booth, then promised to bring his sweet tea on her way back through.

Pulling his phone from his pocket, Reese took a seat, keeping his back to a couple of guys chatting in the booth next to his. It didn't take long before Rachel hurried back over, passing over a glass of tea and taking his order for a chef's salad with ranch dressing on the side. She gifted him with another smile, then went about her business, leaving Reese to have dinner alone as he did most nights.

It was actually how he preferred his meals. Trying to hold up his end of a conversation at this point in the day was tedious. Hence the reason he stopped in here, grabbed a table for himself, and kept his attention from straying by scrolling through his social media accounts on his phone.

Only this time, while he was scrolling, minding his own business, he was distracted by the conversation taking place behind him. He'd caught sight of Brantley Walker, one of Travis's many cousins whom he'd met only recently, but he hadn't recognized the guy sitting across from him.

"You seen Cyrus since you've been back?" the other guy asked.

"Yep. He stopped by last night, in fact."

"You two seein' each other?"

Well, that clarified one thing for Reese. Brantley Walker was gay.

Not that he was the least bit concerned about anyone's sexual orientation. To each his own.

No, he'd been more curious as to Brantley's relationship with Jessie James, the gorgeous woman Brantley had introduced to the group at IHOP the other night. While Reese thought he'd caught the guy looking his way a time or two, he'd been more interested in finding out if JJ and he were an item. Looked like the answer was a definite no.

"I wouldn't put it that way, no," Brantley said from behind him.

"Ah." A laugh followed. "Late-night encounter, huh?"

"Somethin' like that."

"Always keepin' your options open, Brantley."

"What about you?"

"I … uh … no. I'm not seein' anyone at the moment. I know it might sound strange, but I've been on a hiatus for a while."

"How long's a while?"

"Sixteen months."

An amused whistle sounded. "Painful."

Reese did his best to ignore the exchange, knowing he had no business listening in on their private conversation. Probably would've helped if he'd brought headphones, because Brantley's deep, guttural tone wasn't easy to ignore. In fact, the man was hard to miss on all fronts. Between his buzz cut, the dark scruff on his jaw, and his nearly perfect features, Reese had found himself looking longer than was appropriate. Especially for a straight guy. Yet there was something about Brantley Walker that drew his attention.

Last night, when he'd been at Curtis and Lorrie's, he'd listened to the stories being told, the questions Travis and his brothers had pelted at Brantley, inquiring about his time in the Navy. A couple of times, Travis had attempted to engage Reese in those discussions, but as was the case anytime he was asked about his time in the Air Force, he did his best to evade. As far as he was concerned, those days were behind him and he had no desire to sit around and stir up memories better left alone.

From what he'd gathered, Brantley had felt the same despite the fact he'd politely responded to each and every one. That was how Reese had learned the man hadn't left the Teams willingly, but rather had been forced out due to an op that had gone sideways, resulting in his medical retirement.

Reese's attention shifted when he heard movement behind him. A second later, he watched as the man who'd been sitting across from Brantley headed for the doors.

"Care to join me?"

The voice came from behind him, causing Reese to turn, resting his arm over the back of the booth. "Who me?"

"Yep. No reason to eat alone."

He considered it for a moment, but rather than tell Brantley he preferred to eat solo, Reese found himself getting up, taking his tea glass with him as he switched seats, occupying the one Brantley's dinner companion had vacated.

Based on what was left on his plate, Brantley had finished off most of his meal, only half a burger and a handful of French fries remaining.

"So, how do you know Travis?" Brantley inquired as he dragged a couple of fries through ketchup.

"I work for him."

Brantley nodded as though that made sense, but he didn't dig deeper. "His family seems to like you."

Reese grinned. "I'm a pretty likable guy."

There was an amused smirk that pulled at the corner of Brantley's mouth. "Is that right?"

"I'd like to think so."

Those steel-blue eyes latched onto his face, remained there for a few uncomfortable beats before Reese felt the need to fidget. Thankfully, the waitress came over, not thrown off by the fact that Reese had changed seats. She delivered his salad, asked if either of them needed anything, and then disappeared to take care of the other customers.

"Watchin' your figure?" Brantley asked as he two-fisted his burger.

"Somethin' like that." Reese popped the egg yolk out of his hard-boiled eggs, set them aside.

"Best part of the egg," Brantley said, as though it was normal to assess a man's eating habits while at the dinner table.

"That why you invited me over? So you could critique my dinner?"

"Maybe." The smile was mischievous.

"You're a lot like your cousin Travis," Reese told him.

"Handsome and smart?"

Reese chuckled, amused by the man. "Nosy as fuck."

Brantley laughed, a rusty sound that was surprisingly pleasant.

"You know I'm not gay, right?"

"Pity," Brantley said easily. "Damn pity."

For whatever reason, he liked that Brantley spoke his mind. Like Travis, Reese wasn't sure Brantley had a filter. And also like Travis, there were shadows in Brantley's eyes. They were buried under the light the guy gravitated toward, likely in an effort to push down whatever darkness haunted him, but they were most definitely there.

"So, that girl at the range…the one you introduced us to at IHOP," Reese prompted. "She a friend of yours?"

"Yep. Known her since high school."

"JJ, right?"

Brantley nodded, wiped his mouth with a napkin before finishing off his tea and placing the glass near the edge of the table for a refill.

"Why? You interested?" Brantley leaned back, rested his arm on the back of the booth. "I could put in a good word for you."

Reese noticed the way the charcoal T-shirt stretched across Brantley's chest. It was something he never noticed, but there was just something about this man that drew the eye. The casual way he moved, the easy smile, those stormy eyes.

"What makes you think I need help in that regard?" Reese shot back.

Another smile, this one revealing dimples.

"How often you go to the range?"

The shift in topic caught him off guard, but he answered without much thought. "Couple times a week. Why?"

"Just makin' conversation."

So he claimed. To Reese, it felt a hell of a lot more like Brantley was trying to burrow under his skin.

And strangely enough, the realization wasn't exactly off-putting.

Although he had no fucking idea why.

Chapter Five

BRANTLEY WOKE A FEW DAYS LATER TO the sound of his phone ringing, the irritating blast cutting through what had been a relatively peaceful sleep. Considering he'd only been out for two hours, he wanted to hurl the thing through the window.

Slapping at the nightstand, he found the damn phone, cursing as he hit the button to take the call.

"Mornin'," came JJ's too-pleasant voice. "Thought maybe you'd want to meet for coffee."

"You realize it's six, right?"

"And the sun's comin' up. Your point?"

Brantley grumbled, biting his tongue just short of releasing a curse.

"Coffee, Walker. At the diner. Seven thirty."

"Yeah," he groused. "I'll be there."

Had JJ been anyone else, he probably would've told her to fuck off. But since he was hoping to stay in her good graces if for no other reason than he didn't have many people in his life who weren't trying to coddle him, Brantley figured he could forgive her this transgression.

Since he had an hour and a half before he had to meet her, Brantley opted for a run, cutting himself off at an hour but improving his pace so he considered it a win. Back at home, he showered, shaved, dressed. He made it to the diner with about ten minutes to spare but figured he could grab them a table, a task he soon realized wasn't necessary because JJ was already there.

He made his way over, his gaze scanning her breakfast companion, taking in the man's ridiculously nice features. The same ridiculously nice features he'd admired over dinner a few days ago. Reese Tavoularis. Guy just seemed to be popping up every-damn-where.

Stepping up to the side of the table, he peered down at JJ, smiled.

"Hey," she greeted quickly, a flush infusing her cheeks. "You're early."

And you're busted, he thought.

"You remember ... uh..."

Oh, he most definitely remembered the man. "Reese." Brantley smiled. "We had supper the other night."

JJ's eyes widened. "Together?"

"No," Brantley retorted. "Separately, but it was memorable." He smirked down at her. "Yes, together."

"Dinner?"

"That's another name for it, sure," Brantley said. "You know, the meal you have at the end of the day."

"I know what dinner is..."

During this little back-and-forth, Reese had gotten to his feet, held out his hand.

Only because he offered, Brantley shook it, holding on for a second longer than was probably appropriate.

"Good to see you again," Reese stated, taking his hand back.

Most definitely, but not for reasons Reese was likely thinking.

"Any reason you failed to mention you had dinner with Brantley last night?" JJ asked Reese.

"Not last night," Brantley corrected. "Monday."

"Oh, 'cause that helps." JJ huffed, staring at Reese before her gaze shot to Brantley. "You coulda called, dished."

"Nothin' to dish about. Two guys sharin' a table rather than eatin' alone," Brantley explained.

"Yeah, right."

"It's true." Reese's smile was sexy, even if it was directed at JJ and not him. "Completely harmless."

Yes, harmless. Such a shame.

"Sorry, I guess the time got away from us," JJ said by way of apology, obviously realizing she was getting nowhere with this topic.

"I'm a few minutes early," he admitted. "I'll just wait."

"Don't be silly," she said quickly. "Sit. Please."

Though he considered rejecting the offer, Brantley found himself pulling out a chair, easing down into it. He glanced between the two, wondering if this breakfast was their way of parting ways after a night rolling around. Funny that he found himself a tad jealous. Not of Reese. No, he was jealous of JJ for having an opportunity he would never have.

Kinda pathetic, he knew, but he didn't give a shit. It had been a damn long time since he'd had this sort of reaction to a man. Yeah, he knew Reese Tavoularis was straight. So fucking what? Didn't diminish the erotic fantasies a bit.

Reese waved the waitress over, then passed her his credit card before she even got the check out of her pocket.

"Add on whatever he's havin'," Reese said.

The waitress glanced at Brantley. He gave her a quick wink and a subtle shake of his head. "Just a cup of coffee, thanks."

Before she left, the waitress gave Reese a good once-over. Seemed to be an epidemic and Brantley certainly wasn't immune to it.

"Who paid for dinner the other night?" JJ asked when the three of them were alone.

Brantley frowned, trying to catch up. "What?"

"Dinner. You know, the meal at the end of the day? Who paid?"

"I did." Not that he understood why that mattered.

"Hmm."

"No hmm. Just two—"

"Oh, yeah. I heard you. Two guys sharin' a table, blah, blah, blah." Her attention turned to Reese. "Are you headin' to work from here?"

"Yep." He glanced at his watch. "'Bout that time."

Brantley had intended to sit quietly, but curiosity got the better of him. "You work for Travis at the resort?"

"No. Walker Demo."

Why that made him feel better, he wasn't sure, but he played it off. "Ah." He nodded, sat back. "Gotcha."

Reese glanced between him and JJ, clearly not sure what to say. But Brantley could see the curiosity in his gaze. He wanted to know if Brantley had been lying about her being just a friend.

"Don't worry," Brantley offered. "Not here to poach. Like you assumed the other night, you're more my type than she is."

To his surprise, Reese didn't balk at the statement. Instead, he offered a smile. "Is that what I did? Assume?"

Brantley grinned. "If I recall, you're the one who blurted you weren't gay."

He was aware of JJ following their banter with keen interest. Thankfully, it was cut off when the waitress returned with Reese's credit card. Once he'd scribbled his name on the receipt, he set the pen down, smiled at JJ.

"Thanks for joinin' me," he said, as though he didn't care that Brantley was sitting there with them.

"No problem. Thanks for buyin'."

"Maybe we could do this again sometime."

JJ smiled. "Maybe."

Reese looked back at him. "Good to see you again, Brantley."

"Likewise."

To avoid appearing too interested, Brantley didn't turn to follow him as he moved toward the door, although he wanted to. Badly.

JJ, on the other hand, wasn't quite as subtle. Her gaze steadily followed Reese as he made his exit. When she peered back at him, her cheeks were pink and there was a brilliant smile on her face.

"Sorry," he told her again. "Didn't mean to interrupt."

"You didn't," she said easily. "Honestly."

"So you're tellin' me that glassy-eyed look isn't his doin'?"

JJ's eyes widened. "Oh, God, no." She glanced over her shoulder, back. "You thought…?" A soft chuckle escaped. "Definitely not like that."

"And why not?"

"Well, for one, he's a baby."

Brantley frowned.

"He's thirty, Brantley."

He barked a laugh, couldn't help it. "In my book, that makes him eligible."

Another blush infused her cheeks. "Trust me when I tell you, I have no interest in him like that. He's six years younger than me. Far too young."

Brantley nodded his thanks to the waitress who delivered his coffee. He picked up the cup, sipped. "Well, I can tell you, he's not too young for me."

"And up until you walked up, I would've told you you didn't stand a chance," she said with a grin.

Rolling his eyes, he took another sip of coffee.

"Seriously. Did you see the once-over he gave you?"

"From where I stood, he only had eyes for you."

She chuckled. "Anyway … I didn't ask you here so we could gossip about boys."

That pulled a smile from him. "So why did you drag my ass outta bed?"

"First of all, you're usually up at four, so I didn't realize you'd be in bed."

"Late night," he admitted.

"Cyrus?"

The gossip mill really did run rampant in Coyote Ridge.

"No." He didn't bother telling her he'd spent the night alone, suffering from one of the headaches that knocked him on his ass and made him wish for death. No sense ruining a perfectly good morning.

"And two," JJ continued where she'd left off, "I figured I'd given you the cold shoulder long enough."

"You think?"

This time her smile was sheepish as she ducked her chin, her fingers digging into her paper napkin.

He set his mug down, gave her his full attention. "What's on your mind, JJ?"

She exhaled slowly, then lifted her gaze to meet his. How, he didn't know, but Brantley suddenly knew what she was going to say. Before the words could come out of her mouth, he held up a hand, shook his head. If he'd known she was going to bring Dante up, he would've declined the invitation.

Then again, she probably knew that.

"You're datin' him, aren't you?"

"Brantley, I need you on my side here."

Narrowing his eyes, he took a slow, cleansing breath. "Why, JJ? Tell me that?"

"It's the way it's always been meant to be."

"Even after what he did to you?"

"He didn't hit me," she bit out.

"Which, I hate that I'm sayin' this, isn't the worst of his transgressions, JJ. The cheatin', the lyin'. You're willin' to forgive him for all that?"

"Yes, actually. I am." JJ's hand settled on his wrist. "I know what you're thinkin'."

"Do you now?" He pulled his arm from hers, grabbed his coffee mug. "And what might that be?"

"That he's not good enough for me. That I should be with a man who puts me first. That you'll rip him to pieces if he ever hurts me again."

"Yet you won't listen to a word I have to say, right?"

"Dante and I have been spendin' more time together. Not just work."

Funny that the guy hadn't mentioned it. Of course, Dante wasn't a complete idiot. The admission would've come at the risk of a black eye.

"And?"

"And he's been patient with me. I told him I was gonna date other people."

He remembered that she'd been on a date the night he saw her at IHOP.

"But it's not what I want, Brantley. I want to give this a shot. Dante's not the same selfish asshole he was when we dated before. That was a really long time ago. People change."

As much as he wanted to argue, he couldn't. It was true. People changed. And admittedly, after the conversation he'd had with Dante, he could see it, too. The man had changed. Perhaps Brantley'd go so far as to say he had evolved.

Looking into her eyes, he studied her for a moment. "You're a big girl, JJ. I can't tell you how to live your life."

"No, you can't. But I want your support. Now that you're back … my world has righted itself somehow."

He smiled at that. "Because you can't quit me?"

"Exactly." Her hand rested on his wrist once more and this time he didn't pull away. "You're my best friend, B. Always will be. And I'd be lyin' if I said I didn't want you to watch my back."

His gaze dropped to her hand as he placed his over it. "I'll always have your back," he assured her.

He noticed the tension ease out of her shoulders. She'd been worried about his reaction and he wasn't sure if that was good or bad. He only hoped Dante was having the same concerns, because Brantley would not sit idly by this time.

"He hurts you…" he said gruffly.

"I know." A brilliant smile tipped her lips. "He hurts me, you'll hurt him."

"He won't recover from it, JJ." He chugged the rest of his coffee. "You might want to remind him that."

"Oh, trust me, he knows."

AS FAR AS REESE WAS CONCERNED, IT had been a damn good day. Started out with breakfast with a beautiful woman and ended with him bringing on another job, which would ultimately be a positive on his paycheck when it was completed. And now he had one final check-in before he kicked off his weekend with a couple of hours at the gun range.

Pulling down the dirt path leading to the big metal building that housed Walker Demolition's mechanic shop, Reese scanned the vast acres of farmland that branched out in all directions. The Walker land, which at one point had encompassed the whole of Coyote Ridge, seemed to go on forever even if it was only a fraction of what it had been. The small town Reese had grown up in was formerly known as Granite Creek, back before Curtis had it renamed for his beautiful bride. Someone probably should've told Curtis that he set the bar extremely high for the rest of the cowboys who didn't have a damn town of their own to rename.

But whatever.

If Reese remembered correctly, that story was something they were teaching in school these days, the history of what had once been owned by the Walkers in its entirety. Of course, the Walker generosity had ultimately allowed for the land to be parsed, sometimes sold, other times given away, until it became what it was today: a small town consisting of … well, hell, he wasn't the Census Bureau. He had no idea how many people made up the town, but it was enough to still be considered small.

Reese brought his truck to a stop, glancing over at the bay door, which was open. This was another of the Walkers' legacies, a demolition company formed by none other than Curtis Walker's oldest son, Travis. It had since changed hands because Travis had moved on to bigger and better things. And Reese was in charge of the whole kit and caboodle, hence the reason he was stopping by.

Just inside, he could see someone moving around. After tapping on his horn to alert them to his presence, Reese climbed out of his truck and sauntered toward the door.

"This is fair warnin'," he called out, pausing before he went inside. "If anyone's naked in there, speak up now so I can take my ass elsewhere."

A laugh sounded before Kaden Walker appeared in the doorway. "Beau and Ethan aren't here."

Translated to: the risk of naked men galivanting around was thankfully null.

Reese exhaled in relief. He could still remember the last time he'd stopped by to check on things. He'd found the two men in a compromising position. And while he didn't give a shit what they did, he had encouraged them to put a do not disturb sign on the door because there were some things that shouldn't be witnessed by others. It probably wouldn't've been so bad if Ethan and Beau hadn't been like family to Reese. In fact, he'd go so far as to say it might've been a bit … intriguing.

Not that he would think too long or too hard about that. Reese had never gotten off on seeing two men together, yet he still could see it in his head and his reaction wasn't an adverse one.

Shaking off the thought, he turned his attention to Kaden. "Where's Keegan?"

"He ran up to help Lorrie with the kiddos. She's havin' Kate and Mason for a sleepover. Keeg offered to pick 'em up."

Reese peered around the shop. "You need any help in here?"

"Nah. All good. Was about to shut it down. Why? You got somethin' for me?"

"Nope. Figured I'd stop by, tell y'all I was cuttin' out for the weekend."

"Big plans?"

Reese grinned. "If sittin' at home with a cold beer's considered big, then sure."

"Great minds think alike. That's been my plan all week."

"And you think you'll get Keegan to sit at home for even a minute?"

"I bought him a game for the Xbox. Until he gets bored with it, I'm golden."

Funny how Kaden spoke of his identical twin like he was referring to keeping a five-year-old boy entertained instead of a thirty-seven-year-old man.

"Well, if you're all good here, I'm tappin' out till Monday," Reese told him. "See you then."

"Have a good weekend."

"You, too."

Fifteen minutes later, Reese was behind the wheel, making his way through Coyote Ridge to the highway that would lead to the neighboring town. Considering how much time he'd been spending at the gun range lately, Reese probably should consider opening one of his own. Hell, he had nothing better to do. When he wasn't working, he was doing exactly as he'd told Kaden, sitting on his ass.

Sure, there were the times when Travis reached out and asked Reese to do something for him. The requests usually revolved around doing some digging and then confronting whoever it was Travis had it in for. Thanks to all those favors, he'd had his fair share of run-ins with the riffraff. And Travis definitely owed him. Reese figured he'd be sitting high on the hog in his golden years when he cashed them all in.

The thought made him smile.

Not that he had any intentions of cashing in his favors with Travis. The man was a good guy, one Reese highly respected, and if he asked for something … well, there wasn't much Reese wouldn't do for the guy. Or any of the Walkers for that matter. He considered them family.

Speaking of family…

Reese hit the button to call his brother, fully expecting the damn thing to go to voice mail as it had too often in the past year. Z's entire world revolved around Sniper 1 Security, and it seemed the jobs he was taking these days were keeping him out of the country with his husband, Ryan Trexler.

"What's up, kid?" came the gruff voice through the speakers in his truck.

An automatic smile curved his lips. "Been a long damn time since I was a kid."

"You'll always be a kid to me."

Of course he would. Z took the big brother schtick seriously. "Long time no talk."

"How's it?" Z asked. "You keepin' yourself busy or what?"

"Mostly. You? How's married life?"

"Fucking epic."

That made Reese smile. He'd always admired his brother's ability to go after what he wanted. And Z hadn't let anything stand in his way when it came to him wanting RT.

"Have you heard from Jensen?" Z inquired, referring to their baby sister.

"She called last week. Said she was keepin' busy."

"All that schoolin's not good for the soul."

No, it probably wasn't. Then again, Reese knew their sister was all about working her way to the top of the food chain. Why she'd decided to go into psychology, he would never know.

"Anyway, I was just checkin' in," Reese told Z. "Thought I'd catch you stateside."

"Good call. We're up in Boston right now. Long-term assignment. Won't be back for another month."

"Well, when you do get back, maybe we can meet up. I'll head to Dallas, spend a few days."

"Sounds like a plan. You keep your nose clean, kid."

Reese grinned. "Yeah. You, too."

The call disconnected as Reese was pulling into the range's parking lot. There were half a dozen or so vehicles parked on the dilapidated asphalt, including one he recognized from earlier that morning at the diner. The big black Chevy had a United States Navy sticker on the back window and a chrome toolbox in the bed, which made it stand out.

He grabbed his bag from the back seat and found himself smiling, though he wasn't exactly sure why. Maybe because he looked forward to chatting it up with Brantley Walker? Only, he couldn't figure out why that would make him happy. Sure, the guy was a SEAL and he probably had quite a few stories he could offer up. Those that weren't classified, that was. But since Reese was Air Force, he had his own. They could likely fill a few hours swapping war stories, if the guy was up to it.

The thing was, ever since he'd been introduced to the man at the impromptu trip for pancakes, Reese had found Brantley strangely taking up a lot of his brain space. Then came an unexpected dinner with the Walkers, an encounter over a meal at a shared table, and a right place, right time coffee with JJ giving Brantley shit. And perhaps that was the reason he'd been hoping to run into him again. Bottom line was: he liked the guy.

From a friendly perspective, of course.

When he stepped inside, the sales floor was empty except for one customer and one clerk, both of whom were chatting it up over a Ruger sitting on the glass case that held numerous others. Beyond them, at the counter to register for the range, there were two clerks and four customers. When Reese stepped up, all eyes shifted to him, which wasn't unusual. Being that he towered over most men, he tended to draw attention everywhere he went.

"Tavoularis," one of the clerks called out. "Good to see you, man."

"You got anything open?" he asked, making conversation while he stood at the back of the room.

"We're full up here for the next two hours. But I've got a spot for you."

Knowing the guy was referring to the private range, which was underground, Reese gave a nod. "I'll take it." He canted his head toward Brantley, who was standing near the wall waiting his turn. "I'll take the SEAL with me, if you don't mind."

"Not at all. It'll free up a lane up here. Need ammo?"

"Yep. Put me down for six boxes."

"I'll bring 'em down for you."

"Thanks." Reese turned to Brantley. "Come on, Navy boy. Let's see what you've got."

The look on Brantley's face was one Reese had seen before. That slow smirk, the slight tilt of his lips gave him an edge that Reese found oddly intriguing, though, again, he had no idea why. Never in his life had he found a man attractive, but there was something about this guy. Probably had to do with the fact he was a bona fide badass and Reese couldn't deny admiring him for it.

Yes. A badass. He'd go with that.

"Anyone ever tell you it's a helluva lot cheaper to make your own ammo?"

"Too time consumin'," he replied.

"What branch were you in?" Brantley asked as Reese led the way through the employee-only door, then down a set of stairs.

"Forty-ninth Security Forces Squadron," he said easily.

"Air Force." Brantley smirked.

"Fulfilled my contract. Officially out," he noted.

"You see action?"

"More than I cared to," Reese told him, shrugging it off because he rarely talked about his time in the military. He'd gone in as a tribute to his brother, who hadn't been able to serve because of a medical condition. And while he had given it his all, Reese had known he wouldn't be career military.

"Never woulda guessed this was down here," Brantley stated as they stepped through a heavy, windowed door into an anteroom.

"It's not open to the public," he explained. "Roger keeps it open for military only."

Usually he would've donned his ear protection like the sign instructed, but there was no one else down there at the moment, so he stepped through the next door, holding it for Brantley. Once they were both inside, he stepped out of the way, allowed Brantley to pick a lane he was comfortable with. Reese took the one on his left, set his bag down, and pulled out his weapons.

"How long've you been comin' here?" Brantley asked, retrieving his ammo and setting the plastic cases on the small counter.

"Since I got back, so … years."

"Nothin' closer, huh?"

"Unfortunately, no. I was just thinkin' I should open one of my own."

"Yeah?"

"If I had the drive, maybe I would."

Brantley peered over, those blue-gray eyes that were a sure sign of the Walker gene pool skimming over him briefly.

Reese pretended not to notice. Or tried to, anyway. There was something in that quick sweep that sent a frisson of heat through him. It was a foreign feeling, at least in this situation. Although there'd been a couple of times in his life when he'd noticed a man on a visceral level, never once had he considered himself attracted to one. Yet he couldn't shake the strange sensation when he was around Brantley.

Probably overthinking it, he figured. He was curious, that was all it was. Curious to hear about Brantley's last mission, the one that had brought him stateside permanently. The one that had ended his career as a SEAL and placed him back in the civilian world. Aside from the bits and pieces he'd gathered during that Sunday dinner, Reese didn't know much about Brantley. But there was no denying he wanted to.

Once he was set up, Reese walked over and snagged several targets, passing a couple to Brantley before pinning his up and sending it down the lane on the electronic cable hanging overhead. He heard the door open behind him, noticed the clerk setting the additional boxes of ammo at the back. Reese nodded his thanks, retrieved the boxes, then turned his attention to the lane. He stepped up so the partition separating the lanes blocked his view of Brantley.

"Let me know when you're ready," he called out as he put his ear protection on, followed by the clear glasses to protect his eyes.

A few seconds later, there was a light knock on the partition. Reese knocked back, giving the signal he was a go.

For the next hour and a half, the only sounds were the echo of gunfire and the ping of brass casings bouncing on the concrete. They didn't attempt conversation, but it wasn't necessary. They weren't here to chat, and Reese would've been fine no matter who was in the lane next to him. Interesting that he was glad it was Brantley.

Damn near perfect for a Friday night.

Chapter Six

"HOW ABOUT A BEER?" BRANTLEY OFFERED WHEN they headed out into the parking lot nearly two hours after he'd walked into the range.

"You buyin'?"

"Yeah. Provided it includes dinner."

"Pushin' it, Navy boy."

Brantley smirked at the younger man. "Just hungry."

Reese's light brown gaze swung over his face. "Provided you know what's not on the menu."

Yeah, he liked this one, all right. "If I was hittin' on you, you'd know it."

"Fine. Dinner. I know a good steakhouse not too far from here."

"I'll follow you," Brantley said before heading for his truck.

As he drove, he found himself smiling. Reese Tavoularis was unexpected to say the least. And no, Brantley wasn't talking from an intimate perspective. From what he could tell, the guy was definitely straight. Even if there might've been a hint of curiosity behind that inquisitive gaze, he knew better than to entertain the notion. Brantley had long ago decided to keep his intimate encounters on an even keel. He preferred men who both knew what they wanted and didn't see things that weren't there. Men who were open to a sexual partner who didn't play games or hint for more than a few hours of intense pleasure. It was the very reason he got along so well with Cyrus.

As for Reese… Brantley wasn't opposed to some flirting. Especially since Reese seemed to expect it but wasn't put off by the notion that he was hanging out with a gay man.

It was a rarity for him, actually. During his time in the military, no one suspected he was gay. Or if they had, they didn't let on about it because that was how it worked. Sticking your nose in someone else's business could reveal secrets you didn't care to uncover. It was one thing if your buddy came out with it. Past that, you minded your own damn business.

And Brantley had allowed everyone to think the alpha male was straight because that was the assumption. He stuck to the story that he wasn't interested in a relationship and kept his intimate encounters on the down low so as not to raise unnecessary questions. And because of that, he hadn't been able to be himself. Not entirely, at least. So this was refreshing.

They arrived at the restaurant roughly twenty minutes later. It was busy, which was par for the course on a Friday night, and Brantley had to wonder if Reese would be able to bypass the line here, too.

He got his answer a few minutes later when he was following Reese to the bar, peanut shells crunching beneath his boots while a variety of wild animal heads stared down on them as they walked. It was your typical Texas steakhouse, he figured.

Sliding onto a stool on the far side of the room, he made sure his back was to the wall. He'd already identified all the exits as had been beat into him over the years. Even if there weren't any tangos lurking, Brantley was still not taking any chances. His self-preservation instinct would no longer allow it.

The bartender ran by, muttering that he'd be right with them. There was a couple sitting across from them, on the opposite side of the bar. Not far from there, a trio of guys who were paying attention to one of the half-dozen televisions mounted on the wall. Around them were two- and four-tops filled with customers who were getting their Friday night dinner on and harried waitresses moving to and fro.

He glanced over to see Reese skimming the menu as though he had no idea what he wanted. If Brantley was right, the guy had his favorites planned out already and this was just his way of easing into conversation.

Brantley decided to kick it off. "I know your brother."

"Figured you did." Reese smirked. "Any chance you dated him in high school?"

Well, that explained why Reese was so chill on hanging out with a gay man. His brother was clearly out to his family and Reese was evidently cool with it.

"Nope. More like casual acquaintances. Didn't even realize he was gay. We graduated together."

A waitress started past them but drew up short, offering to get them drinks. When they both answered with beer, she moved around behind the bar and took care of the order.

"Yep. He was out of high school when I went in." Reese nodded to the waitress. "Thanks."

"Anytime."

Brantley took his beer, watched the woman as she tried to get Reese's attention before she finally gave up and wandered off.

"Z's up in Dallas now," Reese explained. "Works for Sniper 1 Security. Married Ryan Trexler a few years back."

"Everyone's gettin' married these days," he said absently. "Never in my life did I expect my cousins to settle down. Especially not Curtis's boys."

Reese chuckled. "Now they've got a couple dozen rug rats between 'em, too. What about you? Got any nieces or nephews?"

"My oldest sister Sadie's got two girls. Tori's got one boy. The rest of 'em are single. Well, except for Cal. He just got engaged."

"I heard that. I remember Cal, but he was a couple of years ahead of me. I've talked to him a few times since I've been back, though. He's been with April a long time, huh?"

"Few years now."

The bartender stopped by, looking downright frustrated that he had to take the time to jot down their orders. Because he was in such a hurry, Brantley took his sweet time. Reese opted for top sirloin, medium rare, with double mashed potatoes. Because he was trying to be cognizant of how much junk he ate, Brantley opted for chicken breast and a side salad. The bartender talked him into applesauce as a side, so he figured why the hell not.

"He was flirtin' with you."

Brantley took a swig of his beer, cut his gaze to Reese's. "No, he was tryin' to gauge our relationship."

"Our?" Reese's eyes widened. "As in you and me?"

"Yup." He chuckled. "Don't worry. I'll make sure he knows you're spoken for."

"Yeah. Thanks." Reese took a long pull on his beer. "So, what're you up to now that you're back for good?"

That was the question that seemed to be on everyone's mind. They wanted to know what Brantley's intentions were and he almost considered lying but then figured it would be pointless. He detected only sincere curiosity on Reese's part, so he answered with, "No idea."

"You're gonna get bored."

"Sounds like you're speakin' from experience."

"Oh, I am. I've been back a few years now and it takes a lot to keep my mind at ease."

"What about Walker Demo? What do they have you doin'?"

"Right now, I'm runnin' the place."

"It's not enough?"

Reese picked at the label on his beer, glanced at Brantley. "Between you and me, no."

"It's not easy, is it?"

"No, it's not," he said, clearly picking up on Brantley's reference to being out of the military. "You spend all your time knowin' exactly what you're doin' until one day it's all gone. The routine's now yours to manage."

"But you don't miss it?"

"Certain things, sure."

Brantley glanced at the television on the wall. "I'd still be there if they hadn't sent me on my way."

"I heard you were injured. Your family was worried about you."

"They're still worried." Brantley tipped his beer back, wondering if they should be.

"So, tell me about JJ. You two seem close."

Clearly Reese had understood his need to change the subject. The comment had Brantley grinning.

"We're close," he conceded. "She's like a sister. I dated her brother back in high school. Thought for a while we'd make a go of it. He ended up dumpin' me when I went into the Navy." Brantley stared off into space. "He took his own life."

"Man, I'm sorry. I had no idea."

"Most people don't talk about it."

"Why'd he do it?"

"He was bipolar. Spiraled. Before anyone realized how dark he'd gotten, it was too late."

"In case you hadn't noticed, I'm shitty date material," Reese tossed out.

Brantley chuckled. "This a date?"

"No. I'm just tellin' you why I'm still single."

"I figured it was because you hadn't found the right … person yet."

To his surprise, Reese laughed at that.

Two hours later, Brantley stepped into his empty house. He'd parted ways with Reese, having enjoyed dinner more than he'd expected to. Part of him had been tempted to invite the guy over for another beer, but he'd refrained. No sense beating a dead horse. For whatever reason, he was attracted to a straight man, but that didn't mean he was an idiot.

Plus, he didn't have time to entertain shit like that. Certainly not when it would have him spinning his wheels, never gaining traction.

After a quick shower, he padded naked to his bedroom, snagged the remote, and fell into bed. Before he turned on the television, he checked his phone.

It was then he noticed he'd gotten a text from Reese, which was both unexpected and oddly comforting.

Thought about headin' to an outdoor range tomorrow. If you're interested.

Are you asking me out?

The response was immediate: Keep dreaming, Navy boy.

Not wanting to risk offending Reese, he dropped the flirting and went with: I'm game. You wanna pick me up? Or am I driving?

I'll drive. How's ten sound?

Perfect. See you then.

Setting the phone on the nightstand, Brantley stared up at the ceiling, the television forgotten. His brain had its own slideshow going now, memories of the evening on a quick replay. In every mental image, he saw Reese and that ridiculously attractive grin of his.

It was enough to have Brantley reaching down, palming his cock. He stroked slowly at first, closing his eyes and giving himself over to fantasy. It was a waste of time, but his cock didn't seem to mind the attention, so he went with it. Thoughts of Reese's mouth … those full lips wrapped around him had Brantley's breath hitching. It was too easy to think about Reese, probably because he knew there was nothing to fear. The guy had already stated he wasn't on the menu and Brantley respected that.

He opened his eyes so he could watch his hand moving up and down his shaft, wishing like hell it was Reese's hand teasing him. Pleasure coursed up his spine, drawing his eyes closed once more. Letting the fantasies take flight, he imagined getting Reese beneath him, trailing his mouth over that enormous hard body, then letting the man return the favor. He even entertained the notion of turning over, letting Reese fuck him hard and fast. Brantley didn't prefer to bottom for anyone, but if the situation was right…

Brantley grunted as his cock jerked in his fist. He could practically feel Reese's hard cock sliding deep inside him, pressing against his prostate, making his eyes cross with a pleasure he hadn't known in a damn long time.

"Fuck…" His breaths were sawing in and out of his lungs, his hand pistoning over his cock until he couldn't refrain any longer.

Thank God there was no one else there.

Otherwise, they would've heard him cry out Reese's name when he came.

REESE WASN'T SURE WHAT IT WAS ABOUT Brantley that had him wanting to spend more time with the guy, but that seemed to be what was happening.

After they'd gone to the outdoor range and spent the better part of the morning firing long-range rifles, he felt as though he was learning more about Brantley Walker with very little effort. For example, the guy was a fucking amazing shot. So much so, Reese had conceded to the guy when Brantley had suggested a contest. Although he prided himself on being better than many, he knew when to give up the ghost.

After Brantley had finished showing off, Reese had taken him back home, intending to drop him off. Only, he had accepted Brantley's invite for lunch, which they'd had over conversation in Brantley's kitchen since the guy didn't have a dining room table. Or a couch, for that matter.

"All right," Reese said, grinning as he scanned the space. "What's up with the lack of furniture?"

"There's furniture where it's necessary."

"Such as?"

That cocky grin made an appearance. "The bedroom."

Pretending not to notice the innuendo, Reese replied with, "So you furnished the bedroom, why not the rest of the place?"

"It was my intention, until Travis started harpin' on me about gettin' a couch. Figured it would serve him right."

Reese laughed. "Because he's affected by you not havin' a couch."

"Touché."

"And the dining room table?"

"No need for one." Brantley nodded to the barstool that Reese had vacated. "Got more than enough seating."

Okay, he'd give the guy that much.

"No TV."

"Oh, I've got one." Brantley's grin was one he'd come to expect. It was ripe with flirtation. "In the bedroom. Wanna check it out?"

"No, thanks. I'll pass."

"Thought so." A dimple flashed. "Offer's open anytime."

Reese shook his head. "Don't give up, do you?"

"Not when I want somethin', no."

Pretending not to understand, Reese moved to the back door, peered through the glass. "You plannin' to do anything with the land?"

"You mean like grow corn? No. Just like the space. Can't hear my neighbor and he can't hear me."

"Makes sense. What's in the barn?"

"My cache of dead bodies," he said deadpan.

He grinned because he was quickly learning Brantley's easy quips, expecting them, even. "Do you keep the heads on or off?"

"I'll show you."

Surprised but not disappointed, Reese waited for Brantley to open the sliding glass door, then followed him out onto the porch. They strolled across the calf-high grass, moving along what appeared to be a path being worn into the ground by frequent use.

As they neared the big red barn, Reese's attention was drawn to the eaves, where he spotted two security cameras mounted. Before he could ask why they were there, he noticed Brantley keying in a code on a keypad, then using his palm to unlock the door.

"All that for—" He cut off his own words when Brantley slid the barn door aside to reveal two solid steel doors.

Definitely not your average barn.

The not-averageness extended to the inside. Reese stepped into the air-conditioned interior to see it was most definitely not a barn. There were no stalls, no feed, no animals, and certainly no dead bodies. The floor was smooth concrete, the walls insulated and sound-proofed. The ceiling was composed of the HVAC system as well as well-placed lighting.

"This your bat cave?" he teased.

"Like I said, I haven't figured out what to do with the rest of my life. In the meantime, I've been tryin' to fill the endless hours. This is what was born of that."

Like the house, there wasn't much furniture in the space. In fact, there was nothing aside from the long table that held three flat-panel monitors that were propped up at an angle. Not even a chair. Well, there was the wooden ladder that led to what Reese figured was originally a hayloft. Only there wasn't any hay, or anything else, for that matter, at the top of the ladder. Just a lot of empty space.

"Well, if your goal was to look the part of a high-tech guru, you nailed it." Reese turned his attention to Brantley. "You know how to use this stuff?"

"I can hold my own."

Interesting.

Reese got the feeling if he ever thought he'd peeled back all the layers of Brantley Walker, he would soon learn there were a million more.

"What?" Brantley asked.

It was then Reese realized he'd been staring at the man. Shaking his head, he quickly looked away. "It's cool. I'll give you that."

"Like I said, I've got nothin' to do with my time. Originally thought about convertin' it to livin' space. Started up there before I changed my mind. Figured maybe this would turn into somethin' later on down the road."

"I hope it does. Truly." Because Reese knew all about the need to find a place in the world. He'd spent the last few years attempting to do the same. And while he appreciated Travis Walker's generosity in giving him a job, he knew it wouldn't hold his interest forever. Then again, it wasn't like he'd been pursuing anything else. Somewhere along the way, Reese had gotten comfortable in this half-ass existence he'd built.

Something chimed, drawing Reese's attention. He looked over to see Brantley pulling his phone out, checking the screen.

"Looks like I've got company," he said, his tone telling Reese he hadn't been expecting whoever it was.

Rather than wait for Brantley to lead the way, Reese headed for the door, smiling when he realized they'd been locked in.

"Hope like hell you thought to incorporate a bathroom in this joint. You get too many guests locked in, things might get ugly."

"Full bath," he said easily as he used his palm to unlock the door. "Plus a kitchen."

"Your very own panic … barn."

Brantley shot him a sideways smirk before leading the way outside. Reese waited while he locked up behind them.

"So when you're not sleepin', and you're not sittin' on one of your two barstools, and you're not camped out in your bat cave, what do you do?"

"Not a whole helluva lot."

"Good to know. Next time I need a partner at the range, I'll hit you up."

"Anytime," Brantley said, grinning.

They had just reached the back deck when a man wearing a backwards baseball cap sauntered around the side of the house. His eyes instantly jumped between Reese and Brantley, landing on Brantley before a wide grin formed.

"Hey," Brantley greeted the visitor. "Cyrus, meet Reese Tavoularis. Reese, meet Cyrus Jernigan."

Ah. This was the Cyrus he'd overhead Brantley talking about that night at the diner. Based on the heat he saw in Cyrus's gaze as it raked slowly over Brantley, their mutual friend hadn't relayed to him the fact they were only friends.

Reese offered his hand, noticed how Cyrus thrust his hand out and gave a rather forceful shake.

"Nice to meet you." The comment was pleasant enough, but Cyrus's eyes reflected his obvious question as to what Reese was doing there.

"What brings you by?" Brantley asked, motioning for them to go inside.

"Just thought I'd check in. See how you're doin'. We didn't get a chance to do a whole lotta talkin' the other night."

Reese fought the urge to grin. So that was jealousy sparking fire in Cyrus's green eyes.

"Want a beer?" Brantley said in response.

Cyrus quickly offered a confirmation while Reese figured now was the perfect time for his departure.

"I should probably be headin' out." He spared a quick glance at Cyrus. "Nice to meet you."

"Same."

Brantley moved toward him. "I'll walk you out."

His first instinct was to tell Brantley not to worry about it, but something inside him—some foreign emotion that seemed a hell of a lot like jealousy but couldn't possibly be—had him biting back the words.

Once outside, Reese stepped off the front porch. "Boyfriend?"

"Who, Cyrus?" Brantley chuckled. "No. He's just a friend. An overprotective one."

He was more than that, but Reese didn't bother to say as much. What Brantley did in his spare time was none of his business. Certainly not when it came to his romantic entanglements.

"Well, thanks for hangin' this mornin'. And thanks for puttin' my ass to shame out there."

"To shame?" Brantley's smile was wide and made the dimples in his cheeks flash. "Hell, I wasn't even tryin'."

"Sure you weren't."

"Don't believe me?"

Reese cocked an eyebrow, earning another laugh from Brantley.

"Maybe we can do it again sometime," Reese told him, then realized how it sounded. "I … You…"

Another brilliant smile from Brantley, along with, "No need to explain. I had a good time. Maybe we can check out paintball next time."

"Ah. Paintball. Now you're suggestin' I let you shoot me."

"Perfect way to spend a Saturday, no?"

"No. Probably not." Reese grinned back, knowing full well he would make the effort to go if the opportunity arose.

Before Brantley could say anything more, Reese noticed Cyrus standing just inside the house, his face appearing through the screen door.

"I won't keep you from your company."

To his surprise, Brantley didn't even bother to look back. His gaze remained locked on Reese's. It was Reese who forced himself to walk away. And though he did, he couldn't help wondering when the next time he'd see Brantley again would be.

Or what Brantley and Cyrus would be doing once they went back inside.

The last part … yeah, he decided he wouldn't think too long or hard on that, either.

Chapter Seven

One month later, September

"I STILL CAN'T BELIEVE YOU TOOK A day off to let me shoot you," Brantley told Reese as they stood in his kitchen while burgers cooked on the grill just outside the back door.

"Okay, for the record," Reese stated, "I cut out early. Not the same as takin' a day off."

"Early? You call leavin' at ten in the mornin' early?"

Reese grinned, his hair a wild mess from the helmet he'd worn during their paintball match. "As a matter of fact, I do."

Brantley took a long pull on his beer, noticing the green paint that was practically glowing behind Reese's ear. It took tremendous willpower not to reach over and wipe it away. Somehow he managed to keep his hands to himself though. No sense ruining what was quickly becoming a damn good friendship.

After finishing off his beer, Brantley tossed it into the recycle can. "You mind keepin' an eye on those burgers while I hit the shower?"

"Sure thing."

"Unless you wanna join me," he teased, his gaze swinging to Reese's to catch his reaction.

As usual, Reese's expression remained neutral while his cheeks turned an interesting shade of pink. "Keep dreamin', Navy boy."

"Oh, I will. Trust me."

With a laugh, he sauntered down the hall to his bathroom. It took him six minutes to complete his task of showering and getting dressed. When he returned to the kitchen, he found Reese on the back deck, flipping the hamburger patties.

"That was fast," Reese said when he stepped inside, pulling the glass door closed.

"I'm efficient like that. What time is it, anyway?"

"Two thirty." Reese skimmed a hand over his hair, his fingers finding the green paint. "You mind if I borrow some of your hot water so I can get this shit outta my hair?"

"Go for it." Brantley nodded toward the hallway. "Guest bath's stocked."

Reese's eyebrows rose toward his hairline. "You stock your guest bath, but you can't buy a couch?"

Smiling at the jab, Brantley cocked an eyebrow. "Need me to wash your back?"

The barked laugh followed Reese as he spun around and made his way down the hall.

While Reese did his thing, Brantley cut up an onion and a tomato, chopped some lettuce, and grabbed a couple of pieces of cheese as well as a variety of condiments. By the time his friend had returned, hair still wet and his feet bare, Brantley had pulled the patties off the grill and set them on the island.

Without a word, the two of them prepped their burgers before digging in. Reese took a seat on one of the barstools while Brantley propped himself against the kitchen counter. As was the way of hungry men, neither of them said a word as they ate. Brantley downed one burger and a single patty without bread while Reese finished off one and a half before sighing contentedly.

"Man, next time I'm in the mood for a good burger, I'm gonna be on your doorstep."

"You're welcome anytime, just bring the meat." As soon as the words were out of his mouth, he smirked.

"Anyone ever tell you you've got a dirty mind?"

Feigning innocence, Brantley blanked his expression. "What ever do you mean?"

Reese rolled his eyes, then got to his feet. He walked around the island with his plate, flipped on the water.

"I'll get that," Brantley argued.

"You cooked, I'll clean," Reese countered.

"Is that right?"

"It's called being a good houseguest."

"So now you're a guest?"

"Okay, friend. Whatever. Drink your beer, Navy boy."

With his attention on his task, Reese didn't notice the way Brantley was eyeing him. Of course, Brantley knew it was a wasted effort, but he couldn't seem to help himself. From the moment he'd first seen Reese, the man had caught his attention. And since the morning when Brantley had intruded on Reese's breakfast with JJ, they'd spent quite a bit of time together. A solid month had passed since that day, and their friendship was growing, almost as though they enjoyed one another's company.

Truth was, Brantley did enjoy spending time with Reese. The guy was easy to be around. It required little effort, which was a plus as far as he was concerned. The problem was, Brantley couldn't deny the intense physical attraction. One-sided, of course, but there, nonetheless. Had Reese been interested, there was no doubt they'd already have been naked together and likely tested every flat surface in his house for sturdiness. And at moments like this, when his body hardened with the urge to touch, to taste, to explore, boundaries meant very little.

"Expectin' someone?" Brantley asked when he noticed Reese's gaze continuing to dart to the back door.

"Just figured Cyrus'll show up and chase me off with a stick."

The mental image made Brantley chuckle. "Cyrus is harmless."

Granted, Reese wasn't aware that Cyrus enjoyed getting a rise out of him. He was pulling off the jealous lover perfectly, despite Brantley's repeated requests for him to cut it out. It was a wasted effort, but Cyrus didn't seem convinced.

"So, you two a thing?"

It probably shouldn't have made him feel good that Reese was asking the question. Especially since he'd asked it before.

"Not a thing," he said, leaving it at that. He knew it wouldn't be wise to inform Reese that he and Cyrus were fucking. Or that the last couple of times Cyrus had been there, Brantley had fantasized the man was Reese beneath him. Yeah, he'd be keeping that to himself, thank you very much.

"Does he know that?"

Grabbing his beer, Brantley moved around the island so he could look at Reese while he finished up the dishes. "Are you jealous, Tavoularis?"

Reese didn't look up, but Brantley noticed the smile. "Not even a little."

"No?"

When those pretty brown eyes lifted, Brantley swore he saw a hint of desire glittering there.

"Hey, I'm not one to judge," Brantley teased, holding up his hands. "You wanna admire this, who am I to stop you?"

Another eye roll was Reese's response.

It was then Brantley realized that he wasn't imagining the chemistry between them. No, maybe Reese wasn't gay, but he was certainly interested. In what, he didn't know. And it wasn't like Brantley would act on it. If and when anything ever transpired between him and his newfound friend, Reese would have to be the one to put the moves on him.

Of course, that thought had his cock thickening behind his zipper.

As though timed to save Reese from an awkward encounter, the man's cell phone rang. He quickly shut off the water, dried his hands, then grabbed his phone.

"Yeah?"

Brantley watched Reese's expression turn dark in a matter of seconds.

"Fuck. Yeah, okay. I'll be right there."

The phone hit the counter with a clatter and then Brantley was watching Reese dart back down the hall to the bathroom. When he returned, he was wearing his boots.

"What's goin' on?"

The man didn't have a chance to respond before Brantley's phone was ringing, his sister Bryn's number flashing on the screen.

"Hey, sis," he said by way of greeting.

"Brantley, you need to get to Travis's. Right now."

His gaze shifted to Reese's face as he spoke. "What's goin' on?"

"Travis's daughter … Kate…"

"What about her?"

"She's missing."

The hair on the back of his neck stood on end, his mind shifting into gear, preparing for the mission, whatever that might be. His brain instantly clicked on an image of Kate, Travis's five-year-old daughter. He could see her smiling face, hear her sweet giggle, and his chest tightened with fear. It was a welcome sensation because he knew it would successfully knock everything else from his mind, bringing clarity so he could do what needed to be done. Again, whatever that might be.

"Brantley? Did you hear me?"

"Yeah. I heard. I'm headin' there now." Brantley was on his feet, saying goodbye to Bryn before racing down the hall to grab his boots and his firearm. He was sliding his belt on, affixing the holster when he saw Reese standing in the kitchen, his expression hard.

"You drivin' or me?" Reese prompted.

He was surprised that Reese would consider going together, but he didn't question it. "I'll drive."

Without a word, Reese started for the door while Brantley snagged his sunglasses and keys, followed his friend outside.

"Who called you?" Brantley asked as his tires kicked up gravel in their wake.

"Ethan. You?"

"Bryn." He put the pedal to the floor, the truck's engine roaring with power as he flew down the dirt road that would lead them into Coyote Ridge.

"She give you any details?"

"Nothing except Kate's missing."

Reese exhaled and Brantley could feel the calm that was coming over him. The man might've been out of the military for some time, but it was obvious he still remembered the tools of the trade.

Reaching for that calm himself, Brantley shoved everything from his mind and focused on driving.

TRAVIS WALKER STOOD ON HIS FRONT PORCH, hands planted on the railing, head hanging down. His mind was spinning a million miles a minute, his heart pounding uncontrollably. His fingers curled around the wood and he could feel the power flexing in his arms. The need to rip the porch apart tore through him, forcing him to take deep, calming breaths.

Fear coalesced with pain as he thought about that fucking phone call he'd received. *Mr. Walker, we don't want to alarm you, but … well, Kate's missing.*

How the fuck could they think delivering that news over the phone was a good idea, much less add *we don't want to alarm you* as a way of breaking the ice?

Goddammit.

His entire world had stopped at that moment. The earth ceased to spin, the wind choked out. Hell, he was surprised the sun was still shining and that his heart was still beating.

Inside the house, he could hear his wife's terrified sobs and desperate pleas for someone to find their daughter, his husband's gruff voice as he attempted to calm her down. Somewhere behind him, Sheriff Endsley was on his phone, barking orders as he reached out to the appropriate departments for assistance. Although they didn't have an exact time when Kate had disappeared, they knew it had been at least three hours.

Three. Fucking. Hours.

Every second felt like an eternity as they stood around with their thumbs up their asses. Waiting when they should've been doing. And for what? What the fuck were they waiting for? He wanted some fucking answers. Anything to tell them where Kate was. There was plenty of speculation from the principal, the school counselor, even the fucking deputy who'd been jotting down information.

Maybe Kate wanted to play hide-and-seek.

Umm, no. His daughter was a hell of a lot smarter than that.

Maybe Kate saw someone she knew at the capitol, left with them.

Umm, no. Those who knew Kate were a hell of a lot smarter than that.

Maybe, maybe, maybe. What it was was a bunch of fucking bullshit meant to calm the waters.

Too late for that. This was the eye of the storm, a parent's worst fucking nightmare. Travis's chest was heaving, his panic a living, breathing thing. Kate was missing.

Knowing it would do no good to lose his shit, he tried to focus on what they did know while forming a plan to get his daughter back.

According to the details they'd received from the frantic teachers at Kate's school, all the kids had been accounted for after their brief lunch break during the field trip to Austin's capitol building. It was a trip the kindergarten class at Coyote Ridge Elementary took every single year without incident. And, according to the teachers, another head count had been done before they'd left the capitol grounds, but somewhere there was a mix-up. It wasn't until they returned to the school that they realized they were down one child.

A mix-up, they said. Like they grabbed the red marker instead of the blue one.

For. Fuck's. Sake.

And his daughter was the one to go missing.

Not that he wished this on anyone. He didn't. God knew he would move heaven and earth to help anyone locate their child, but for this nightmare to make it to their doorstep…

He took a deep breath, exhaled slowly, stared out at the trees lining the property.

Travis knew better than to think Kate had simply wandered off. His daughter knew the dangers of the world because they'd had those discussions. Stranger danger was a topic they covered frequently and their five-year-old knew it well. She was a curious child, but she was also smart. No, Kate didn't simply wander off.

A tortured wail sounded behind him, drawing him to his full height.

He marched inside the house, making a beeline for his wife. Gage was holding Kylie against him while she sobbed uncontrollably. When Travis met Gage's eyes, he could see the terror there, knew his husband was doing his best to hold himself together.

Placing a hand on Kylie's back, Travis simply wanted her to know he was there. She immediately pulled away from Gage and spun around, slamming into Travis's chest. He wrapped a hand around her head, held her steadily while he fought to breathe through the panic that had threatened to suffocate him from the moment he'd gotten the call. He'd been at the resort with Gage when the school had contacted him. Within minutes, he and Gage had been in his truck heading to the school. Not long after that, the sheriff, who had come to meet them, decided it would be in everyone's best interest if they took it back to the house. Probably had something to do with the fact that Travis threatened to obliterate the principal for allowing this shit to happen.

A hothead, they called him.

Yeah. So?

"What's bein' done to find her?" Gage demanded, his words directed at the sheriff.

Jeff Endsley wasn't only the sheriff of Coyote Ridge. He was also family, related because Jeff's daughter Kennedy had married Travis's brother Sawyer. On top of that, Jeff was the husband to the Walker family's longtime friend Mack Schwartz. No, Jeff wasn't only here in an official capacity, but Travis knew as well as anyone that they needed him to be. Right now, emotion didn't need to be a factor in locating Kate.

"We've issued an Amber Alert," Jeff noted, his tone calm and cool, a professional to his core. "I've sent her picture out to every law enforcement agency in the vicinity. I've also contacted Austin PD and the Department of Public Safety since it appears she was taken while at the capitol building, requested they do a room-by-room search. It's being set up."

A knock sounded on the front door. Travis kept his hands on Kylie, keeping her shielded against his chest as he glanced over to see his father walking into the house. Although he knew Curtis had no answers for him, Travis couldn't deny that seeing his father was a relief. He'd grown up worshipping the man, still did. And he knew there was nothing Curtis Walker wouldn't do for his family.

"Where's Mom?" he asked.

"She's with Kennedy and Beau. They're picking up all the kids, taking them back to her place. Zoey's on her way over there, too."

Travis nodded, grateful his mother had thought to do so.

"You have to find her," Gage demanded, his voice trembling as he spoke to Jeff. "You've got to find our baby."

Travis's stomach clenched at the pain he heard. As was always the case, Travis wanted to fix this. For Kylie, for Gage. But most of all, for Kate. He wanted to march out that fucking door, find his daughter, and bring her home safely. He wanted to ease everyone's pain because there was so much of it, and in an effort to maintain his sanity, Travis wasn't even considering how terrified Kate must be. They had no idea where she was, who had her, or why.

"We're doin' everything we can," Jeff assured him.

"Not good enough!" Gage snapped.

Curtis walked over to Gage, set a hand on his shoulder, then gently steered him around before placing a comforting arm around him. Travis watched as his father hugged his husband, doing what was necessary to offer comfort even though it would do nothing to fix the situation. But it was obviously what Gage needed because it was then that the man broke down.

Travis's heart squeezed tight in his chest as he watched Gage, a former police officer, one of the strongest men Travis knew, buckle beneath the onslaught. In Travis's arms, Kylie was doing the same.

Son of a bitch.

No way could he fucking sit here and do nothing. It wasn't in his DNA.

Reluctantly, he eased back from Kylie, urging her back into Gage's arms when Gage managed to pull himself together.

"Where're you goin'?" Gage asked when Travis snagged his truck keys from the table.

"I can't just sit here and—"

A firm hand settled on his shoulder. "Take a breath, boy."

Travis turned to look in his father's eyes, saw the strength he'd always admired in the man.

"I can't, Pop. I can't just sit here. Kate's out there…" His nostrils flared as emotion threatened to strangle him. "She's out there and I'm goin' to find her."

The hand on his shoulder tightened when he attempted to turn. Travis knew it was wrong to shove it off, but he tried. Failed.

Another hand landed on the other shoulder, his father turning him so they were nose to nose.

"Right now, you're needed here." Curtis's voice was low, firm. "There's no sense in you goin' off half-cocked. It won't do a damn bit of good for you to go plowin' over the people who're workin' to find Kate. Let them do their jobs."

Travis knew his father was right. Hell, he didn't even know where to go. The capitol? And then what? Kate wasn't there. In his gut, he knew she wasn't there.

The keys he'd picked up were slid from his hand, then deposited in Curtis's pocket, out of reach.

"I've got another set," he grumbled, feeling recalcitrant.

"Take a breath, boy," Curtis repeated. "Let's put our heads together and figure this out."

Swallowing past the lump of emotion lodged in his throat, Travis nodded. He would stay. Not because his father told him to. No, he would stay because he knew that his wrecking ball charm was the last thing anyone needed right now.

He exhaled slowly, nodded to his father. "Fine. I'll stay." He narrowed his eyes. "Just know it's gonna fuckin' kill me to do so."

"Trust me, boy. I know."

As they all stood there feeling helpless, Travis's brothers began to arrive. Sawyer, Braydon, and Kaleb showed up first. Ethan, Zane, and Brendon weren't far behind. He caught bits and pieces of information as Ethan relayed that he'd started calling family, letting them know what had happened and that they needed all hands on deck.

"What can we do?" Sawyer asked Jeff, leading the pack that faced off with the sheriff.

"Right now, I've ordered searches at the capitol building. They'll be going over video footage to see if they can locate who she left with, where they went."

More pain squeezed his insides as he thought about some motherfucker taking his daughter. Rage damn near blinded him, but he fought it back. It was useless at the moment, and the last thing he wanted to do was scare Kylie more than she already was.

"Jessie's on the way over," Braydon said as he approached.

Travis nodded. "Did you call Joe and Melissa?"

"Yep. Joe's scheduled to be home in a couple of hours. Melissa's on her way over."

Being that Joe was an airline pilot, they were lucky Kylie's father could get there quickly. In the meantime, he knew Kylie's stepmother would be able to provide some support.

There was another knock on the door, Travis's attention darting in that direction, as though whoever it was might have his daughter with them.

The sheriff opened the door, stepped back so the newcomers could come inside. Although he recognized them both instantly, it took a second to register why they were there.

Glancing back, he saw Gage had noticed them, too. Though he hated to do it, he passed Kylie off to Curtis, then strolled over to greet Brantley and Reese.

"My sister called," Brantley said, offering his hand. "She's got a friend who works at the school."

Travis nodded, understanding, then shook Reese's hand as well.

"Well, come in," he said softly. "We don't have a lot to go on, but—"

"We're not here to stay, Trav," Brantley said, his voice low, as though he didn't want anyone to overhear.

Travis frowned, confused.

"It looks like you've got plenty of support," Reese said. "We're gonna be your boots on the ground. Just need to get whatever information you have to know where to start."

Travis's sharp inhale was full of emotion as he stared at the two men.

"What do we know?" Brantley asked, stepping in as though he was born to lead.

The fact that he said "we" was telling. When it came to the Walker family, that was what they were. A collective unit, a whole.

"Not a fuck of a lot," Travis grumbled.

"We're doin' everything we can right now," Jeff said, marching over as though he feared they were going to go rogue.

The sheriff knew them well.

"With all due respect, sir," Brantley said, addressing the sheriff, "it's not nearly enough. Until Kate's back where she belongs, it'll never be enough."

Everyone in the room went silent, hearing the clipped edge on Brantley's tone. It was in that moment Travis saw the Navy SEAL, the man who was used to walking into the action, not sitting on the sidelines waiting for it to find him. The difference between them was that Brantley could do so with a level head while Travis tended to lean toward explosive.

"But I'd like to hear what 'everything' entails," Brantley continued when the sheriff didn't say anything.

Jeff glanced at Travis. He nodded his head, urging the sheriff to relay the details. To his credit, Jeff started from the beginning, disseminating every pertinent detail from the point where they believed Kate to have gone missing until now.

"I hate to insinuate this," Brantley stated, turning his attention to Travis. "But do you think this could be personal?"

Gage muttered a curse, and Travis exhaled slowly. "Anything's possible. I've made a lot of friends over the years, but I've made just as many enemies."

Travis wouldn't pretend he was a saint. He'd called in many favors and he hadn't hesitated to reach out to those who could get shit done. He had friends in both high and low places. Everyone from the governor of Texas to a mob boss up in Dallas. And during times like this, he wouldn't hesitate to call in every fucking favor he'd ever garnered.

"But no ransom calls?" Reese inquired, his eyes narrowed.

Travis shook his head. "Not yet."

Brantley nodded. "Unless you have somethin' else for me to do, I'm gonna head over to the capitol, see what shit storm I can stir up there."

"I'll go with you," Reese said. "I've got a couple of friends in APD and my brother can call in a few favors. There'll be no shit storm. We'll do a sweep of the building, check their security feeds, see if we can determine anything."

"We've already asked for security feeds," Jeff told them. "At best, we're looking at tomorrow morning."

"Not good enough," Brantley said, his face expressionless. "I've got ways of gettin' things done."

Travis was stunned speechless. At the moment, he couldn't think beyond his own fear, much less come up with a plan to do what was necessary to bring Kate home. Considering he was always the first to lead the pack, it pained him to feel so helpless.

"We've got you," Brantley said softly, putting a hand on Travis's shoulder. "Just keep us updated and we'll do the same."

Travis nodded.

"I really think you need to let law enforcement handle this," Jeff intervened, although there wasn't much conviction in his tone.

"We won't get in their way," Reese assured him.

Before Jeff could say more, Travis put a hand out to silence him.

"Check in often," Travis told them.

Both men nodded, then turned and left the same way they'd come in.

"Travis, I'm not sure this—"

"How many missin' kids' cases have you handled?" Gage bit out, his voice low, his fury evident.

Jeff's eyes widened, sorrow replacing his frustration. "More than I wanted."

Travis knew that could've meant one or one hundred. And while he trusted Jeff to do what he could, Travis knew law enforcement had its limits. They would do things by the book, one step at a time. And that was fine for many things, but when it came to missing children … fuck the book.

"Let them do their thing," Curtis said, his hand on Travis's shoulder once more. "We'll work it from here."

His father had a way of calming him, even during a time when calm wasn't in his dictionary.

The door opened, Mack strolling in, Jessie not far behind. More people arrived, the house filling with those who wanted to help, everyone attempting to get an update, to find out what they could do.

Travis appreciated everyone, but he couldn't think, could hardly breathe. His heart was lodged securely in his throat as he thought about his little girl. He embraced the pain, gave himself some time to breathe through it because the time would come when he had to shove it down and take matters into his own hands.

After all, Travis had learned long ago … if you wanted shit done, you had to do it yourself.

Then again, he got the feeling Brantley might be the next best thing.

Chapter Eight

BRANTLEY WASTED NO TIME GETTING THEM DOWN to the capitol. Not an easy feat on a Tuesday afternoon, the city flooded with people going about their regular routine. Traffic was a bitch, the streets clogged as businessmen and women headed home for the day.

"Did you ever come to the capitol for a field trip?" Reese asked from the passenger seat.

"Probably. Don't remember that far back."

"I don't either, but I assume we would've made the trek, right? How the fuck is it possible that the teachers chaperoning miscounted the kids? Isn't that like their priority? Ensuring they keep all the kids safe?"

Brantley knew all those questions were rhetorical. Reese was working through this, and evidently, pelting one question after another was his process. Right now, blaming anyone seemed like a waste of time. The objective was to find Kate. They could deal with the how and why after the fact.

"What'd Z say?" In times like these, Brantley knew it paid to have an in with the appropriate people, which was why he was grateful Reese was with him.

"He's callin' in a few favors. Askin' for us to get access to do a search."

Probably wouldn't help because he had to believe the APD and state troopers were capable of doing their jobs, but it would go a long damn way to making Brantley feel better.

Ten minutes later, they learned that Z had come through for them. As they strolled into the capitol building, they were escorted by one of the troopers assigned to the building, a man who explained he would accompany them on a full sweep while the Austin Police Department finished up their initial search.

"Have you been on duty all afternoon?" Brantley asked.

"Yes," David Zeck confirmed. "Since early this morning."

"Did anything out of the ordinary happen here today?"

"No. Normal day. Lots of visitors moving through."

"No fire alarms pulled, no metal detectors going off unnecessarily?"

"Standard day," he said, his patience admirable. "And since we learned of the missing girl, we've been scouring the building top to bottom. They've checked everything."

"Well, we're gonna check it again," Brantley stated, leaving no room for argument.

"Understand." David motioned for them to follow. "As soon as it was brought to our attention, we did a full sweep of the building. There were three field trips here today, all elementary schools."

"No one else missin'?" Reese inquired.

"No. We contacted the other two schools. They confirmed all their students are accounted for."

Which likely meant this was personal. Brantley figured there'd been somewhere around one hundred students wandering the halls of the state capitol. The odds that Kate was randomly selected by the kidnapper were slim. If that were the case, they would've grabbed the first kid available. Otherwise, it would've been all based on timing.

"What about video footage?" he asked, stepping into what appeared to be the security office.

"We monitor the grounds and the building day and night. There are hours of footage from a couple dozen cameras. Our techs are currently sifting through them."

"No issues with the cameras?" Reese asked.

David cleared his throat.

Brantley stopped, waited for the officer to tell him what had his shoulders tensing.

"The cameras at the back exits, as well as one overseeing the staff parking lot were disabled for at least fifteen minutes during the time we believe she disappeared."

Inhaling deeply, Brantley leveled his gaze on the man. "Please tell me this is information that's been relayed to the necessary authorities."

"Yes, of course."

The way David's eyes shifted slightly to the left told Brantley he was lying. This was information they were keeping to themselves. At least for now.

"I want to see the footage," Reese stated.

"Unfortunately, that's not something we can provide."

Before Reese could counter, Brantley put a hand on his shoulder, halted him.

"If you don't mind, we're gonna give ourselves a tour," he told the officer. "If there's anyone you need to notify, you should do so now."

With that, Brantley turned and walked out of the security office, Reese keeping pace beside him.

"I coulda—"

Brantley cut him off by raising a hand even as he pulled out his phone. He brought up his contacts, found JJ's number, and dialed.

"Hey, handsome. To what do I owe the honor?"

"I need a favor," he said easily, peering around at the wide hallway, the white walls, and the various paintings hung throughout.

"Whatcha got?"

"I need to see the video footage of the cameras at the capitol. From roughly noon today until now."

JJ choked on a laugh. "You're kidding me, right? Brantley, what—"

"There's a kid's life at stake here," he growled softly into the phone. "I need you to do whatever it is you do to find her."

"Oh, my God, Brantley."

Feeling shitty for not easing her into it, Brantley exhaled and offered a quick explanation of what they'd learned about Kate Walker's disappearance.

"They confirmed she was with them for lunch, but at some point after that, she disappeared. Find whatever you can, JJ. And if you do get a bead on her, get me the information on the vehicle she left in and where they went."

"Of course," she said quickly. "I'll do what I can. But you should know, I don't have the necessary tools at my disposal right this minute."

"Go to my place," he insisted. "You'll find what you need in the barn. Use your date of birth to get in. I'll set the code up now. I need this, JJ. There's no time to waste."

"Absolutely. I'll hit you back when I know something."

Brantley disconnected the call, tucked his phone in his pocket, and turned to see Reese staring at him.

"Well, that's handy."

He smiled, but there was no humor in it. "JJ's got skills."

"Sounds like it."

He took another quick look around. "Let's do this, shall we?"

Two hours later, they'd made a trip through every office, every storage room, every nook and cranny in the building, and as Brantley expected, there were no signs of Kate. His anxiety level had ratcheted up a few notches during the search, as had his anger. It wasn't that he thought he was some sort of superhero who could find a lost kid because he willed it to happen, but Brantley wanted some sort of lead to go on.

Anything.

Based on the last time the teachers had seen Kate, she'd been missing for roughly six hours and no one had heard from the kidnapper. He did not want to think about what that could possibly mean. At some point since he'd heard the news, he had started banking on this being a kidnap and ransom scenario. The asshole who took Kate would call Travis, make his demands. At that point, Travis would give the assholes what they wanted, and Kate would be returned safe and sound.

If this wasn't a ploy to extort money from Travis Walker, then that meant the little girl was in serious danger. He refused to consider what that bastard might've done to Kate during the time she'd been—

His cell phone rang as they were getting into his truck. Brantley could feel Reese's eyes on him, which was why he chose to take the call through the Bluetooth in the truck.

"Yeah, JJ. Whaddya got?"

"First, let me say, you've got some magnificent toys here, Brantley. I'm a little pissed I didn't know about 'em before now."

Attempting to rein in his patience, he exhaled heavily.

"Okay, sorry," she said quickly. "I was able to hack into the cameras. They've got plenty of them, I might add. And all seemed to be working fine with the exception of several leading out the back of the building and a couple in the parking lot. They lost the feeds for sixteen minutes."

"That's what we were told," he said, pulling his truck out of the parking lot so he could wind his way back to the highway.

"There's no way that wasn't planned. Whoever took Kate had an extraction plan and they took the cameras down for their getaway. However…"

Brantley could hear her typing, waited.

"I compared a shot of the parking lot before the cameras went down to one when they came back online. There are three vehicles missing in the later picture. A grey Ford Expedition, a blue Altima, and a silver Audi. The Altima and Audi are registered to state employees."

"And the Expedition?" Reese inquired.

"Oh, hey," JJ said, clearly surprised by the voice.

"I've got Reese with me," Brantley explained. "What do you have on the Expedition?"

"No plates, of course. Kidnapper knew what she was doing. And the image I've got is grainy at best, but I can make out a blond woman in the driver's seat."

Brantley glanced at Reese, then back to the road. "A woman?"

"Yeah. Unfortunately, I don't have the necessary software for facial rec, and even if I did, I don't think it'd be enough to go on."

"Can you send me a picture of the woman? I'll take it back to Travis, see if he recognizes her."

"Yep." There was a slight pause. "Done. Oh, and I reached out to Dante, explained what was going on."

"What can he do?" Reese asked.

"Dante's the governor's son," Brantley explained. "And the guy JJ's dating."

"Ah."

"We're headin' back now," Brantley told JJ. "Gonna stop at Travis's, show him the picture."

"If you don't mind, I'll just stay here," JJ replied. "Keep diggin'. Not sure it'll help, but I feel like I've got to do somethin'."

"I appreciate it," he told her. "See you in a bit."

He disconnected the call and passed his phone to Reese. "Check out the image."

"You think I'll recognize her?" he asked, taking the phone.

"You never know."

Brantley drove in silence for a few minutes, attempting to keep from violating too many traffic laws as he headed back to Coyote Ridge. Thankfully, the toll road would take them most of the way, the eighty-mile-per-hour posted speed limit his friend.

"I got nothin'," Reese noted, referring to the image he was looking at. "Mind if I shoot this to Z? I know Sniper 1's got some nifty software. I'll see if they can get a hit."

"Go ahead."

At this point, Brantley would do whatever it took to take something back to Travis.

IN ORDER TO SEND THE IMAGE, REESE had to pull up Brantley's text message app. He'd had every intention of sending the picture to his phone so he could shoot it over to Z. He hadn't planned on opening the app to find it was on an ongoing message thread between Brantley and Cyrus.

It was a huge invasion of privacy to read the conversation on the screen, but he found himself doing just that. What that said about him, he didn't know. Nor was he sure he wanted to know.

Evidently, Brantley and Cyrus were spending quite a bit of time together. The last message had been from Cyrus, letting Brantley know he would be stopping by. That had been last night a little after ten. The response from Brantley was what he continued to stare at, his mind whirling.

Door'll be unlocked. No talking tonight, Cyrus. Your mouth's gonna be plenty busy.

His breath caught as an image of Brantley and Cyrus flashed in his mind. But it wasn't heat that inundated him. No, Reese would have to say his immediate reaction bordered on jealousy. For some fucking reason, he didn't like the idea of Cyrus paying late-night visits to Brantley.

Of course, that made absolutely no sense. Brantley could do whatever the hell he pleased. Reese didn't have any claims to the man. Hell, he was straight, for fuck's sake. Why the hell should he care that Brantley was getting it on with another man?

"You okay?"

Tearing his eyes from the screen, Reese glanced out the window to see they were about to exit the toll road.

"Yeah. Sorry."

He cut his eyes to Brantley, noticed the man was watching him, a frown marring his forehead.

"Took a minute to save the image so I could forward it," he lied even as he did just that. A second later, he texted the picture to himself, noticing Brantley hadn't deleted their text thread, which had grown longer over the last month or so. Not a huge consolation, considering.

After passing back Brantley's phone, Reese pulled out his own. He sent a quick message to Z, informing his brother of what he needed, then put his phone away. He stared out the window, trying to erase the image of Brantley and Cyrus from his brain.

It wasn't working.

In fact, that foreign sensation continued to intensify. Jealousy, anger, he couldn't really tell the difference. Or maybe it was simply frustration over the fact that his wires had gotten crossed somewhere along the way. There was no way he was thinking about Brantley as anything more than a friend. No way the mere thought of Brantley and another man would bother him. It wasn't like he wanted the guy.

You sure about that?

With a heavy exhale, he tried to remember what they were doing. The more pressing matter of a missing girl.

"What's on your mind, Reese?"

The sound of Brantley's voice surprised him, making him flinch.

"Hey, now," Brantley said softly as he reached over, touched Reese's arm.

The warmth of his hand drew Reese's attention, had him staring at the that big hand curling around his wrist as it offered a reassuring squeeze.

"We're gonna find her. Bring her home safely."

Brantley had misunderstood Reese's response. Thank God for small favors.

He was still staring at Brantley's hand on his arm, wondering why the fuck he didn't pull away. There was nothing sexual about the touch, but the man's mouth could've been on him for all the heat that slammed through him.

Not that he wanted that.

He didn't.

What the fuck?

"I know. We'll find her," he echoed.

Brantley's hand disappeared and Reese instantly felt the absence of his touch.

By the time they arrived at Travis's fifteen minutes later, Reese had managed to get himself under control. He chalked up his reaction to the shocking events of the day. Finding out Travis's daughter was missing had taken its toll on him, and it was his inability to do anything to fix it that had him seeking solace where there shouldn't be any.

However, his reaction hadn't gone unnoticed by Brantley. The man was watching him closely, as though he was worried he would go postal at any given moment.

"JJ was able to get this image from the security cameras at the capitol," Brantley said to Travis and Gage.

He went on to explain the way the cameras had been taken offline, then brought back up. How JJ had compared a before and after to identify the three vehicles that had left the premises during that time. It was actually a pretty simple yet brilliant way of making the deduction. Reese was impressed. Mainly because no one else had thought of it.

"Do you recognize her?" Brantley asked.

Travis stared at the image on the phone screen for long seconds. "No. I don't."

He passed it over to Gage, who gave it the same assessing review before shaking his head.

"You're thinking a woman kidnapped my daughter?"

"I'm not thinkin' anything right now," Brantley said quickly. "But this is what we have. Could be nothing, but I'm gonna follow it until it fizzles out if that's the case."

"Should we provide the image to the sheriff?" Reese prompted, looking more to Gage for a response since he was a former police officer.

"We can, but he won't be able to do anything with it. You have nothing to show she left with that woman at all. For all we know, she was dropping someone off or had some other business inside."

"Okay, but I've asked my brother to run the image in their system. See if they can get a hit on it."

"Doubtful," Gage mused. "The image's too grainy."

"Right now, even the smallest lead is still a lead," Brantley declared, his voice firm, as though he needed Gage to hear his intentions. "It's worth a shot."

"You're right." Gage stepped up next to Travis, their shoulders touching.

Reese had always admired the way the two men were so easy with their affections. Both for one another and for Kylie. Although Travis had hidden who he was for a long time, when he finally accepted what he wanted, he hadn't tried to keep others from figuring it out.

And oddly, Reese had found himself jealous of Travis a time or two. Not because he was married to a man and a woman—the best of both worlds according to some—but because he went after what he wanted. There were times Reese wondered if the guy was superhuman, lacking the doubt and uncertainty the rest of them were plagued with.

"JJ's back at my house doing some more digging," Brantley offered. "I figure we'll head back there, see how we can help."

It was then Reese saw the fear in Travis's eyes. The man was hanging by a thread. Not surprising because his daughter was still missing and the only thing they had to go on was a fucking grainy image of a blond woman who no one recognized.

"Sheriff Endsley get anything?" Reese asked.

"They've gotten an influx of calls in response to the Amber Alert. People claiming they've seen Kate. Nothing's panned out yet."

"We'll keep looking," Brantley assured him. "Anything you need, call me. I don't care what time it is. I don't sleep much as it is."

Reese watched as Travis easily hugged Brantley. It was a testament to how close their family was. Which was another thing Reese envied about Travis. He had the love of his family and they were all there, nearby at all times. Something that wasn't the case for Reese. Hadn't been for a long damn time.

"Let me know if you hear something," Brantley stated, then shook Gage's hand.

Reese said his goodbyes to both men, then stuck his head in the kitchen, noticed all the women and men crowded around Kylie. She looked as though she was hanging by a fragile thread, too, and any minor tug would send her spiraling. He couldn't imagine how hard this was for her. Hell, Kate wasn't his daughter, but his own fear was prevalent.

Not wanting to interrupt, he returned to see Brantley had stepped outside. He found him waiting, leaning against the chrome grille of his big Chevy. When he saw him approaching, Brantley pushed off the truck and headed for the driver's side.

Neither of them said much during the few minutes it took to get from Travis's to Brantley's. Once the truck came to a stop, Reese quickly got out, feeling the need to move around. He wasn't sure what it was but being in a confined space with Brantley was … it was getting to him, that was what it was doing. Every second he was with Brantley, he was wrought with confusion.

"All right, Tavoularis. What's up with you?"

Reese spun around to face Brantley. "What are you talkin' about?"

Brantley sighed, putting his hands on his hips, his T-shirt stretching over his chest muscles. Probably not something Reese should've been noticing, but he was. Again.

"Ever since you snooped in my phone, you've been … upset."

"Upset?" He snorted. "Why the fuck would I be upset?"

"You tell me."

Frowning, Reese mirrored Brantley's stance, facing off with his hands on his hips.

"You have somethin' to say to me?" Brantley prompted.

"About…?"

"I don't know. Maybe the text messages you read."

For a brief moment, Reese considered denying the accusation, telling Brantley he'd done no such thing. Problem was, Reese wasn't one to lie. Certainly not about shit that meant nothing.

He sighed, dropped his arms. "I just didn't realize you and Cyrus were … so close. Took me by surprise. That's all."

In the twilight, Reese could see the smirk on Brantley's face, the glitter in his eyes as he took a step closer.

"What makes you think we're close?"

"He's your booty call, Walker."

That fucking half smirk tilted the corner of Brantley's mouth, his dimple winking back at him. "And this bothers you?"

"Hell no," he said a bit too quickly.

Brantley's gaze scanned his face slowly, pausing on Reese's lips.

For the first time in his thirty years, Reese felt a stirring inside him. It wasn't the pull that was foreign. No, it was his strange attraction to this man. This man, for fuck's sake. No denying it freaked him out a little, but he wasn't the sort to make excuses. Yes, he was attracted to Brantley. It made no sense whatsoever, but it was a fact, nonetheless.

But like everything else, it would pass.

Fixing his gaze to Brantley's, Reese held his ground, realizing the man had stepped closer. He would not be intimidated. Not like this.

"Tell me, Reese, would you prefer you were the one I was texting?"

Those words were said in that invariably low rasp, the sound scraping over Reese's nerves in a way it shouldn't have.

There was maybe an inch difference in their height—Brantley just a hair shorter—which meant they were eye to eye, nose to nose, chest to chest. Thinking about the logistics of them coming together in an intimate manner … it should've pissed him off, had him stumbling back. It didn't.

"I noticed you're not sayin' no, Tavoularis."

He wasn't. But he should've been.

The distance between them diminished until they were practically sharing air. Reese knew he wasn't the one who'd moved closer, but he wasn't stepping back, either. He wanted to say it was pride that kept him rooted in place. He wasn't about to let Brantley bully him.

But no, that wasn't it at all.

For some fucked-up reason, Reese wanted to know just how far Brantley would push.

Chapter Nine

CHRIST ALMIGHTY.

Brantley's adrenaline had spiked the instant he'd seen the glitter of a dare in Reese's golden eyes.

The man was so close he could feel Reese's breath fanning his face. It would be the work of a moment to close the scant few inches and press his lips to Reese's. But as much as he wanted that, he wouldn't dare. He was not about to take advantage of the moment. They were both worked up from events of the day. The fear for Kate's safety was making him see things that weren't there.

Realizing he had to get a handle on this situation, Brantley leaned back, let his gaze drop to Reese's mouth briefly before returning to hold the man's intense stare.

While he wasn't going to take what he wanted, he wasn't above pushing to see which direction it might be leading.

"What is this, Reese?"

That golden gaze dropped to his mouth and Brantley felt his lungs constrict. Oh, yeah, he could see the curiosity there. And there was no ignoring the temptation the man presented. Brantley wouldn't deny he had a thing for the guy. Hell, he'd been fucking Cyrus nightly in an effort to expel Reese Tavoularis from his thoughts. It wasn't working, but that didn't mean he wasn't doing his damnedest.

"Are you jealous of Cyrus?" He wasn't sure why he was provoking him, but he couldn't seem to stop.

He noticed the tic in Reese's jaw. "I don't know."

Shocked to the soles of his boots, Brantley took a step back, then another, attempting to grasp what he'd said. "What?"

"You asked, I answered."

Yeah, he'd answered in a way Brantley hadn't expected. This was not the way he'd envisioned this playing out. Sure, he enjoyed flirting with Reese, messing with the guy because he knew Reese could handle it. But he certainly hadn't expected such a candid response.

"Surprised?" Reese taunted.

Shaking off the weird vibe he was getting, Brantley forced a smile. "How 'bout we pretend this conversation never happened."

"I didn't figure you for a coward, Walker."

Okay, now. That got his hackles up, had him stepping in, this time moving in so that his lips were dangerously close to Reese's.

When the man's breath hitched, Brantley realized he'd been pushing him for this response. Reese wasn't lying when he said he didn't know if he was jealous, but he wasn't going to make a move. Which meant he was forcing Brantley to make it.

"You're throwin' mixed signals here," he countered hotly, "and I damn sure don't appreciate it."

The sound of tires on gravel had Brantley's shoulders tensing even as Reese leaned over, peered around him.

"Looks like your boyfriend's here. It's almost like he knew this was gonna happen."

"What was gonna happen?"

Reese's gaze bounced back and forth over his face, but he didn't answer the question. Instead, said, "Probably should back up now. Wouldn't want Cyrus gettin' any ideas."

Because he was never one to do what people expected, Brantley leaned in a little more, keeping his voice low when he said, "You're right. He's a booty call. He comes over late, lets me fuck him until we're both exhausted, then he falls asleep in my bed."

There was a soft growl coming from Reese, which, if truth be told, was the response Brantley had been hoping for.

"You wanna know if I enjoy it, don't you?"

Those brown eyes glittered as they narrowed.

"I do, Reese. It gives me a chance to live out my fantasies."

"Fantasies?"

Cyrus's car door slammed shut and Brantley knew he was heading toward them.

"Yeah. Because when I'm with him, it's your mouth I imagine wrapped around my dick." He dropped his voice another octave. "It's you I'm fuckin', Reese. Every. Goddamn. Night."

Reese's sharp inhale was drowned out by Cyrus's greeting just as Brantley was stepping back, putting space between them. Brantley turned to face his friend, gave him a friendly smile.

"What brings you by?" he asked, ensuring his tone lacked any of the hunger he had for the man behind him.

"I heard what was goin' on." Cyrus glanced between them. "With Travis. Thought I'd stop by, see if I could help."

"I appreciate it." He glanced back at Reese. "You stayin' or you headin' out?"

Reese's eyes had hardened, and Brantley fully expected him to bow out. He'd understand because what had just transpired between them had been spurred by something out of their control. He wasn't going to hold this over Reese and he prayed like hell Reese would do the same. Last thing he wanted was to lose a friendship over some misguided emotion.

"I think I'll stay."

Surprised but not disappointed, Brantley offered a small smile. "I was thinkin' I'd order pizza. You hungry?"

"Starving," Cyrus replied, evidently thinking the question had been directed at him.

"Good. I need to check on JJ first. Then I'll place the order. Go on in. I'll be there in a few."

He could tell Reese didn't care to go in without him, but Brantley didn't give a shit. Right now he needed a minute to pull himself together. He was reeling from his admission, pissed at himself for letting Reese push him that far. What the man was up to, he had no idea, but he didn't like this shit. He wasn't interested in games and clearly Reese was maneuvering chess pieces to suit himself.

By the time he reached the barn, he had managed to calm down. When he found JJ sitting in front of the monitors, on a trash can she'd overturned, he couldn't help but laugh.

"You owe me a neck rub," she said easily, her eyes still on the screen in front of her as she hooked her hand over her neck as though it ached.

"Me?"

"Yeah." JJ huffed, peered up at him. "The least you could do is get appropriate seating in here."

"It's a work in progress," he said defensively. "Find anything else out?"

Her disappointment rang out when she said, "No."

When she hung her head, Brantley walked around behind her, placed his hands on her shoulders, rubbed firmly. She let out a soft moan, dropped her head forward to allow his hands to move over the tense muscles.

"Do the police have anything yet?" she asked.

"No. We stopped by Travis's, showed them the picture. No one recognizes her."

"I didn't figure they would. Her face is too obscured. I'm tryin' to clean it up but…"

"We're not expectin' you to be a miracle worker, JJ."

"Maybe not, but I've got to do somethin'."

Brantley understood her desire to solve this, because he felt the same.

"You know who's also a whiz on the computer?" JJ prompted, lifting her head and shrugging her shoulders.

Releasing her, Brantley took a step back. "Who?"

"Cyrus."

It was true. Cyrus was a software engineer, had skills to rival JJ's and a different sort of experience.

"Are you suggestin' he work with you?"

"I'll take anything right now, Brantley. Anything that'll give me a thread to pull."

Understanding, he nodded. "Well, why don't you take a break. I'll order pizza, you can toss your ideas at Cyrus. See what he thinks."

"Cyrus is here?" she asked, grinning.

"He is."

"And Reese?"

"Yeah. Why?"

"And you're not worried about that dynamic duo?"

Brantley frowned. "What are you talkin' about?"

"Oh, come on, B. I know Cyrus as well as you do." She stood, grinned. "Okay, maybe not quite as well, but I know he's got a mischievous side."

"So?"

"You don't see it, do you?"

"See what, JJ?"

"This thing with Reese."

"There's no thing with Reese."

"Isn't there?"

Frustrated with the circuitous route of this conversation, Brantley motioned for her to head to the door. "No, there's not."

"Then you're blind. But whatever." She headed for the door. "But we both know Cyrus likes to fuck with people and he's gonna pick up on Reese's fascination with you sooner or later, if he hasn't already. And you know what that means, don't you?"

"Right now, JJ, I don't know a fuckin' thing. You're twistin' my brain in knots with this shit."

"As soon as Cyrus realizes he can get a rise outta Reese, he's gonna go for the jugular. You know there's nothin' serious with Cyrus, and Cyrus knows there's nothin' serious, but that doesn't mean he won't play it up for the audience."

"Well, he'd be wastin' his time with Reese. The guy's a friend." He would've said a straight friend up until ten minutes ago. Now he wasn't so sure.

"You go on dates with all your guy friends? Spend all your time with them?"

"I am not spendin' all my time with him." Okay, fine, he sounded extremely defensive here.

Clearly she noticed because JJ chuckled as they stepped out into the night. "Whatever you say."

"How 'bout you drop the subject and I'll spring for cinnamon bread."

JJ grabbed his arm, threaded hers through, and peered up at him with wide eyes. "You really are my hero."

"I thought that was Dante's status," he grumbled.

"Speaking of…" JJ released him. "He told his dad what was going on. Governor Greenwood wants him to keep him apprised of the situation."

Brantley wasn't sure how that would benefit anyone, but he wasn't going to argue the point. The more people who were working on this case, the faster they could get Kate home. Which was the only thing that mattered.

"You don't think this is random, do you? That woman takin' Kate from the capitol? Seems too well-planned."

"No, I don't think it's random. Just a gut feelin'." And yes, he did believe that woman had taken Kate. They had no hard evidence to confirm his suspicion, but Brantley wholeheartedly believed she was the key to all of this.

"Well, I don't think your gut's ever steered you wrong."

Brantley wasn't so sure about that, but he tended to listen to it.

And right now, there wasn't much else he could do.

Unfortunately.

TRAVIS PACED HIS LIVING ROOM, BOOTS SHUFFLING over the hardwood, hands fisting and unclenching at his sides, anger coalescing with fear, worry superseding anything and everything, threatening to morph into a full-blown panic.

As of half an hour ago, four of his children had been put to bed. Four, not five.

And because of that, he knew there would be no sleep for him tonight. Instead he would pace the house in the event the fucking kidnapper called, praying they would.

When he wasn't pacing, he was glancing at the picture he'd had Brantley send to him. The one of the woman they suspected had taken Kate out of the capitol. His gaze skimmed past the woman in the driver's seat, as though it would allow him to see his little girl somewhere behind her. Was she buckled in safely? Or had the woman had to do something to restrain her?

The thought of Kate tied up had a sob escaping. He prayed like hell Kate came home safely. There'd better not be a single bruise marring her flesh, otherwise there would be hell to pay.

"Hey."

The gruff greeting had Travis turning to see Gage stepping into the living room. His eyes were bloodshot from the tears he'd shed throughout the afternoon. His hair was sticking up because he'd run his fingers through it from the stress of it all. Of course, Travis figured he looked no better. God knew he felt like warmed-over dog shit.

"Hey." Travis glanced back down at the phone, then resisted the urge to throw the damn thing through the window.

It was then his own tears emerged like a flood. The pain in his chest threatened to take him out at the knees.

"Baby…" Gage was instantly there, holding him up off the floor as Travis let the fear and anger merge into a storm that had been building all day.

His heart was breaking, cracked right down the fucking middle at the thought of Kate out there by herself. No one to hold her, to tuck her in, to tell her they loved her.

"Where is she? God, where is she, Gage?" he sobbed, his arms wreathing his husband as though he was a lifeline.

Rather than offer placating words, Gage cradled the back of Travis's head with his big hand, holding him tightly, keeping him together while he himself was splintering on the inside.

As much as Travis needed him, he knew it wasn't enough. Right now, their wife was in their bed, likely tossing and turning as she was forced to sleep thanks to the sleeping meds the doctor had given her. It had been the only option in keeping Kylie from losing it. The only option because Travis hadn't brought their daughter back to them.

How the fuck did people deal with this? He knew Kate wasn't the only child to go missing. He knew there were hundreds, maybe thousands of parents who endured this living hell every year, some never getting closure. His heart ached for them, but deep down, he prayed they weren't one of those parents. He wasn't sure he could go on without Kate. Along with the other four, they made up the whole of his heart.

"Shh," Gage whispered. "I've got you."

Yeah, he did.

But for the first time since he'd fallen in love with the man and woman who completed him in ways no one else ever had or would, Travis hated to admit … it wasn't enough.

ᴀ𝑒ℓ

REESE WAS SITTING ON THE COUCH, WHICH doubled as a bed in his small studio apartment. With a pillow under his head, his legs stretched out, he stared at the laptop propped on his thighs.

He'd been home for about an hour, having spent most of the evening at Brantley's with Cyrus giving him the stink-eye for being there. It was the only reason he'd stayed for so long, trying to wait out the other man. Something inside him had hoped Cyrus would leave, but he didn't know why he gave a fuck.

Except that darkly possessive need hadn't abated, no matter how much time had passed. The more Cyrus seemed to be sticking around, the worse it got until finally Reese risked doing something that was absolutely, positively asinine. In an effort to save face, Reese had been the one to jet, instead telling Brantley he'd be in touch if he heard anything from Z.

He hadn't. Heard anything, that was. Z had kindly checked in to let him know they were running that woman's face through their software and reaching out to people they knew in the area to see if she was anyone they'd run across before. So far, nothing.

And Reese felt as helpless as everyone else.

So, plagued with thoughts of Kate, the little girl who affectionately referred to him as Uncle Reese although there was no relation, he'd been staring at his laptop wondering what else he could do. Where he could look, what earth he could plow up to find the little girl with the quick smile and a million questions. He couldn't count how many events he'd spent with the Walkers, how many times he'd seen one or more of those little ones run by, giggling for one reason or another.

To think someone would want to harm a single hair on their heads…

Reese sighed, forcing his hands to relax from the fists they'd balled into.

Just another reason he would never be having children.

His thoughts drifted to his own parents. Thomas and Cindy had been phenomenal parents, giving their all to their three children. It still pained him to think his father had died without seeing them one last time. Back in 2011, Thomas had been in a car accident that had left him in a coma. For years, they'd prayed relentlessly that Thomas would open his eyes and come back to them.

He never had.

Years of waiting, watching over him, praying had turned into weeks of discussion, a final agreement to remove him from life support being the consensus. It had been a gut-wrenching decision for all of them, but in the end, Reese had known it was the right thing to do. The hope had shifted to grief as the four of them stood over Reese's father while the doctor shut down the equipment. Not long after, Thomas had left them for good, taking his place among the angels.

And while he was gone, he was definitely not forgotten. Every now and then, Reese would talk to his dad as though he was still here. Probably had to do with the fact he'd sat at the man's bedside for years doing exactly that.

"We could use your help now, Dad," he said to the empty space. It was no longer the one he'd grown up in. After his father passed, it had been too difficult for Reese to remain there. His mother had sold the house and Reese had gotten an apartment in one of the two complexes in Coyote Ridge. It had been pure luck that it had come available when he'd needed it. Then again, he'd always wondered if Travis had had something to do with it.

For a few minutes, he shared the details, speaking them aloud as though Thomas Tavoularis could possibly hear and assist in some way.

"They're my family, Dad," he whispered. "They've become my family over the years."

Like Z, who had the Kogans and Trexlers for his extended family, Reese had the Walkers. Although he hadn't expected to get caught up in their world, he would admit he appreciated them. Their love and support helped him get through every cold, bleak day as well as the days filled with sunshine.

His cell phone chimed, the sound overly loud in the otherwise silent room. He lunged for it, praying it was a text from Travis to let him know Kate had been found safe and sound.

No such luck, he realized when he saw the message had come from Brantley.

You awake?

Reese debated on whether he should respond. It would be in his best interest to allow some distance to grow between them. After their encounter earlier, he knew he was getting dangerously close to altering what he'd been sure was a pretty straightforward existence.

Problem was, he didn't want distance from Brantley. In fact, he'd go so far as to say he wanted more time with the man. If for no other reason than to figure out what the hell was going on.

Selfish? Yeah, probably.

With a resigned sigh, he typed in a response: Yeah. Any news?

Can I call you?

Call him? Reese wasn't sure he wanted to hear Brantley's voice. Not right now while the memories were so fresh in his mind. However, if it pertained to Travis, he wasn't about to say no.

Rather than respond, he hit the button to place the call.

"Hey, man," Brantley greeted, his voice sounding strained. "You okay?"

"I … uh … yeah. Just a headache."

He'd thought Brantley had been acting off earlier. It had seemed to come on suddenly, while they'd been eating pizza. Reese had noticed his quick smile had dimmed and he'd started to retreat from the conversation. Now it all made sense.

"Did you take somethin' for it?"

"Not yet. Will. Once I can."

Reese sat up straight, staring at the dark television in front of him. "What does that mean?"

"I get 'em all the time. Compliments … of the mission gone sideways. Nothin' to worry about."

Reese wasn't buying that, but he didn't say anything.

"Just wanted to tell you I'm sorry 'bout earlier. I shouldn't've said the things I did."

Brantley's words were slurred, but not like he'd had too much to drink. Reese could hear the pain in his voice.

"Are you at home?"

"Yep."

"Is Cyrus there?"

"Sent him away," Brantley muttered, followed by a whispered mumble that sounded oddly like, "Not you."

No, he wasn't touching that with a ten-foot pole, but he did say, "I'm comin' over."

Brantley didn't respond, but Reese could hear him breathing, knew he hadn't hung up.

"I'll be there in ten. Stay where you are."

A grunt was the reply he heard before the line disconnected.

Reese got to his feet, tucked his phone in the pocket of his athletic shorts. He took the time to snag a T-shirt from his dresser, pulled it on, then tugged on a pair of Adidas he kept near the front door. He didn't bother with socks, instead grabbed his keys and locked up.

He made it to Brantley's in just under ten minutes, pulling into the drive to see the house was dark and only Brantley's big Chevy was parked in front of it.

Hoping the door was unlocked, he double-timed it up the porch steps, yanked open the screen, tried the knob. He was grateful it opened because it meant he wouldn't have to pick the lock to let himself in.

Rather than shout his presence, he kept his voice low, warning Brantley not to shoot him.

He found the man in his bed, a blanket pulled over his lap, his chest bare. The room was dark save for moonlight that slipped in through the cracks in the blinds over the two single windows on each side of the bed.

"Where's your meds?" he whispered, placing a gentle hand on Brantley's shoulder.

"Bathroom," came the mumbled response.

Reese set his keys and phone on the dresser, made his way to the bathroom. He found a prescription bottle in the medicine cabinet, skimmed the label. It was prescribed for pain and appeared to be full.

Looked as though Brantley had an aversion to pain pills. Probably fucking sucked in times like this.

He shook out the correct dose, then headed to the kitchen to retrieve a bottle of water. He cracked the lid open on the return to the bedroom.

"I want you to take this," he urged, keeping his voice low.

Brantley didn't move, but Reese could see his face was pinched with pain.

Easing onto the edge of the mattress, he slid one hand beneath Brantley's neck and lifted him so he could get the pill down him.

He knew better than to ask questions because noises alone would make his situation worse. Reese had witnessed his mother enduring migraine headaches for years and he remembered the debilitating state she'd be in during an episode.

Good thing he didn't need to talk to do a few more things to help the guy. The pain pill would hopefully do the trick. The problem was, it would take time. Until then, he needed to keep Brantley comfortable, ease him somehow.

Then he recalled his mother putting cold soda cans against the back of her neck. He remembered asking her why the first time he'd witnessed it. She'd said something about the pressure and the cold provided more relief than anything else she'd ever done.

Reese made another trip to the kitchen, found an energy drink in the refrigerator. Figuring it would work just fine, he returned to the bedroom and into the attached bath. He grabbed a washcloth out of the towel closet, got it wet with cold water, then wrung out the excess.

This time when he returned, he didn't say a word. He walked around to the side Brantley was on, maneuvered him until he had the cold can beneath his neck, the pillow adjusted to allow his neck to rest against it, then placed the washcloth on his forehead, ensuring it covered his eyes in the event the moonlight was too much stimulation for his battered head.

Brantley didn't speak, but his breathing was still labored, his bare chest rising and falling as Reese observed. Yeah, so his gaze lingered on all that smooth, sun-bronzed skin, along the contours of his pectorals, past the small, dark nipples, lower … down to the thin trail of hair that disappeared beneath the sheet.

There was a niggling in the back of his mind that told him it wasn't normal for him to be ogling this man, but the rational side of his brain said he wasn't hurting anyone.

It wasn't like he hadn't seen a man before. Hell, he'd been in athletics in school and then in the Air Force for eight years. He'd been around plenty of half-dressed men. Funny how, before now, he'd never had any sort of reaction to one. Not so much as a stirring in his blood.

That wasn't the case with Brantley, and he had no fucking clue what it all meant. Worse, what he should do about it. If anything.

If he was smart, he'd walk away.

Too bad smart seemed to have left the building.

Chapter Ten

BRANTLEY WOKE IN A QUIET ROOM, HIS brain foggy but his headache blessedly gone.

As was the case anytime he recovered from the sort of pain that assaulted him without warning, he took his time opening his eyes, not wanting to do anything that might bring the fucking agony blazing through his head again.

He heard someone breathing deeply nearby and he tried to think back to the events of last night. He remembered having pizza with his friends. A hint of animosity flickering between Reese and Cyrus. Reese had left shortly after the meal, JJ next. Then Cyrus had made his usual attempt to seduce him, but by that point, Brantley'd been in too much pain.

The headache had been his excuse for not taking Cyrus up on the offer, but Brantley knew it had been more than that. Reese's admission that he didn't know if he was jealous or not... Yeah, no matter how hard he tried, Brantley couldn't stop thinking about that.

By the time Cyrus had taken his leave, the headache that had come on strong had blazed through his head, making lights and sounds unbearable. His bed had been his only destination but that was about where it all got fuzzy.

Had Cyrus come back to check on him sometime during the night? Given him the medication that would put him under, the same meds he refused to take because they weren't his thing and he damn sure had no intention of making them his thing?

Brantley shifted, turning his head toward the heavy breathing. It was then he realized there was a washcloth covering his eyes. He dragged it off his face but kept his eyes closed. The room brightened significantly behind his closed lids, which he took to mean it was morning.

He reached over, letting his hand move along the arm he located first. His hand brushed fingers, slowly sliding upward over a wrist, higher. He felt the forearm and realized there was no way that was Cyrus. Too much muscle.

"Please tell me you're not gonna feel me up in my sleep."

Brantley smiled at the familiar rasp of Reese's voice. A frisson of warmth curled within him at the thought of Reese in his bed.

"Not unless you want me to," he said, his voice gravelly from sleep.

"Mmm."

His brain registered that as a noncommittal mumble. His body … not so much. Without moving his hand from Reese's arm, Brantley turned toward him, eyes slowly coming open to peek at the man.

Reese was in his bed, propped up on a pillow as though he'd been reclining against the headboard initially but had slowly slid down until he was on his back.

"Did you take advantage of me?" Brantley teased. "Because I feel as though you might have."

"Keep dreamin', Navy boy," Reese said, his eyes still closed, face relaxed.

That frisson of heat from a few moments ago turned into an inferno. Brantley's body blazed to life, his blood churning faster in his veins at the sight of the sexy man in his bed. Sure, it was innocent, to a degree. While Brantley was naked beneath the sheet, Reese was wearing a pair of shorts and a T-shirt, his body laid out over the sheet, ensuring they weren't touching.

But there was a fucking sexy man in his bed. The very man who should've been running scared after their heated conversation yesterday. Brantley wasn't sure if he should be glad or worried that Reese was there now.

"You took care of me," he said softly.

"I did."

"Why?"

"Why not?"

"How'd you know?"

"You called me."

Brantley grinned. "Did I?"

"Yep." Eyes still closed, Reese stretched. "Went on about how you were sorry for bein' a total dick."

He chuckled, relieved when the move didn't make his head throb again. He figured it was safe to say the headache was gone. For now, anyway.

"How often do you have them? The headaches?"

"Three or four times a month," he admitted. "When it first happened, they were every couple of days."

"My mom used to have migraines. Figured some of those techniques would work."

Not sure what techniques he was referring to, Brantley decided he didn't need to know the details. The fact that the man had come over in the middle of the damn night and tended to him… He didn't want to get his hopes up, but damn it, he couldn't help it.

Maybe that was the aftereffects of the drugs talking. It wasn't like Brantley was looking for someone to take care of him. He was content with what he had going with Cyrus. Several nights a week they would get together, Brantley would fuck Cyrus senseless, they would go their own ways and meet up when the need arose again.

Or rather, he'd been content. Right up until Reese Tavoularis had come into his world and seemingly found a permanent place there. Now Brantley didn't know what the hell he wanted.

Reese shifted, his head turning as his eyes opened, peering right into Brantley's face. "You're still touchin' me."

Brantley glanced down at the hand he still had on Reese's arm, then back to meet Reese's stare. "You haven't pushed me away yet."

"I know."

There was a wealth of concern in those two words. As though Reese was aware things were … progressing.

"Have you ever been with a man?" Brantley dared to ask, keeping his tone inquisitive as he slowly pulled his hand away.

"No."

Surprised by the immediate response and the easy way he answered, Brantley continued to stare.

"Ever had the desire to?"

"No."

Brantley broke the eye contact, letting his gaze trail down to Reese's shoulder as the answer he'd expected but had hoped not to hear penetrated his brain.

"Until you," Reese whispered.

His attention shot right back to Reese's face. The man was still staring at him, his face frozen in a grimace as though the admission hurt him.

Those golden eyes left his as Reese turned to stare up at the ceiling. "It makes no fuckin' sense, Brantley. I don't understand it."

"But you want to?"

"Not really, no. I want it to go away. I prefer my uncomplicated existence."

"And being with a man would be complicated?"

"For me? Yeah."

"Why?"

"It's not that I find it taboo or anything. It's just … it goes against everything I've ever believed about myself."

Brantley remained where he was, wanting Reese to elaborate because he wanted to know more about the man.

"That mornin' you came to the diner," Reese continued, "when I was havin' breakfast with JJ, I was plannin' to ask her out. She's more my type, Brantley."

"She's a lot of men's type," he acknowledged.

"And I can honestly say, we would've had a damn good time. I'd looked forward to it, the anticipation building as we shared breakfast. Talking was easy, her laughter more so. I was locked in."

Brantley watched Reese as he worked through it; all the while he held his breath, wondering what the fuck was coming next.

"Then you walked up to that fucking table."

The anger he heard was muted but it was there, simmering beneath the surface.

"That night we all went to IHOP, the first night I met you ... I couldn't take my eyes off you. Figured it was a fluke. Then I saw you leavin' the range with JJ ... somethin' seemed different. Inside me." The words came out softly, on a huff of frustration. "Whatever it is, it's growing ... stronger. It confuses the fuck out of me." Reese closed his eyes. "But it was the day we spent at the range that clinched it. Since then, I've spent too much fuckin' time wonderin' when the hell I'll get to see you again." He huffed again. "Fucked up, I know."

"And here you are," Brantley said, keeping his tone light. "In my bed."

Reese chuckled, turning his head and opening his eyes again. "And not making any move to leave it."

Brantley stared, wondering what the hell Reese was getting at. If anything.

"Last night, when you said what you said about, you know, you fantasizing ... I was pissed. More so at myself because I didn't put you in your place. I'm not supposed to give a shit who you're fucking, or who you're thinkin' about when you do."

"But you do." It wasn't a question. Brantley already knew the answer.

Reese barked a laugh. "I'm fightin' it, trust me. Then you called last night, and I heard the pain in your voice, knew something was wrong. I didn't even think about it. Just got in my truck, drove my ass over here, and took care of you. I could've left—should've. But here I am."

They were both silent for a few minutes, but there was no awkwardness.

"I'm not gonna make a move on you, Reese," Brantley finally informed him. "I'm not that guy. What I told you yesterday … about my fantasies … that was all true. Doesn't mean I'll act on them. As far as I'm concerned, you're a damn good friend and I don't intend to fuck that up."

Reese's eyes moved over his face. "And if I make a move?"

Brantley's cock jerked at the thought. "If you're askin' if I'll turn you away…" Brantley grinned. "You'd have to make the move to find out."

REESE WASN'T SURPRISED BRANTLEY WAS PUTTING IT all on him.

Did he want to make a move?

Yes and no.

As he lay there, staring at Brantley's face, his hair mussed from sleep, the stubble on his jaw darker today than yesterday, he couldn't deny he was tempted. Probably a lot of people in the world would've been. Even from a straight man's eyes, Brantley Walker was nice to look at. One of those guys who exuded power and a raw sexuality simply by breathing. And though Reese had never had an intrinsic attraction to a man, he wasn't surprised he did with Brantley. Animal magnetism, he believed it was called.

And the urge to explore him on a physical level was potent. Not all that different than what he'd felt for various women in the past. The idea of pressing his lips to Brantley's, feeling him move against him, hearing the heated moans as he got worked up … it was simple lust. A natural response.

Problem was, this was dangerous territory. Reese could cop to the fact he was drawn to him, but that was a far cry from wanting to be intimate with the man.

What happened if he kissed Brantley and hated it? Where would that leave them?

He did have an answer for that because he'd spent endless hours thinking about it. For starters, there would be a huge rift between them that would threaten the fragile relationship they'd established up to this point.

Was that a risk Reese was willing to take?

For fuck's sake, the guy had become his closest friend in the past month and a half. And while Reese had plenty of acquaintances, he didn't have many friends. No one he spent a lot of time with. And this friendship … it was growing because they had so much in common. And being around Brantley was easy. Even now, when Reese should've been freaked out that he was lying in bed with a naked man.

"I don't wanna fuck this up," Reese said softly.

"Then don't."

Shaking his head, he tore his gaze away from Brantley and stared up at the ceiling fan. "Is it really that easy for you?"

"What?"

"The no-strings thing? You and Cyrus … you might not see it, but that man has it bad for you. Yet, as an outsider, even I can see the feeling's not mutual. I don't want to be that guy for you."

Brantley sighed. "It's all an act, Reese."

"What is?"

"Cyrus doesn't have feelin's for me any more than I have them for him. We're friends. Damn good friends. Cyrus is one of those guys who'd lay down his life for me. I feel the same for him. But there's never been the illusion our friendship would morph into anything else."

"Then why—"

"Does he act like he's jealous? He's tryin' to get a rise outta you, Reese. That's all it is."

The fact that Reese had taken the bait … that was telling, right? Had Reese not wanted something from Brantley, he wouldn't have cared.

Brantley rolled to his back, stretched. "I'm not pushin' you, Reese. I don't want to fuck this up, either. I need a friend like you in my life."

Rolling his head, he turned his attention away from the drywall. "A friend like me?"

"Yeah." Brantley glanced his way again. "One who doesn't coddle me. You don't hover and worry. I've got enough of that in my life, so it's rare to be around people who don't treat me like I'm gonna break. I appreciate it."

"So what you're really sayin' is you don't wanna fuck me?"

Brantley laughed, a deep, throaty sound that had Reese's entire body hardening.

"Oh, I wanna fuck you. Nine ways to Sunday, in fact. I'm just good at self-restraint."

Yeah, clearly.

Brantley sat up, dropping his legs over the side of the bed. "You hungry?"

He was, sure. But rather than allow the subject to drop, for them to move on with the rest of the day, pretending this never happened, Reese didn't respond. Not with words.

Rather than take the out he was being handed, Reese's hand shot out and he gripped Brantley's arm, dragging him back down to the mattress. There was no resistance on Brantley's part; the man just let himself be manhandled until he was pulling his legs back up, his attention shifting to Reese.

Reese rolled to his side, propped himself up on his elbow, leaning over Brantley.

"You can't undo this." Brantley's softly spoken words were a warning.

Oh, he was well aware of that.

Still, he didn't stop.

Their eyes met and held as Reese leaned in, closing the distance between their lips. Time seemed to stand still as Reese's mouth eased over Brantley's. No hesitation, no second-guessing. He went full throttle before he could change his mind.

Brantley's lips were warm and smooth and surprisingly soft, but they weren't pliant. The only reaction was the tension that coiled in his hard body. Reese felt Brantley's restraint, knew the man was going to make him work for it.

Figuring he'd crossed the line already, Reese moved into a better position, propping up his upper body by planting his hands on either side of Brantley's head, holding himself there as he dared to slide his tongue over Brantley's lower lip.

"Kiss me back, dammit," he grumbled, lifting his head and meeting Brantley's eyes.

"You sure you want that?"

Reese narrowed his eyes and spoke the truth as he knew it. "I wouldn't be here if I didn't."

"Be careful what you wish for," Brantley whispered.

It took a moment for the words to register, but then all thought fled. In an unexpected turn, Reese ended up on his back, Brantley mirroring Reese's previous position, suspended over him. This time when their lips came together there was no hesitation on Brantley's part.

Christ Almighty.

When Brantley's lips parted, allowing Reese entry, he could taste passion blazing and it went right to his bloodstream like a drug. All of his senses seemed to heighten, the way a drug addict's might when they took a hit.

Their tongues collided in a slow but exquisite mating, Reese's hands cupping Brantley's face, holding him in place. Sure, he was currently on the bottom, but he had no intentions of giving up control.

But as quickly as it had heated, the kiss morphed, shifting into an exploration of tongues. Brantley was kissing him in a sensual manner that had Reese's balls tightening, a lightning bolt arcing along his spine. He briefly wondered if he could come from the perfection of that kiss.

Aside from keeping their lips melded, Brantley didn't move to touch him in any other way. His hands were fisted on the bed, holding him up so Reese maintained control of the kiss. It was a concerted effort, he knew. Brantley wasn't used to letting go of the reins, but he was doing so for Reese.

This was different than any kiss Reese had ever experienced before. Hotter, more intense. He didn't expect the onslaught of emotions. Confusion warred with desire, but he didn't try to pull away. He didn't want to stop. And when Brantley moaned softly, Reese did the same, groaning low in his throat as the sensations rippled through him.

The moment eventually came to an end when Brantley lifted his head.

Reese stared up at him, unable to look away as his lungs worked overtime to fill.

Brantley's smirk was slow and sexy. "You good?"

"Yeah," he said in a rush. "I'm … better than good."

The glint of heat in Brantley's eyes sent another bolt of lust through him, but Reese resisted the urge to kiss him again. For now, he was satisfied. Either he would continue to want more or he would chalk up the experience to curiosity.

"I'm gonna shower, then I'll make eggs and bacon."

"You shower, and I'll make breakfast."

Brantley nodded, his gaze dropping to Reese's lips once more. While he wouldn't have pushed him away, Reese exhaled his relief when the man moved, crawling out of bed and padding naked to the bathroom.

Upon his retreat, Reese took the opportunity to watch him stroll away. His gaze slid down Brantley's impressive back, observing the sexy flex and pull of his muscles, over the various scars that decorated his skin, then pausing on his firm ass.

Yeah, Reese was definitely better than good, but that didn't tell him a damn thing about what the future held.

Not that he was thinking about the future. No, the here and now seemed more pressing.

Dropping back onto Brantley's bed, Reese stared up at the ceiling, a smile pulling at his lips.

That kiss…

Twenty minutes later, Brantley joined Reese in the kitchen.

Not sure what he was expecting, Reese waited for the weirdness to encompass the room, to chase out the laid-back chill he'd had going on since he came in here to make breakfast, but it didn't. In fact, it felt like any of the other times they'd shared a meal. Granted, there was still the underlying desire to kiss Brantley again, to feel his lips, to taste the mint of his toothpaste.

He refrained, offering a smile as he passed over a plate with toast, egg whites, and six pieces of bacon.

"You're servin' me too?" Brantley asked with a smirk, his gaze sweeping over the plate. "Careful now. I could get used to this." When he looked up, he was still smiling. "Well, except for the egg whites. Not sure why you gotta go and ruin a perfectly good egg."

"Healthier."

"So I hear."

"Don't worry, next meal's on you and I'm expecting steak."

Realizing how that sounded, Reese ducked his head, chuckled.

Brantley took a seat, grabbed his phone, and glanced at the screen as he picked up his fork.

"Anything from Travis?"

"No." Brantley lifted his head, met Reese's gaze. "You?"

"No. I shot him a text to check in but haven't heard back yet."

"Anything from your brother?"

Reese shook his head, bit off a corner of his toast, chewed.

They ate in silence for a minute or two before Brantley asked, "What time do you have to be at work?"

"Nine," he said, glancing at the clock. "I doubt anyone else is there, but I'll check in, make sure nothing pressing needs my attention. Then I figured I'd head over to Travis's. See how I can help out."

Brantley opened his mouth to say something, but his phone chimed, snagging his attention.

"It's JJ," he said, staring at the phone, his shoulders squaring as he sat up straight. "She's got somethin' on that blonde."

Feeling a sense of hope, Reese chased his toast with coffee, wiped his mouth. "She say what?"

"She's on her way here now."

Reese nodded, took a few more bites of his eggs, then more coffee. A minute later, he'd cleared his plate.

"I better head home. Shower. You'll call me when you know somethin'?"

"Yep," Brantley said around a mouthful of bacon.

And that was how Reese kicked off the first day of what he figured was going to be an altered reality.

Interesting that he wasn't put off in the least.

Chapter Eleven

"YOU LOOK BETTER THAN YOU DID LAST night," JJ noted upon her arrival at his house shortly after Reese left.

Brantley ran a hand over the scruff on his jaw, offered a pleasant smile. "I feel better than I did last night."

Her head canted to one side, then the other as she seemingly studied him. "I'd go so far as to say you look … happy." Her tone shifted to rampant curiosity. "Why do you look happy, Brantley?"

"It's a new day," he said, motioning toward the back door so he could lead the way to the barn.

"It is." Her gaze dropped to his gesturing hand, then back to his face. "You'll tell me eventually."

"Right now, I'm hopin' you'll be tellin' me somethin'." He urged her toward the door with a hand on her back. "Somethin' about this blonde."

JJ's expression instantly sobered and he understood her reasons. As it was, the headache had caused Brantley to lose precious hours he could've spent looking for Kate. Now that he was fully functioning again, there was no time to reflect on anything other than the missing girl who had been gone for roughly twenty hours.

"Anything from Travis?" she inquired. "Did the kidnapper call?"

"No. He called me a few minutes ago. Still nothing from the sheriff, either."

"Fuck," JJ hissed. "We have got to find this little girl. What if we're off here? What if this woman had nothing to do with it? What if it was a random kidnapping? Some pervert saw the perfect opportunity and pounced?"

"This wasn't random, JJ," he assured her because that was something he truly believed. "We need to keep tugging on this thread. See what unravels. What did you find?"

"Okay, well…" JJ stepped out of the way so he could slide the barn door back, revealing the doors leading inside. "You probably won't like this, but since we had nothing to go on with the exception of a grainy image and no motive, I decided to do some digging."

Brantley peered down at her as they crossed toward the row of monitors.

"On Travis."

That pulled him up short, had him turning to face her fully.

"I told you you wouldn't like it, but really, Brantley. I had to do something."

He understood that. As it was, he felt entirely inept because they hadn't uncovered anything on who might've taken Kate, where she was, or why someone would want to snatch her during a field trip to the state capitol. The only thing his gut was telling him was that this wasn't random. Kate had not been taken by some creep who wanted to get his hands on a little girl. That was the only thing keeping him calm right now.

"And I didn't exactly dig into Travis, per se. More like his resort."

"Alluring Indulgence? What does that have to do with Kate's disappearance?"

JJ stepped up to one of the monitors, tapped her fingers over the screen. "Well, I figured if this was some sort of retaliation against them, then it seemed pretty straightforward to think it would be someone from the resort. They are an invitation-only establishment and they cater to some well-known names. But it wasn't the famous people I was looking into. I was able to hack their system—"

"I did not hear that, JJ."

"Fine." She forced a smile. "I was able to obtain the information I needed, and I started using the list of people who'd been to the resort and pulling up information on each of them."

"Lookin' for what?"

"Anomalies. People who'd experienced some sort of major life event recently. Brushes with the law, divorces, lost their job. That's when I found this."

She punched a button and an image came up on the second screen.

"This is Juliet Prince, the former wife of Nicholas Prince, a wealthy businessman on the Gulf Coast. And by wealthy, I mean Forbes-worthy. Guy owns a chain of casinos and hotels."

The details were simply white noise, his focus on learning who the woman was, because from where he was standing, there was most definitely a resemblance to the grainy image they had. "You said former wife?"

"As in recently divorced because Mr. Prince evidently decided he required a more updated version and he has since sent Juliet on her way, replacing her with the recently divorced, and decidedly younger, Andrea Nolan, whom he met at … drum roll, please … Alluring Indulgence."

Brantley frowned. "You're tellin' me that this woman might've kidnapped Travis's daughter because she's pissed that her husband left her?"

"If only it were that easy." JJ frowned. "Not only did he leave her for a woman he met at Travis's resort, the prenup she signed left her with absolutely nothing. No houses, no cars, nothing. How he managed to slight her like that, I don't know, but she got fucked in the deal. Royally.

"But that's not the worst part. The husband also got sole custody of … wait for it"—she tapped another key on the screen, pulling up another image—"their five-year-old daughter, Lani. Mr. Prince accused Juliet of being an unfit mother and he used his millions and a handful of ruthless lawyers to ensure the courts saw it his way, too. So much so, she's been reduced to supervised visitations only."

Brantley did not like the direction this was taking. If the divorce was true, Juliet might have taken Kate as revenge against who she saw as the one responsible for her failed marriage. But if Juliet was hurting because the relationship she had with her child had been destroyed… That complicated matters. It meant there would be no ransom because Juliet wasn't looking for Travis to financially atone for what she would see as his transgression. She would be looking to replace the daughter she'd lost.

"As for the unfit claim," JJ continued, "there wasn't much in that."

Brantley frowned.

"I'm tellin' you this to reassure you. If Juliet is the one who took Kate, I don't think she'll hurt her."

At least they hoped not.

"Do you have an address for this woman?" he asked.

"Not a current one, no. I found her parents, called them last night, and pretended to be an old friend from high school. Juliet's mother said her daughter didn't live there, but she would pass on a message next time she talked to her. And yes, before you ask, I gave her my real phone number. Figured what the hell. Maybe she'll call. If she does, we can locate her that way." JJ took a deep breath. "I was able to get several addresses for the ex-husband."

"I need to pay this guy a visit."

"Easier said than done. He resides in Mississippi near the casinos he owns, but he's got houses all over the country. One in Denver, another in Atlantic City, two in California, and an apartment in New York. Oh, and one right here in Austin. Might make more sense to loop in the local police in each of the cities."

Brantley shook his head. "Right now, the only person who needs to be brought up to speed is Travis." Leaning over, he kissed the top of her head. "Send that info to my phone, please."

"Will do. And while you're doin' that, I'll see if I can get a lock on Mr. Prince's whereabouts."

Without wasting any more time, Brantley hurried back to the house. He grabbed his keys and his sunglasses and was in his truck within minutes. He had Siri transcribe a text to Reese, letting him know what JJ had discovered.

Before he'd made it to the main road that would take him to Travis's, his phone was ringing.

"Hey," he greeted Reese. "I'm headin' to my cousin's. JJ's tryin' to get a bead on the ex. The guy does have a house here in Austin. Figured I'd head over there, see if maybe Juliet Prince is holed up there without her husband's knowledge."

"I'll meet you there, and I'll go with you."

It wasn't like he was going to decline the assistance. While Brantley could easily handle it himself, he was looking forward to working alongside Reese. He wasn't sure what it was about the man, but the more time Brantley spent with him, the more he was drawn into his orbit.

"See you in a few," he said before disconnecting the call.

TRAVIS WAS SITTING ON HIS FRONT PORCH, watching Kylie pace nervously back and forth. She'd been out here for the better part of the last hour, her anxiety level rising with every passing minute. Unable to soothe her with words and promises, Travis had opted to keep her company instead, hoping against hope that his fucking phone would ring, and he'd get some information. Any information, being that he had a couple dozen people looking into his daughter's disappearance, along with the police and the local sheriff. No one was giving him any answers and it was all he could do not to lose his fucking mind.

Kylie pulled up short, her attention swinging to the drive as a big black Chevrolet came toward them.

"It's Brantley," he told her as he got to his feet.

"Does he know somethin'?" she asked, her voice thin and reedy but filled with hopeful anticipation.

"I don't know, baby. Let's go find out."

Taking her hand, he led her down the steps as Brantley was pulling to a stop behind Gage's truck. Travis watched as his cousin exited the vehicle, pulling off his aviators and sliding them into the neck of his T-shirt.

"Hey," Brantley greeted, his face pinched with concern as he glanced back and forth between the two of them. "Any news?"

A wave of disappointment rocked his foundation. Here Travis had been thinking Brantley had come by to tell them something. Trying to hide his despondency, Travis shook his head, locking on Brantley's gaze. "Not yet."

"Well, I might have somethin'."

Kylie's breath hitched, her hand squeezing Travis's as hope slammed into them both.

"Because there was nothin' to go on and JJ's not one to sit idly by, she started lookin' into your business dealings," Brantley explained, his voice level and even.

Travis didn't ask what that meant. At this point, he didn't fucking care if she'd hacked his fucking financials. If it would bring Kate home safe and sound, he'd give her access to whatever she wanted.

Brantley pulled out his phone, tapped the screen a few times, then passed it over.

"Do you recognize them?"

Taking the phone, Travis kept it down so Kylie could see it, too. On the screen was a man and a woman, both dressed to the nines with that forced air of happiness worn by unhappy couples surrounding them. They looked vaguely familiar, but he couldn't place either of them.

"It's possible," he answered. "Why?"

"That's Nicholas Prince and his ex-wife, Juliet. He's a casino mogul in Mississippi. They've both been to your resort, though when they came, I don't know."

"And this means what?" Kylie asked, staring up at Brantley as though he held the key to their happiness.

The screen door squeaked behind them, drawing Travis's attention over his shoulder. Gage appeared, his eyes instantly scanning the scene as he made his way down to where they were.

Travis passed him the phone, nodded toward the image on the screen.

"That's Nicholas Prince," Gage stated. "He and his wife visited the resort last year."

"Correct," Brantley noted, then nodded toward the phone. "That woman bears an eerie resemblance to the grainy image of the woman we suspect might have Kate."

Gage leaned in closer to the phone, narrowed his eyes. "I agree."

All eyes shifted back to Brantley.

"From what JJ was able to dig up, Nicholas and Juliet have since parted ways. Sounds like he might've met a younger version while he was visiting AI, realigned his priorities. She got the shit end of the deal, left with nothing. He's now married to the new woman and, as of recently, has acquired full custody of his and Juliet's five-year-old daughter."

Travis didn't need to be a rocket scientist to put the pieces of that puzzle together. "And you think she might have my daughter?"

"I do," Brantley concurred, taking the phone back from Gage when he passed it over.

"Do you think…?" Kylie gasped.

Travis knew where her thoughts had gone.

"Do I think she took Kate out of revenge?" Brantley nodded. "Partly, yes. However, based on what we have to go on, I don't think Kate's in any immediate danger."

"Because you think she took our daughter not only out of revenge but as a replacement for her own," Gage mused.

"Correct."

While Brantley tapped on his phone again, the sound of tires on gravel drew their attention. Travis noticed Reese pulling the red Walker Demolition dually up the driveway.

"JJ doesn't have a current address for the woman, but she has located several homes Nicholas Prince owns, including one here in Austin."

When Brantley paused, Travis looked his way.

"With your go-ahead, I'd like to pay the man a visit, see if he can tell us where she's at."

"Do you know where he is?" Gage inquired.

"No. JJ's lookin' into that. As soon as she has contact info, I'll send it your way. But even if he's not here in Austin, that doesn't mean she's not. It's possible Juliet's hidin' out there, lyin' low if her ex is off galavantin' elsewhere. And if not, someone at the estate might know somethin'."

"It's a good place to start," Gage said.

Brantley held Travis's stare. "Wherever you need me ... all you have to do is say the word."

Travis saw the determination in his cousin's steel-blue eyes. It was the same look he saw in every pair of eyes he'd made contact with in the past twenty-four hours. Everyone he knew was willing to do what was necessary to bring Kate home.

"We have to find her," Kylie whispered. "I…" Kylie let out a pained sob and Travis pulled her into his side, wrapped his arms around her, and nodded to Brantley.

Had it not been for the fact everyone was insisting he remain here—no doubt inspired by his father—he would've been the one tracking down this lead. But rather than galivant across the country, Gage was holding him to his promise to sit tight. There was nothing to say that this wasn't a fool's errand. It could be a simple coincidence that this woman had been at the state capitol at the same time Kate disappeared.

Which meant, if Brantley was wrong, they could be dealing with another situation altogether. Something random and the thought of that ... it was terrifying.

"Hey," Reese greeted as he approached.

Brantley's phone rang and suddenly everything seemed to stop, including the birds in the trees. It was as though the universe was waiting for answers the same way they were.

Travis watched as Brantley took the call and turned away from them, pacing toward his truck.

"Brantley filled me in," Reese said, as though clarifying why he was there. "I figured I'd go with him to check out the residence. See what we can find."

Travis glanced at the man who'd become one of his closest friends over the years. He had depended on Reese, asked him to do things he didn't trust others to handle for him. And not once had Reese let him down. So it made perfect sense that he would want to help in this matter.

But what didn't make sense was what Travis sensed going on between these two men. He'd noticed the way Brantley's eyes had trailed Reese's movements when he approached. Even now the man seemed to be quite enthralled by Reese's appearance. Though he was on the phone a few yards away, he was keeping a close eye on Reese.

Had Travis not had more pressing things on his mind, he probably would be able to put the pieces of that puzzle together. Unfortunately, nothing mattered right now except bringing his baby girl home.

And he prayed that was what was going to happen. Soon.

~e~

REESE STOOD WITH TRAVIS, KYLIE, AND GAGE, waiting for Brantley to end the call. He was doing his best to keep his eyes from wandering over to Brantley, but it wasn't easy. From the moment he'd pulled into the drive, he'd been fixated on the man.

Not that Brantley looked any different than he had when Reese left him a few hours ago. Well, aside from the sheer intent he could feel coming off the man in waves. Didn't surprise him since it seemed Brantley and JJ had come up with the first real lead that might bring Kate home.

Reese got the feeling that was normal for Brantley. When the man set his mind to something, he didn't stop until he'd accomplished his task, no matter the cost. The guy was a SEAL after all. They were an intense bunch. And even as a civilian, no longer in the Teams, Brantley wouldn't have lost that ingrained instinct to complete the mission.

No one would've guessed the guy had been laid out flat with a brain-searing headache the night before. Reese remembered the way Brantley had moaned during the night, his pain a tangible thing. It had been enough to have Reese feeling helpless. Not something he was familiar with when it came to other people. It was the reason he had stayed, remained close, eager to get Brantley through the worst of it.

Or so he continued to tell himself.

Yep, and he was definitely back to the denial phase of his new realization. He was once more refusing to believe he had stayed because he'd wanted to sleep in a bed with Brantley, to remain close for his own comfort. No, he was not thinking along those lines because they made absolutely no sense.

"JJ's gonna send you the contact numbers she came up with," Brantley told Travis when he returned to their side, disconnecting the call on the way. "She's also got several addresses, including his Austin residence. He lives out off of Bee Caves."

Reese peered back at Travis, waiting to see what the man wanted them to do. But it wasn't Travis who spoke up.

Gage's voice was deep and commanding when he said, "While we work to get in touch with him, see if he can give us his ex-wife's information, you two go to his Austin house. If she's hidin' out there…"

"Then we'll find her," Brantley said quickly, accepting the orders easily. "We'll keep you in the loop."

Reese was surprised when Brantley spun around and headed for his truck without waiting for more information. Then again, he'd gotten his orders, so evidently, he didn't need to know the other details. They'd be forthcoming.

Because he knew he'd be left standing there otherwise, Reese said a quick goodbye and strolled over to the passenger side. He'd managed to make it into the truck before Brantley was shoving it in reverse and heading out.

"You really think this woman has Kate?"

"I do," Brantley replied, his voice firm. "I don't believe in coincidences, Reese. That woman wasn't simply at the state capitol yesterday because she had business there. If I had to guess, she's been keeping close tabs on Travis for some time."

"Because she blames him?"

"Exactly." Brantley cut his eyes to Reese quickly, then turned back to the road. "She's pissed her husband left her. Maybe because he's got another woman, maybe because he left her with nothing. Regardless, she needs someone to blame for that. Probably had some plan to get back at Travis all along. Then she lost custody of her daughter…"

"Insult to injury," Reese muttered.

"This woman's at the end of her rope. Heartbroken, angry. Then she realizes she has the perfect opportunity to put the hurt on the man she believes is responsible and solve her emotional crisis at the same time. If she can't have her own daughter, she'll get a substitute."

"You don't think that's a stretch? I don't see normal people just jumping up and stealing someone else's kid because someone took theirs away."

"Normal people don't usually have everything ripped away from them in the blink of an eye. Her husband, whether she loved him or simply appreciated him for what he could afford her, was supposed to be hers. We know that he was into kinky shit, otherwise, he wouldn't have come to the resort."

"Maybe it was her idea," he replied, playing devil's advocate.

"Possible but doubtful. And that's not a sexist statement. I'm sure there are plenty of women who're the dominant in their relationship. I figure if she'd been the one to suggest it, they'd still be together. My guess is, he brought up the idea, convinced her it would spice up their marriage. They went, did whatever it is that's done there. Had some fun, swapped partners in the heat of the moment. Juliet probably enjoyed it until she realized her husband's attentions had strayed elsewhere."

"Swapped partners?" Reese chuckled. "Is that what they do there?"

Brantley glanced his way again. "I don't know. Ever been?"

"No. Not into that."

"No?"

Reese shifted his gaze to the window, stared out at the road in front of them as he thought about Cyrus and Brantley. "No. I don't like to share my toys."

Brantley chuckled. "Is that what I am to you?"

He could hear the teasing in the man's tone, knew Brantley was simply trying to lighten the mood despite the gloomy situation. Though they hadn't talked about what happened this morning, it was definitely sitting between them. Would be until they addressed it. And God knew Reese had spent more than his fair share of time thinking about it. In fact, he'd done little else for the past couple of hours.

"You think she's still in Austin?" he asked, wanting to get them back on the reason they were here now.

"No."

Reese's head snapped over, his eyes locking on Brantley.

"I don't think she'll go anywhere her ex might find her."

"Makes sense," he said, mulling over that information. "If she plans to keep Kate as a replacement for her daughter, she'll go somewhere no one knows her."

"But she'll need to feel safe," Brantley noted. "Wherever she goes, it'll be someplace she can blend in, but she'll be familiar with it. Or close to a place she is."

"Which means we need to know who this woman is," Reese said, holding out his hand.

Brantley glanced over at his hand.

"Your phone. Let me call JJ, have her start diggin' up as much info on this woman as she can."

"You sure you can handle lookin' at my phone again?"

Reese snagged the phone. "Depends. Were you thinkin' about Cyrus when you kissed me this mornin'?"

Brantley chuckled. "If I recall correctly, you kissed me."

"Is that a yes or a no?" he demanded, surprised by his own need for clarification.

That handsome face sobered when he looked at Reese again. "Cyrus who?"

There was a strange warmth that settled in Reese's chest, but he ignored it. Right now was not the time to venture down that path. Despite his denial, he still wanted to kiss Brantley again to see if it had been as good as he thought, but there was a time and place for shit like that.

Here and now was certainly not it.

Chapter Twelve

THE THIRTY-MINUTE DRIVE TO WEST AUSTIN was done mostly in silence after Reese had placed the call to JJ.

Brantley had listened with half an ear as Reese talked, his mind bouncing back and forth between the encounter in his bed that morning and what was going on now. It wasn't easy to stay in the moment even if he knew it was where he needed to be.

Problem was, every time he thought about that kiss, his body hardened. His cock was rigid, his hormones rioting just from the memory of Reese's mouth. Firm, hesitant, eager. Not to mention hot. So. Fucking. Hot. He longed for the next one, found himself praying Reese would want to explore this, all while recognizing the man had already started to pull back.

Brantley had played out the fantasy of what might've happened if he'd taken the lead rather than allowing Reese to control the pace. In his version, he would've been sliding deep inside the man, taking him with a passion that had eluded him for so long. The urge was so potent Brantley was surprised he even recognized it. It surpassed any of the urgency he'd experienced before.

"We're not gonna find her here," Reese said.

The words pulled him out of his thoughts as he guided his truck into the wide circular drive of Nicholas Prince's home, with its fancy, if not gaudy, water feature centered in front of the enormous mansion on the hill. From behind, he knew there would be a phenomenal view of the lake, the water spread out for miles. It was the view people paid for here, something that was unique to this area, but he seriously doubted the house lacked any of the luxuries accessible to the wealthy.

"Well, we're here, so we'll see what we can find out."

Ten minutes later, after they'd sauntered up to the front door, knocked, and had a brief conversation with a very unhappy majordomo who managed the place while his rich employer was away, Brantley accepted that Reese was right. They wouldn't find Juliet or Kate here, of that he was certain. Based on the response from the man they'd all but interrogated, he was not Juliet's biggest fan, so even if she did stop by, he would not be offering her safe harbor.

And now they could mark this residence off their list and hope that Travis and Gage would get somewhere with the rest of the locations JJ had dredged up. If they were lucky, Nicholas Prince would give them some input on where Juliet might go if she wanted to stay off the grid.

"Where to now?" Reese asked when they were back in the truck, winding their way down the hills toward the highway.

"You're the one who talked to JJ. What'd she say?"

"That she would trace the woman back to birth if that was what it took."

And Brantley knew JJ wasn't exaggerating. The woman was nothing if not meticulous when it came to digging up information on people.

"Well, I guess we'll go back to my place, see if she's found anything else."

"Y'all are close, huh? You and JJ?"

"To a degree, yeah. We kept in touch while I was away, saw each other every now and again when I stopped in on leave."

"You ever date her?" Reese asked.

Brantley laughed, catching Reese's gaze. "No. I've never been with a woman. Never had the desire to be."

"So you've always known you were gay?"

"Always. From the time all my friends started checkin' out the girls in the fifth grade, I knew I had no interest."

"But you don't think it's one way or the other for everyone?"

Brantley focused on the road. "Of course not. I don't think there's a sexuality playbook. I think some people know from a young age whether they're gay, straight, bisexual, or transsexual. Others learn from experiences what they're open to, what they need."

"Yeah, I suppose you're right."

"I'm not tryin' to be right," he said, reaching over and touching Reese's hand. "If you're questionin' what happened this mornin' or you think you owe me an explanation, forget it."

"I am questioning it," Reese countered, his voice harsher than before. "Never in my life have I lusted after a man. And this mornin', I was kissin' you."

Brantley knew he could turn this into a joke, tease Reese until the mood lightened, but he got the feeling Reese needed to work through this logically.

"Did you enjoy it?" he asked, ensuring Reese heard his curiosity and his sincerity.

He felt those golden eyes move to him, but Brantley didn't look over. He realized he wanted to hear Reese's answer because it mattered to him.

"At the time, yeah."

A surprising disappointment flooded him.

"Now that I've had time to think about it, I want to blame it on … a dry spell."

Brantley pulled up to a red light, peered over at Reese. He let his gaze drop to the man's mouth before shifting his attention back to the road. He would not make this about himself. Brantley had no confusion over what he wanted. What he'd wanted all along. But he could not force Reese on this. The man would get to where he was meant to be one way or another.

"But I know that's just a bullshit excuse," Reese said softly.

After taking a deep breath, Brantley let it out slowly, not wanting Reese to hear the relief he felt.

They were both quiet for the last ten minutes of the trip. By the time Brantley pulled into his driveway, he was expecting Reese to jump out of the truck as soon as it came to a stop. When he didn't, Brantley shut off the engine, unhooked his seat belt, waited.

"Brantley?"

Keeping his eyes forward, Brantley pulled off his sunglasses, set them on the dash, and rested his hands on the steering wheel. "Look, Reese. I don't know what happened this mornin' for you. I know it was a pleasant surprise for me. But I'm not—"

"Brantley."

Shocked by the demand in Reese's tone, he looked over, saw that Reese was leaning over the center console.

"I figure there's only one way for me to know what I felt."

"How's that?" Yeah, his voice was all raspy and shit. So what?

Reese's eyes lowered to his mouth at the same time he reached for Brantley, his hand sliding behind his neck, tugging him toward him.

He didn't resist, not minding in the least that Reese wanted to manhandle him. However, he didn't initiate the kiss, figuring this was another of Reese's experiments.

"It doesn't feel wrong," Reese whispered, his breath fanning Brantley's lips. "But it's foreign to me."

"What is?"

"Wanting someone like this."

"Someone?"

Reese's lips brushed his and a blaze instantly ignited in his veins, swimming through his body at an alarmingly high rate of speed. More electricity sizzled down his spine when Reese licked his way into his mouth. Their tongues met, tangled. Slowly at first, then moving more intently. Searching, seeking, exploring. Brantley tried to hold back, to give Reese the reins, but he couldn't. Although he would not push the man, he wasn't above finding his own pleasure in the moment.

It was his taste, he decided. Peppermint, to be exact. It was addicting, the combination of mint and man, a slow seduction that kept him captivated, made him want only this. More would be overwhelming, but this … the way Reese kissed him so fervently, with such care and leisure, as though he wanted to be right here, right now … it was unlike anything Brantley had ever experienced.

"Christ," Reese muttered, tilting his head and leaning in.

Brantley felt the shudder go through Reese, his body hardening all the more. To know Reese was turned on by this, craved it … that was enough to have his cock throbbing against his zipper.

They were inhaling one another at that point, their mouths fused together, Reese's hand curling tightly behind his neck as though he feared Brantley would move away before he was ready.

Little did Reese know, but for the first time in a long damn time—maybe ever—Brantley had no desire to go anywhere. In fact, he could easily see himself content to let this play out at its own pace.

After all, who knew where it might go.

REESE KNEW HE WAS PLAYING WITH FIRE. More than likely, he would get burned, but not even the risk of incineration could get him to stop. Never had he been so drawn to any one person— man or woman. Never had anyone made him ache this desperately, feel this much.

And it wasn't that he hadn't had his share of lovers. More than, in fact. But not a single moment stood out to him the way this one did. Only a kiss, at that. But it was enough to hold him there, suspended in time for eternity.

They were both panting by the time their lips separated, though Reese wasn't sure who drew back first.

"What did you mean," Brantley rasped, "when you said someone?"

Reese met his eyes, searched them, tried to find the solitude he could sense behind the tumultuous storm brewing there. There was no doubt in his mind Brantley was a test he would never pass, but maybe the tutoring would be worth it.

His breath slammed into his lungs when Brantley's hand lifted, then so very gently cupped the side of his face. It was a move he never would've expected from such a hardened man, but it was a comfort, nonetheless.

"I've never wanted like this. Not even a woman," he admitted, the words escaping on a rough whisper. "And kissing you … it's all I can think about. Your mouth…"

Why he was rambling, especially waxing poetic about a kiss, Reese didn't know.

The smile that pulled at Brantley's mouth was so full of promise and mischief, he couldn't help but return it.

"And to think … it's just gettin' started."

That was one way to look at it, sure. Reese knew there was more exploration needed before he could go all in with whatever this was, but he was certainly on board with the idea.

A knock sounded and they both jumped apart. Reese felt the heat consume him, his face likely red from embarrassment. There, standing in front of Brantley's truck, was JJ. She was smiling, her gaze bouncing between them before she shouted for them to get a room.

Fuck.

"Relax," Brantley said, smiling over at him as he exited, closing the door gently behind him.

Easier said than done, Reese thought as he sat there, trying to get his body under control.

Taking deep breaths to slow his respiratory system and settle his heart rate, Reese finally got out of the truck, sauntering around to meet JJ and Brantley in front of it.

Thankfully, JJ didn't launch into some curiosity quest, choosing rather to get right to what mattered. "So, I did some more digging like I told you I would, and I came up with some information that might help us."

Reese was grateful she was talking to Brantley and not looking at him.

"Juliet Prince, whose maiden name is Aronda, was born and raised in Kentwood, Louisiana. Yes, before you freak out, it is the hometown of Britney Spears."

Her excitement at the fun fact made Reese grin. He got the sneaking suspicion Brantley was one of the few people on earth who didn't know who the famously infamous pop star even was.

JJ winked at him, then looked back to Brantley and continued, "Anyway. Juliet grew up in Louisiana, but her family spent a lot of time on the Mississippi shores. From what I can tell, they enjoyed vacationing there every year. It was during one of those trips that Juliet was introduced to Nicholas Prince. Seems the good businessman had been doing some vacationing himself. Which actually translates to cheating on his second wife after he stumbled upon the much younger Juliet. Who the hell knows what an eighteen-year-old girl saw in a man twice her age, but from all accounts, it was love at first sight."

"And this means what to us?" Brantley asked, nodding for JJ to lead the way into the house.

Reese followed at a respectful distance, which worked for him, twofold. One, it allowed him to get his bearings, which were still off-kilter thanks to that mind-blowing kiss. And two, it gave him a chance to ogle Brantley from behind without anyone realizing.

He noticed the way Brantley's big hand held open the screen door, his long fingers curled around the edge. It brought to mind the way he'd touched Reese's cheek. It also had him thinking about what those hands would feel like on him.

Reese had to adjust himself as he walked, cursing the damn Wranglers he wore. If this kept up, he'd have to make some serious adjustments to his wardrobe.

"Her upbringing is really no concern," JJ answered, "other than the fact that we've learned that Juliet loves the beach. I'd go so far as to say she's obsessed with it. When she married Nicholas—"

"Wait." Brantley pulled up short when he stepped into what should've been a dining room if it'd had a table. "You said we've learned." His dark eyebrows rose. "Who's we, JJ?"

Reese was impressed by the way she didn't back down, holding her ground against the much larger man.

"We," she bit out. "As in Dante and I. I needed help. He offered."

"I thought you were gonna get Cyrus to help you."

"I asked. He had somethin' else to do but promised to stop by when he could."

Curious as to the battle brewing behind Brantley's blue-gray gaze, Reese remained at a distance, watching the pair face off with one another. For a brief moment, he thought Brantley was going to launch into a tirade. Instead, he took a deep breath, his shoulders visibly relaxing.

"Is Dante here now?"

"He is," she answered quickly and without concern. "He's in the barn. I came up to the house because I saw your truck pull up on the cameras. When you didn't show up, I thought maybe you needed help." JJ's gaze swung around to him and she smiled brightly. "I realized quickly that you definitely did not need my help, but by then, I'd already made the trek."

Reese felt his ears catch fire, and rather than stand there beneath her scrutiny, he marched around them into the kitchen. Grabbing a bottle of water from the refrigerator, he turned his attention out the back door. It wasn't until he was taking a drink to cool the heat in his throat that he realized how easily he moved around the place. Almost as though he was familiar there.

Of course, he was. More so than he probably should've been.

"Could you give us a few minutes?" he heard Brantley tell JJ. "Then we'll meet you in the barn."

There was no response from JJ, or if there was, it was too low for him to hear. A minute later, JJ crossed through his line of sight, out the back door, and headed toward the barn.

"Hey, you okay?"

Reese nodded, knowing the question was for him. He could sense Brantley standing behind him, could almost feel the concern coming off the guy.

"If you're worried she'll say somethin'…"

Reese set the bottle of water on the counter, then turned to face Brantley. "I'm not worried about who knows."

Brantley held his gaze, nodding in understanding.

"I just don't want there to be any confusion."

He watched Brantley tilt his head back just slightly, eyes hooded as he peered down his nose. It was something he did when he was being addressed and he wasn't exactly sure about what the point of the conversation was. Reese had seen him do it a dozen times and he found the move uniquely sexy.

"What confusion might that be?" Brantley asked as he crossed his arms over his chest.

"You and me. Whatever this is … I don't want people to start thinkin' one thing only to learn it's not that."

Honestly, Reese wasn't sure what he expected Brantley to say, but the understanding nod was not on the list. It was as though Brantley was expecting to be the guinea pig and he was on board with whatever Reese said. Probably should've been a relief, but it wasn't. As much as Reese wanted to think like that, he couldn't. He had no idea how to identify or label whatever was going on in his head, but it was more than some experiment.

"Hear you loud and clear," Brantley said, turning away from him. "I'll make sure JJ keeps it to herself."

"That's not what I meant," Reese countered, stepping forward.

Brantley turned back around, seemed to want to say something but refrained and said in lieu, "I'm not here to put pressure on you, Reese. You wanna use me for your own entertainment"—he raised his hands, motioned to himself—"feel free. I'm more than willing."

As much as he wanted to get into a heated argument over what this was or was not, Reese knew now wasn't the time. For one, he fucking had no clue what the hell was going on here. But more importantly, they had a five-year-old girl who was missing. They should be focusing on the mission, not trying to figure out which direction Reese's sexual orientation flag was flying.

"Then we should go hear JJ out," Reese told him. "Figure out what this woman's fascination with the beach has to do with anything."

Another lift of Brantley's chin, a clear sign he was surprised by the quick shift in topic. Reese figured the man wasn't exactly happy about it, but like usual, he was willing to go with the flow.

And that was something they'd have to discuss in the future, too.

Along with the rest of … whatever the fuck this was.

Chapter Thirteen

"WELL?" TRAVIS ASKED HIS HUSBAND WHEN HE stepped into their home office and found Gage sitting at the desk, his head in his hands.

"Haven't heard back. Still waitin' for them to get the message to Mr. Prince. They've confirmed that, yes, he is onboard the ship, but they haven't yet located him," he grumbled as he lifted his head.

Travis's gut clenched when he saw how bloodshot his husband's eyes were. He doubted his were any better, but it pained him to see the man hurting like this. But as much as he wanted to shoulder all the weight, to alleviate Kylie's and Gage's agony, he knew it wasn't possible. The only thing that would give them any peace was for them to find Kate and bring her home.

"What about you?" Gage asked. "Did you—"

His words were cut off by the doorbell chiming loudly.

Gage was instantly on his feet, eyes squinting as though he could see who it was that way.

Travis pivoted and headed for the door. Figuring it was the sheriff stopping by to tell them they hadn't been able to find anything yet—because that was what everybody was fucking telling them—he jerked it open only to come face-to-face with a couple of familiar faces from his past.

Standing on his front porch were Luke McCoy and Luke's husband, Cole Ackerley. Their expressions mirrored the somber mood that had settled over the house.

"Travis," Luke greeted, holding out his hand.

Travis took the proffered hand, but rather than shake, he jerked Luke forward for a hug. Some back slapping ensued, and Travis could feel the comfort the man was attempting to offer.

"What brings you here?" he asked, stepping back and allowing them into the house.

"We heard what was going on," Luke replied. "Figured we'd come down, see if we can help."

Travis exhaled heavily. "I wish I could say there was somethin' you could do, but the police are doin' all they can. Plus my cousin's chasin' down a few leads."

Luke's steady gaze remained on his face. "I was thinking more along the lines of the resort. Thought maybe we could offer our assistance in running it for the time being. Relieving you and your brothers so you can take care of the more important things."

Travis thrust a hand through his hair. "Honest to God, I haven't thought twice about the resort."

As far as he was concerned, the place could go up in flames and it wouldn't make a damn difference to him. Right now, the only thing Travis could focus on was his missing daughter.

"Hence the reason we're here. Just to offer a helping hand."

Peering over his shoulder at Gage, he saw the relief there. If he had to guess, Gage was attempting to keep everything in balance even if it was tearing him apart inside.

"I'm not gonna refuse the offer," Travis told Luke.

Luke responded with a hesitant smile. "I was hopin' you wouldn't. And we've also come bearing gifts."

Frowning, he glanced down at Luke's hands. The man wasn't holding anything, so his confusion was obvious.

"In the way of a private jet. Trent's, actually. He was kind enough to send us down here with it. Said it's at your disposal should you need it. And if you don't, it'll return us to Dallas whenever you say the word."

Trent Ramsey, one of Hollywood's golden boys, as well as a business mogul, had sent his jet. He'd only interacted with Trent a few times and they had some sort of one-sided rivalry—on Trent's side—going on, but the man had offered to help in this crisis. On top of that, Luke and Cole had dropped everything to come down and help out an old friend.

"We've got Xander keeping an eye on Dichotomy and Club Destiny, so we're here for whatever you need, Travis. And Logan and Sam have offered to help in whatever way they can."

Tears filled Travis's eyes as the pain he'd fought to hold back ripped through him. Before he knew it, Gage was there, a wall of support, pulling him in close. Strong arms wrapped around him, and for a couple of minutes, they held each other up.

It wasn't that Luke or Cole or even Trent was offering anything more than everyone else, but it was that they were there when Travis and his family needed them most that brought the flood. That and the fact that with so many powerful people helping, he couldn't deny the hope that flared.

Gage released his firm hold, pulling back enough to look in his face. Those strong hands curled around his neck, his thumbs gliding over Travis's jaw. "We're gonna bring her home."

The promise in his words was so powerful Travis had to believe them. "I know."

It took a minute, but he managed to pull himself together enough to talk to Luke and Cole once more. He found them in the living room, glancing around the house as though taking it in for the first time. Then again, it probably was the first time they'd been there. Most of Travis's get-togethers were held at the resort. Simpler that way.

"We appreciate the help," he told them both. "Sincerely appreciate it."

"Anything we can do, just let us know. We've got some favors due us, so I mean that. If you need us to push someone…" Luke smirked. "Well, you know how much joy I get in that."

Travis smiled and it felt genuine. "Thanks. Helping with the resort is more than enough."

"I think the only thing we need from you is permission to be there," Cole said, speaking for the first time. "I assume you've got someone managing the place in your absence. If you give them the go-ahead, we'll utilize them to get what we need."

"Of course." Travis nodded. "And the pilot and crew … might as well put them up at the hotel in case we need them."

"I'm sure they'll appreciate it," Cole stated. "But we'll warn them ahead of time."

Travis laughed, though the sound was definitely fragile.

ONCE BRANTLEY AND REESE JOINED JJ AND Dante in the barn, she began rattling off more details than Brantley cared to have about a woman who was looking more and more like the one who had taken Kate. And if JJ was right, they'd narrowed down her possible location to more than a few beach towns in Mississippi.

While he wasn't sure how the hell they would cover all that ground easily, Brantley was glad to see they had a direction to go. A mission, so to speak.

Once JJ had finished relaying the information, he'd gotten on the phone with Travis and Gage, passed on what they'd learned, and asked where they wanted them now. They were currently waiting for a phone call with a firm answer.

If they'd had boots on the ground in Mississippi, they would at least have the opportunity to hunt for the woman. Whether she'd taken Kate or not, the only way to check her off the list was to find her and confirm for themselves.

"So, I was thinkin' maybe I could bring a chair from home," JJ mused, knocking on the side of the trash can she was still perching on when she worked.

He pretended to consider that. "And what? You'll drag it back and forth as you need it?"

"It beats the hell outta sittin' on this thing." She shrugged her shoulders and rolled her head on her neck. "Not all that comfortable."

With a heavy sigh, Brantley dug his wallet out of his pocket, produced a credit card, and held it out to JJ. He could feel Dante and Reese watching him.

"What's this?"

"Money," he said as though it wasn't obvious. "Buy some stuff for in here. Maybe another desk, couple of chairs."

Her green eyes brightened. "You're serious?"

"Yeah. It's been my intention all along. Just haven't gotten around to it."

"While you're at it," Reese told JJ, "get him a couch for the house."

JJ's grin was slow and bright. "That's a brilliant idea."

"Don't buy me a fuckin' couch," he stated, turning toward the door. "Don't need one."

"If you expect me to hang around, you do," Reese said, his voice trailing behind him.

"Why would I expect that?" he asked when they'd stepped outside, leaving JJ and Dante in the barn to finish up what they were working on.

He was honestly hoping they wouldn't get back on the subject, because after what Reese told him earlier, Brantley wasn't in the mood to listen to him waffle back and forth about what he might or might not want.

Brantley led the way back into the house, leaving the door open behind him as he headed for the refrigerator, grabbed a bottle of water.

It was true, he'd been disappointed when Reese admitted his confusion. After that kiss in the truck, the one Reese had initiated … well, to be honest, Brantley had started to think this thing between them was growing stronger. Not that a couple of intense kisses made this anything special. He'd been intimate with enough men over the years to know when someone was experimenting. Not all men he'd been with had been decidedly gay, but they'd all been committed to the encounter at the time.

And fine, he had told Reese he was there for his personal use. In his defense, it had been a knee-jerk reaction, something he said off-the-cuff because he hadn't wanted Reese to catch on to the fact he'd been hurt by the idea of what Reese was insinuating. Now that some time had passed, the moment behind them, Brantley wasn't keen on the idea of dredging it up again.

It wasn't that he was looking for a relationship. In fact, he didn't think that was in the cards for him for the future. Admittedly, he'd considered the notion for a few moments. There was just something about Reese. Then again, it could be the fact that he knew nothing would come of this. Reese was curious, not interested. There was a big fucking difference.

"You wanna give me a ride back to Travis's?" Reese asked, the subject clearly dropped and forgotten by him as well.

Good to know.

"Yep."

Snagging his keys off the island, Brantley didn't falter on his way to the door. Outside, he headed right for the driver's door, Reese to the passenger's. Neither of them said anything during the quick trip back to town and over to Travis's. Rather than go inside, see if they'd come to a decision, Brantley simply dropped Reese off, then returned the way he'd come.

Before he'd made it back to Main Street, his cell phone was ringing. He hit the button on the steering wheel to take the call, seeing on the truck's navigation screen that it was Travis.

"Hey, man," he greeted softly.

"High-tailin' it outta Dodge?" Travis retorted. "I saw you drop Reese off. Looked like you were runnin'."

Rather than answer, he grunted. It was the truth, and any lie he tried to tell, Travis would see right through it. The man was nothing if not astute.

"Gotta plan for me?"

"Yeah." Travis's voice was firm, his amusement vanishing completely. "I know it's a long shot, but we talked and figured it would be best for you to head out. To Mississippi. Pick a city to start from, I don't give a fuck. In the meantime, I've got my brothers helpin' out with the search here. We'll cover more ground this way."

"For what it's worth, I agree. Might net us nothing, but it won't hurt to extend the search."

"I don't know why I think you're onto somethin', Brantley, but that's what my gut's tellin' me. I'd go myself, but… Just bring my daughter back to me, Brantley."

Feeling the emotions in those words, Brantley cleared his throat. "I will," he promised.

Sure, it was a tall order and God only knew what was in store for them when they got there, but he knew the only way they were all going to make it through was if they maintained hope.

"There's a private jet waitin' for you," Travis continued. "Figure out where you wanna go, and get the details to the pilot ASAP so he can file the flight plan. I'll have a car waitin' for you, wherever you go. You'll have to drive from there."

With a plan forming, Brantley confirmed, then disconnected the call. Although he hesitated, wondering if he should simply go solo on this mission, he caved, calling Reese to relay the information. Without preamble, he dropped the high-level details.

"I'll meet you at your place," Reese said.

"I'll swing by yours," he countered. "I'm only a couple minutes away. You can pack a bag while we figure out the plan. Need to let the pilot know where we're headed."

"Pilot?"

"Yep. Private plane."

"Yeah … um … all right."

Brantley listened as Reese rattled off the address then disconnected. He entered the details in his navigation, though he knew the vicinity to which he was headed. There were only two apartment complexes in Coyote Ridge, neither of them substantial.

Roughly five minutes later, he was pulling into an empty space in front of Building A, beside Reese's truck. How the man had beaten him there, he didn't know, nor did he care. Probably knew a shortcut.

Not long after that, he was banging a fist on Reese's hunter-green door with its tarnished brass security hole. Across the way, someone stuck their head out but quickly ducked back inside when Brantley turned to look. He turned back when the door opened, Reese walking away as soon as entry was granted.

The chill that greeted him was not from the air conditioning. Looked as though some of Brantley's tension had rubbed off.

Stepping inside, the first thing he noticed was that, unlike him, Reese had a couch. It had seen better days, but he had one. And it was where Reese headed, sitting down directly in front of the laptop that was open on the coffee table.

"All right. Based on what JJ told us," Reese stated, "I've got quite a few places noted on the map. It's probably a long shot, but I say we start with those closest to where she grew up."

"Opposite," Brantley corrected. "Keep in mind, if we're right, Juliet's doin' this because her daughter was taken away from her. If she thinks there's a chance she'll see her again, she'd want to be closer to Lani than to her folks."

"Okay. We'll do it your way. Start in Gulfport, work our way west."

"I'll let the pilot know where we're headed and that we'll be there in"—he glanced at his watch, then started for the door—"forty-five minutes. You call Travis, tell him where to have the rental waiting. I'll meet you at the airport."

"Or I could ride with you," Reese said quickly.

"Nah. I'll meet you there."

Without looking back, Brantley marched out of the apartment, back to his truck. He knew he'd just pulled an asshole stunt, but Reese had successfully stepped on his pride earlier and Brantley needed a little time to get over it.

He only hoped he could do so in the next forty-five minutes.

REESE KNEW HE HAD DEFINITELY PUT HIS foot in his mouth earlier. Now as he parked his truck in an empty spot at the private airstrip in Pflugerville, he figured he would have to apologize. As for whether Brantley would be in the mood to listen, much less accept the gesture, Reese didn't know. However, he was not about to spend God only knew how much time with the man while he was in a mood.

He grabbed his duffel from the back seat, hefted it over his shoulder, then started for the building. He was pulled up short when he heard someone shouting his name, then saw Brantley waving in his direction. Redirecting, he marched over to the private plane that would evidently be making their trip a bit less stressful.

It took effort, but he tried not to appear impressed when he stepped into the cabin, following Brantley. The first thing he noticed was the head room. He didn't have to duck to stroll through.

Definitely not your mother's typical mode of transportation. Everything in the thing was high-end, including the buttery leather seats, the plush carpeting on the floor. There was even a large television mounted in the wall, probably to keep it from taking flight on its own in the event of turbulence.

"May I take your bag?"

Reese turned to see a woman standing behind him. Auburn hair, green eyes, and skin so pale Reese didn't think she spent much time in the sun. She was dressed conservatively, but not in one of those navy getups most flight attendants wore. On any given day, she would've been exactly his type, a woman he would've struck up a conversation with in an effort to determine if she was good company. Today he felt no need to converse, no desire to gauge her interests in the hopes of taking her to bed.

Odd.

"Sure," he said in response to her question.

She took the canvas duffel with a smile, placed it inside a closet near the front of the plane, returning a moment later.

"We're looking at roughly three hours and twenty minutes to get to Gulfport," she said kindly. "Good news is, we won't have to wait to land; however, we are delayed by fifteen minutes in getting in the air. Can I get you anything while you wait?"

"Just a bottle of water," he answered, then glanced over to see Brantley was nursing a beer. "Scratch that. I'll have what he's havin'."

"Absolutely."

When she disappeared to the front of the plane, Reese turned his attention to the brooding man.

"You've been here a while," he assumed, taking a seat across the table from Brantley in a single leather recliner that looked more comfortable than any piece of furniture he owned. As he sank into it, he realized it actually was.

"Had a bag in the truck."

For some reason, that pissed Reese off. The guy could've simply waited. Then again, they would've had to spend time together, and based on the way Brantley was avoiding looking in his direction, that was where the problem lay.

"You still keep a go-bag?"

"Damn straight. Never know when you'll need to jet in a hurry."

The flight attendant returned.

In order to save face for a few minutes and not involve the kind woman waiting on them, Reese decided not to tackle the hard conversation yet. Instead, he accepted the beer, chatted with the woman who had yet to give him her name.

"During the flight, I'll be in my quarters," she explained, glancing between the two of them. "Feel free to utilize the amenities on the plane. In the back you'll find a small office, a bedroom, as well as the restroom. We have Wi-Fi if you need it and just about any movie you could possibly want to watch, including all the new releases. If you need me, simply push that button"—she pointed to a silver button on the wall behind them—"and I'll be happy to get you anything you need."

"I'm sure we'll be fine," he told her when it was obvious Brantley's lack of manners extended to her as well.

"Very well." Her gaze bounced between them briefly before she offered a smile and headed toward the front of the plane.

"Any reason you're bein' a dick to everyone?" Reese asked when they were alone.

Brantley's blue-gray eyes flipped toward him. "Not in the mood for people."

"Look, Brantley, about what I said earlier … I wasn't—"

"Not in the mood for people," Brantley growled, his stormy gaze shooting daggers his way.

So that was how he wanted to be. Fine. Reese could play that game, too.

"In that case, I think I'll relocate elsewhere."

Taking his beer, Reese ventured to the back of the plane. There was more seating in the main cabin, but he chose to check out the office. Inside, there was a small desk and a chair complete with seat belt. The window in this room was a little bigger, but he could close the shade to block out the light, which was what he was looking for.

Placing the bottle into a cup holder, Reese took a seat, belted himself in, and slid the window cover down. Yep, the perfect place to catch a nap. Three-plus hours, she'd said.

Just enough time.

Forty-five minutes later, Reese realized sleeping wasn't on the agenda. The plane had taken off without incident, the pilot coming over the speaker to relay the information about the flight path, their estimated landing time, as well as the weather. At one point, he was almost positive he heard Brantley come back, but he figured that was likely wishful thinking because even though this was a luxury aircraft, the hum of the engines still drowned out any noises on the other side of the door.

They had to iron this shit out between them. For the sake of the op if nothing else. Reese couldn't imagine they'd get much accomplished with Brantley pissed at him for his distasteful comment. He'd been in a panic, scared about what Brantley stirred in him. Telling him he didn't want others to see something that wasn't there … he hadn't meant it. Not really.

Reese stretched when he stood, grabbed his empty beer bottle, deposited it in the small trash can, and headed out of the office. He noticed the main cabin was dark; only running lights along the floor were on, all the window shades battened down. Reese stopped before getting to the front, where he figured Brantley was snoozing. It would be wise to return to the office, hide out for the remainder of the trip, and let Brantley get some sleep.

Right?

Yes.

As for why he didn't move, Reese wasn't sure. Was he seriously going to be a chickenshit? Avoid the confrontation that was inevitable? He needed to smooth the waters with Brantley, if for no other reason than so they could find Kate and take her safely back home where she belonged.

Okay.

He was going to take a seat, wake Brantley, have a conversation.

Taking a deep breath, he started forward, but stopped suddenly when a firm hand landed on his shoulder, urging him back.

His body stilled, his muscles on high alert. The fight-or-flight instinct kicked in, but he refrained from going hand to hand with the man behind him. It was a natural response, but he managed to refrain because he recognized who was behind him. The hand on his shoulder was Brantley's, as was the unique masculine scent that drifted in the air.

Brantley's other hand was on him then, sliding around his waist, his palm flattening on Reese's stomach. He looked down, watching the move, noticing the veins in Brantley's thickly muscled arm. The sight of it was much like the kisses they'd shared. It threw him off-balance for a moment, had his breath hitching.

"We need to talk," Brantley said softly, his voice a soft growl in Reese's ear.

"I agree."

But Brantley didn't launch into a conversation. No, the arm banded around him pulled him back until Brantley's chest was pressed against his back, one arm around his middle, the other hand curling around his throat, tilting his head back.

The move was erotic and sensual, a control thing that he'd come to expect from Brantley. The man had him right where he wanted him. Warm breaths fanned his neck and it was all Reese could do to remain standing. There was something shockingly salacious about this moment, the way Brantley had taken control, holding him firmly but not forcefully.

"I've decided I won't be your guinea pig," Brantley whispered, his words vibrating against Reese's neck.

Reese covered Brantley's arm with his, firmly gripping the thick forearm, ensuring they would not be separated.

"Not expectin' you to be," he admitted. "But I can't make any promises, Brantley."

"Not askin' for any."

The hand on his throat tightened, tilting his head back another inch. Reese sucked in a shocked breath when Brantley nipped his jaw.

"Close your eyes," Brantley instructed.

Without hesitation, Reese closed his eyes, allowed the hard body behind him to hold him up. Not exactly the conversation he'd been expecting…

Warm, smooth lips trailed down his neck, pausing where his neck met his shoulder. Then Brantley's hand fell from his throat, sliding to his hip. The other slipped out from beneath Reese's arm, so he allowed his own to drop to his side.

"What are you feelin' right now?" Brantley asked.

"Tension," he said because it was the truth. His entire body, from the roots of his hair to the tips of his toes, was coiled tightly.

That only intensified when Brantley's hands slid beneath his T-shirt, his splayed fingers gliding over his stomach up to his chest. Although the idea of pulling away, telling Brantley to stop vaguely crossed his mind, words were absent. He was a hot ball of sensation, every inch of him aware of the man standing at his back.

"Do you like my hands on you?"

Reese figured there was no reason to lie. "Yes."

Those hands took a detour, gliding back down until the tips of Brantley's fingers were dipping into the waistband of Reese's jeans.

Christ Almighty.

Reese's lungs worked overtime, his heart hammering in his chest.

"And now?"

"Yes." He wanted to urge Brantley not to stop, but he couldn't bring the words to his lips. While he enjoyed the fuck out of this, there was hesitation lingering. He doubted it would last long, but for now, it was still there, still making him question what he wanted.

Brantley's lips pressed to the back of Reese's neck and he leaned his head down, giving him better access. He moaned as Brantley teased his skin with his tongue, but when Brantley's mouth suctioned to his neck, Reese wondered briefly if he could come from that sensation alone.

"And my mouth? Do you like my mouth on you, Reese?"

"Fuck yes," he hissed, praying like hell Brantley wouldn't stop.

If he did … well, if the man opted to leave him hanging right now, Reese knew he wouldn't be responsible for his own actions.

Chapter Fourteen

BRANTLEY HADN'T INTENDED FOR THIS, BUT WHEN he'd stepped out of the bathroom to find Reese standing before him, it was the first and only thing he'd thought about doing.

Now that his hands were on Reese, he didn't want to let go.

No, he wasn't trying to seduce the guy. Not to the degree they would end up naked, anyway. But he was trying to prove a point, and from where he stood, it was working.

"If it feels good, why does it matter if I'm a man?" he asked, licking his way up to Reese's ear before nipping the lobe gently.

"It doesn't."

"No?"

Reese grunted when Brantley flicked his fingernail over one nipple, then the other.

"Earlier you said you didn't want people to get the wrong impression."

"Correct."

"Meaning you don't want people to think you're gay if you decide you're not."

Another grunt followed, along with a hiss when Brantley tweaked Reese's nipple.

"I want to know what you want from me, Reese."

"Ever occur to you that I don't know?"

He had expected Reese to say that. Even suspected Reese believed it was true.

"You're on the fence," he contemplated. "You're teetering on the edge and you don't know if you should simply fall or jump." Brantley kissed his neck, inhaling that spicy scent he'd come to crave in such a short time. "I want you to jump, Reese."

"Why?"

"Because jumping's a choice."

"And falling's not?" Reese countered.

"No." He let his hands slide down Reese's smooth abdomen, dipping his fingertips in his jeans once more. "Falling's an accident and everyone knows accidents have repercussions."

Expecting a retort, Brantley was thrown off guard when Reese suddenly spun out of his hold, turning around, cupping both sides of his neck in those big, warm hands. Their eyes met, held.

"Jumping has repercussions, too," Reese bit out.

Holding his ground, he stared into those golden eyes, saw the turmoil and the lust. "And you're scared of both." Brantley tilted his chin back, daring him to argue.

"I'm not scared."

"Then what's stoppin' you from touchin' me?" he ground out, lifting his T-shirt. "Touch me, Reese."

They remained like that for long seconds, Reese's hands still curled around his neck, Brantley's legs braced to keep them from falling over, his shirt pulled up to his chest.

"Touch me," he pleaded, his words softer, more urgent. "I'm not askin' for more. Just touch me."

Reese's hands loosened, then started drifting lower. The sensations were fucking amazing and to think they were both fully dressed… And when Reese's bare hands flattened on his stomach, Brantley hissed.

"Is that what you want?" Reese questioned, his words clipped, his hands firmly gripping his waist, fingertips digging into his back as though he was scared to move them.

"You have no fucking idea what I want from you, Reese. This is just the beginning."

"And what happens if I can't give you what you need?"

"Touch me," he growled softly. "Just fuckin' touch me, Reese."

Reese leaned in, nipped his lower lip while his hands blazed a trail up his torso. "What if I can't give you everything?"

"We'll take it slow."

"Doesn't matter how fast or slow we go," Reese said, pulling back enough for their eyes to meet. "Right here and now, I could tell you I'd give you whatever you want. In this moment, it would be the truth. But when the time comes…"

The delicious growl in those words had his blood pumping hot and fast in his veins. It was true, he wanted Reese to commit to seeing where this would go because … hell, Brantley wasn't even sure why it was necessary, but it was.

"Slow," he repeated.

"And you think that's gonna make it easier?"

If he'd thought for one second that there wasn't something more here, Brantley would've backed away, told Reese he had a damn fine point. However, they'd spent too much time together in recent weeks. What was transpiring between them … it surpassed friendship. And he wasn't simply referring to the kissing and the touching. There was more here. He wasn't sure how he knew that, but he did. And Reese … for some damn reason, Brantley knew Reese was the man he could give all of himself to despite his own reservations about relationships.

Sure, it was a scary thought, but one he couldn't ignore. Didn't want to.

Brantley took Reese's hand, tugging it from his stomach and gripping firmly. He stepped back, leading the way to the bedroom.

"What're you doin'?"

Glancing back at Reese, he kept his expression blank. "Trust me?"

Those golden eyes narrowed but Brantley could see the truth in them. He did trust him, and he proved it when he took another step, then another, following obediently.

Once inside the cramped room, which was little more than a bed, Brantley sat on the mattress, tugged Reese's arm until he joined him.

"Right now, the only thing you're gonna do is kiss me. Nothin' more than that."

Reese didn't seem convinced, but Brantley knew he would learn Brantley was a man of his word. He didn't overstep.

He leaned in, inhaling that seductive scent. "Kiss me, Reese."

Although there was a moment of hesitation, it didn't last long. Reese's lips met his and there was an electric storm that ignited in the confined space. It consumed them both, intensifying when Brantley lay back on the bed, pulling Reese with him.

That was where they remained, Reese laid out beside him, their lips fused, thighs touching, hands shifting. Minutes passed as the passion churned. It never got out of hand, but Brantley knew it easily could have. They were both holding back, but it was necessary.

Sliding his hand beneath Reese's T-shirt, he urged the cotton higher. "Take this off."

Reese pulled back, stared at him, his eyes hard, confusion evident.

"I told you, only this. But I want to touch you."

Reese's Adam's apple bobbed when he swallowed hard, but he finally relented, gripping the back of his shirt and pulling it over his head. Brantley took it from him, set it on the mattress at his side.

"Now mine," he instructed.

There was a bit less hesitancy that time, as though Reese agreed with that plan.

Once they were both shirtless, Brantley slid his hand behind Reese's head, pulled his lips back down to his. He explored Reese's mouth with his tongue, mimicking what he would one day do to his body.

"Closer," Brantley urged, tugging Reese until the man was moving over him, straddling his thighs, leaning in.

Up to this point, they'd never been quite this close, this intimate. The previous times they'd kissed, Reese had maintained his distance, which was the reason Brantley urged him closer. He wanted Reese to feel him, to know who he was with at all times.

It was better, but Brantley wanted to feel his heat. He trailed his hands up Reese's sides, watched the man shiver from the sensations, loving the way those golden eyes glittered with barely restrained passion.

He pulled Reese down until their upper bodies were touching, their chests pressed intimately together.

"This is all I want," Brantley promised him. "It's all I'm askin' you to give me."

For now, it was more than enough.

⌒◡◡ℓ

FUCK.

Too good.

Reese wasn't sure why this was the most erotic encounter of his entire life up to this point, but it was. Or, at least, it sure felt like it.

Had touching someone ever felt this fucking good? Having their hands on him? No. Definitely not. His entire body hummed … no, make that vibrated with lust. Beneath him, Brantley was so warm, so hard. Reese could feel the hard ridge of his cock pressed between them, extremely close to his own. It took effort not to grind his hips, to rut against the man just to ease the ridiculous ache.

It probably should've felt strange, but it didn't. The hard planes and angles of Brantley's body were noticeably different than the soft, smooth contours of the women Reese had been with before, sure. But it was a good different. Where he was used to soft sighs and a gentle touch, he got neither with Brantley. Firm hands stroked over his skin, leaving blazing heat in their wake while the hard body beneath him held still, as though he was worried Reese might panic and go running from the room.

Running was the last thing on his mind. For one, he wasn't sure his lungs were working properly. Every time Brantley's hands grazed his bare back, Reese sucked in oxygen like it was scarce. And every time they went dangerously close to his ass, Reese held his breath, praying like hell Brantley would venture just a little lower.

Until finally he did.

Brantley's big hands cupped his ass, gently pulling him closer. Reese grunted as the friction on his cock had him seeing stars. "Don't," he rasped.

The hands released him and suddenly Brantley was staring up at him, confused.

"I didn't mean to stop doin' that," he clarified, sliding his arms beneath Brantley's, curling his fingers around his shoulders, letting the man bear his full weight as he laid out over him. "Just don't make me come like a fuckin' teenager."

Brantley chuckled, his body loosening, hands returning, only this time they slid inside Reese's jeans, those calloused palms scraping sensually on his ass.

"Fuck," he bit out, unable to stop himself from humping the man beneath him.

"Let go, Reese," Brantley urged, his deep voice scraping along every one of his senses.

"Don't … please don't make me do this."

"Never make you," Brantley whispered softly, his lips pressing to Reese's neck, his tongue licking along the underside of his jaw.

Reese was rocking his hips forward, back, the hands inside his jeans holding on but not forcing him. No, Brantley wasn't controlling this, Reese was. It was his movements that were working him dangerously close to the edge.

"Kiss me, Reese. Put your mouth on mine."

He did and when he plunged his tongue inside Brantley's mouth, his hips bucked, and a devastating moan escaped as his cock exploded. He came like a teenager who had no control over his dick.

He went limp, but that didn't seem to bother Brantley. The hands slipped out of his jeans and moved over his back, gentler this time, soothing. Those solid arms wrapped around him, holding him as though he mattered, and the sensation was foreign yet not entirely unwelcome.

Reese was still aware of Brantley's cock, hard and thick beneath his hips. His brain conjured up images he'd never thought would flit about inside his head. He could imagine himself with his lips wrapped around Brantley's thick shaft, sliding over him, taking him in deep… He wanted to taste, to explore, to experience the pleasures he knew could be had with this man.

Again, there was hesitance, though his resistance was dwindling. With every passing second, he wanted more, wanted to know what it would feel like to give himself to a man. No. Not just any man. To this man. Only Brantley.

Another grunt escaped him as he drove the images out of his head. It wasn't that they were inappropriate, but this really wasn't the time or place. His brain wasn't yet on the same track as his body, and until they were aligned, he knew he needed to put on the brakes.

"For the record, that does not qualify us into the Mile-High Club," Brantley said, his voice teasing. "So, we'll have to add that to our to-do list for the future."

Lifting his head, he stared down at Brantley, saw that the guy was smiling as though it didn't matter that his dick was iron hard in his jeans and there was no relief in sight for him.

"The future?"

The teasing glint disappeared, Brantley's face sobering. Uncertainty swamped the heat, strangling it, sending it away, and Reese suddenly wanted to reassure him, to let Brantley know where they stood, because it mattered.

"I'll commit to the future," Reese told him. "If that's what you want. I want to see where this goes, Brantley. I want … to see where it goes."

A slight nod was all he got in return, but he could see the relief in Brantley's stormy blue eyes. Whatever this was … Brantley didn't have to worry because it wasn't an experiment on Reese's part. Well, mostly. There were some things that would require experimentation. Namely when it came to their sexual encounters, because Reese had never been touched by a man, much less done any touching of his own.

However, outside of getting to know him on an intimate level … no experimentation necessary. He knew exactly who he wanted.

Two hours later, Reese was riding shotgun while Brantley drove the black Chevy Tahoe toward the beach.

Before they'd touched down, he'd managed to grab a quick shower and change his clothes in what turned out to be a full bath on the luxury jet. After they had landed, the first place they had gone was Nicholas Prince's main residence. They'd gotten the same runaround as they had at the Austin house, although the majordomo in charge of that domain had been somewhat pleasant, informing them that Mr. and Mrs. Prince were currently on an Alaskan cruise and wouldn't be back for ten more days.

They'd already known this but checking out the house had given them the chance to get a feel for who Nicholas Prince was and what his ex-wife had given up to the younger version of herself. And after seeing a picture of the happy couple in the entryway of the Prince home, Reese decided that was exactly what Meghan Prince was. She had the same blond hair, the same blue eyes, even the pouty lips were the same. So either these two women went to the same plastic surgeon or Nicholas had a type.

When the answers to their questions had dried up, they'd decided to optimize what was left of the daylight hours by flashing pictures of Juliet Prince as well as Kate to people at the local beach, see if anyone had seen them. While every answer they received was in the negative, Reese held out hope.

And while they were pounding pavement—or sand as was the case here—JJ was back at the tech barn doing her thing. The woman truly was gifted with a computer. From what she'd told them, she'd managed to dump Nicholas Prince's phone and she was currently chasing down phone numbers to see if they could find one that might lead them directly to Juliet rather than the scenic route they were currently on.

To top it off, Z had offered to send one of the Sniper 1 Security agents to Juliet Prince's parents' house in Louisiana just to check in, see if they'd seen or heard from their daughter. While Gage had successfully called them and filled them in on their suspicions—something Juliet's parents adamantly denied was even a possibility—everyone was looking for more concrete answers. Since a little girl's life hung in the balance, it only made sense.

And to ensure the Arondas didn't tip their daughter off to the investigation, JJ had managed to tap into their phones, keeping an eye on them that way. Sure, it was illegal, but in the grand scheme of things, who really gave a shit? Until Kate was brought safely back home to her parents, anything and everything was fair game.

"What do you say we swing by the police department, fill them in on what we know, then grab a bite to eat?" Brantley said when they'd once again returned to the Tahoe.

"Provided I pick the restaurant," he said simply because he wanted to harass the man.

"Fine. Where do you wanna go?"

"Haven't decided yet. But I'll let you know soon enough."

Just as soon as he figured it out himself.

THE RESTAURANT REESE SELECTED WAS A SEAFOOD joint near the hotel that boasted they had the best steak and lobster in town. As far as whether they were, Brantley didn't know, but he would take their word for it. Dinner had been good, the company more so.

"Why'd you enlist?" he asked Reese as he stared at the man across the table.

"Because my brother couldn't."

Taking a long pull on his beer, Brantley waited for Reese to elaborate. It didn't take long before he did.

"Z has a congenital heart defect that kept him from going into the military. It was always his dream though it was just out of reach. I looked up to him, thought he walked on water. Still do, most of the time."

"So you figured you'd let him live vicariously through you?"

"Somethin' like that."

"You said you were in for eight years?"

"Yeah. A couple of tours in Iraq, one in Afghanistan. Saw more action than I cared for, figured I'd do it until I no longer wanted to. One day, I woke up, realized I was done with it. Completed my tour, came home. Haven't really thought much about it since." Reese nodded his chin in Brantley's direction. "What about you?"

"I wanted to be a SEAL," he said easily. "The best of the best. My brothers harassed me, said there was no way I'd make it. At that point, I had to prove them wrong. To be a SEAL, I had to enlist."

"What'd your parents think?"

"They supported me." Brantley smiled. "Maybe not completely at first. I think all parents have fears about their children going into the military, but they didn't try to talk me out of it."

"And your brothers? They eat crow when you didn't ring out?"

Brantley laughed. "Oh, yeah. I gave them shit for the longest time. Still remind them."

"You'd still be there if…?"

Nodding, he took another swallow of beer. "Yeah. Thought I'd be there until…"

He let the sentence trail off, not wanting to dampen the mood. Truth was, Brantley had figured he would die in the line of duty. He was a SEAL at his core, a man who needed to complete the mission, to fight for the country he loved. He honestly hadn't considered what life would look like after, until he'd been forced to.

"And now?" Reese asked, drawing Brantley out of his thoughts.

"Now what?"

"What're your plans?"

Brantley glanced around. "No idea."

"You like chasin' the bad guys."

Since it wasn't a question, he didn't respond.

"You're good at it, too."

"I wouldn't go that far." Brantley finished off his beer. "If I'm bein' honest, JJ's the one who uncovered all this. She found the image of the blond, located her, uncovered her truths."

And ultimately broke the case, provided they weren't going down a rabbit hole. There was still the possibility Juliet Prince had no part in Kate's kidnapping and they'd get to the end of the line and find themselves back at square one.

"Ever thought about being a PI?"

Brantley chuckled, shaking his head. "No. Definitely not."

"Why's that?"

"I'd shovel shit for a livin' before I'd arm myself with a camera to catch some asshole cheatin' on his ol' lady."

"Well, when you paint it in that flattering light…"

Shifting forward, Brantley pulled his wallet out of his pocket. Before he could retrieve his credit card, Reese snagged the leather folder with the bill in it.

"I've got this. You can buy breakfast."

Smiling, he leaned back, relaxed. "Two-dollar sausage biscuit sandwiches at McDonald's. You're on."

"You better make good on those promises, Navy boy."

An hour later, Brantley was walking out of the bathroom, the steam from his shower drifting out behind him. His damp towel was wrapped securely around his hips, but not for long. Although he had company, he had no intentions of changing his sleeping habits, which consisted of no clothing. The less restriction, the better as far as he was concerned.

He found Reese propped up in the bed closest to the window, the remote in his hand. He'd changed into shorts and a T-shirt, his feet bare, legs out long over the comforter, looking as relaxed as Brantley'd ever seen him. Well, except for the man's shoulders. They were tense, as though he was gearing up for an attack but not quite sure where it would be coming from.

Rather than join him, Brantley dragged back the comforter on the other bed, flopped down into it, kicking his feet out as he grabbed his cell phone. If he hadn't been watching Reese out of the corner of his eye, he would've missed the relieved breath he'd released.

Yep. The man was still strung tight, despite the orgasm he'd had earlier.

Not that Brantley expected anything less. Hell, he'd been surprised when Reese had offered to share a room provided there were two beds. He figured it had more to do with saving money than wanting to be in close proximity, but whatever. The man was nearby, close enough Brantley could keep an eye on him, yet far enough away to strip away the temptation.

Mostly.

He took a few minutes to type out a message to Travis, let him know what they'd accomplished tonight, who they'd talked to and what his plans were for tomorrow, promising to keep in touch along the way. Once that was done, he hooked the phone to the charger and set it nearby.

Reaching over, Brantley clicked off the lamp on the stand between the two beds. He'd already set his alarm for six since they were still on central time, figuring that would be the perfect time to head out. If all went well—and he prayed like hell it did—they'd have Kate safe and sound by the time the sun went down and Juliet Prince would be behind bars.

Chapter Fifteen

THE NEXT DAY WAS SPENT DRIVING, CHOWING down on fast food, and walking endlessly along the beach while showing pictures of Juliet Prince and Kate to people who all claimed to have not seen either the woman or the child. At least the walking helped to offset their shitty food choices, but other than that, it wasn't doing a whole lot of good.

While they were hitting one wall after another, Brantley wasn't giving up hope. He wasn't allowing himself to be discouraged. Doing so wouldn't help Kate in the long run and that was his only motivation. Finding the little girl, bringing her safely home to her mother and fathers.

It felt as though they'd been driving for an eternity, when in reality, they'd managed to travel a full twenty miles of coastline, the majority of which was spent walking, then backtracking to the Tahoe only to drive down a ways and do it all again. Thankfully, the weather was nice, not unusually hot for mid-September because it was about ten degrees cooler than back in Coyote Ridge. Of course, the humidity was ridiculous, as were the brief, infrequent rain showers thanks to the moisture pulled in from the gulf.

Back in the Tahoe, they'd just driven the Bay St. Louis Bridge via US 90 heading toward the Hollywood Casino Gulf Coast thanks to a lead passed to them by JJ. According to a tip, someone had spotted a woman and child who resembled Juliet and Kate. While JJ hadn't divulged how she'd come to learn of this tip, Brantley wasn't ready to discredit her considering her track record, so they'd packed it up and were on their way.

"It's like we're lookin' for a very specific needle in a stack of needles," Reese grumbled, speaking up for the first time since they'd gotten in the SUV. "How're Travis and them?"

"Hangin' in there," he said, recalling the conversation he'd had with his cousin a few minutes ago. "They're alerting the Bay St. Louis Police Department, cluing them into the Amber Alert and the possible sighting."

"With any luck, they'll be able to help us," Reese stated.

Yeah, that was the plan. But unless they were willing to go door to door, Brantley didn't see this being an easy trek.

"You think she'd bring a kid to a casino?"

"If it means keeping a low profile, maybe," he mused.

Reese grunted. "I'm not buyin' it. If I'm this woman and I've just abducted the kid of a high-profile resort owner who has friends in high and low places, I'm not venturing out into the open. A few months from now, maybe. Right now, I'm hidin' out somewhere, ensuring no one finds me or the kid."

That was a damn good point. "So what're you thinkin'?"

"My bet's on her rentin' a place," Reese said. "Maybe near the beach if she's as keen on it as JJ says. A condo or a beach house. She's got to blend, so it'll be in a rural area. Not too many neighbors to ask a lot of questions. She won't want them chattin' up her kid, findin' out Kate's not really hers."

Brantley pulled off his sunglasses, glanced over at Reese. "Go on."

"JJ said there were a couple of calls made to Juliet's parents that pinged off a cell tower near Diamondhead." Reese had his cell phone in hand, a map pulled up on the screen. "Looks to be a small town. And with its proximity to the Hollywood Casino, it's possible someone around here did see her."

"Put in an address," Brantley instructed, nodding toward the navigation screen.

"Roughly half an hour drive," Reese said as he keyed in the information.

A hop, skip, and a jump from where they were. But with night falling soon, Brantley doubted they'd cover much ground. However, that didn't mean they couldn't scope out the area so they could start their search at first light.

"I say we go in here," he told Reese, nodding toward the hotel in front of them. "Show the pictures just to tie up loose ends, make sure no one's seen them. Then we'll head that way, grab some dinner, drive through the town, see what we can find."

"Works for me."

"Why don't I go in. You call JJ, let her know what the plan is. See if she can do some diggin' on rentals in the area. Maybe find something that's been leased recently. She might've found a place before she made her move, ensuring she had a safe place to go back to."

After getting Reese's agreement, Brantley hopped out of the truck, headed inside the hotel. He found a pleasant-faced woman standing behind the check-in desk, her eyes glued to a computer screen.

"Welcome," she greeted, glancing over at him, her smile widening as he approached. "Are you here to check in?"

"Actually," he said, casually leaning a forearm on the counter, "I was wonderin' if you could help me. I'm lookin' for a friend of mine." He flashed a smile, laid on the country charm. "Actually, she's a friend of my mama's. She was comin' for a visit, said she was runnin' a couple days behind, but Mama hasn't heard from her since then. That was three days ago. You know how it is. Mama's worried about her, asked me if I'd check on her, make sure she hasn't gotten herself in a bit of trouble."

The woman stared back at him, her eyes softened with worry. "Do you know what room she was staying in?"

"See, that's the problem. She told Mama she was stayin' just down the road, but … well, I know Juliet. She likes to, you know, play the tables. She wouldn't want Mama to know that, though."

"I'm sorry, but I can't divulge information on guests."

"Oh, no," he said, offering his best grin. "I wouldn't dare ask for that. I'm just wonderin' if maybe you've seen her around here." Brantley pulled up the image of Juliet on his phone, passed it over.

The woman peered down at the screen, leaned in closer, eyes narrowing. "No. I'm sorry, I haven't seen her." She looked up at him once more. "Then again, it's possible she went to the casino. There's enough people coming and going…"

"Is there anyone I could talk to there? Maybe they'll recognize her?"

She seemed to consider it for a moment, then reached for the phone. "Let me call Rick."

While she placed the call, Brantley waited patiently, glancing around the lobby, pretending to admire the space. He knew this was a long shot, but he was running on the theory they should leave no stone unturned.

A few minutes later, Brantley was wandering over to the security office, where he flashed Juliet's picture at the man he assumed was Rick only to hear that, no, he didn't recall seeing the woman there in the last couple of days, and yes, he was good with faces, tended to remember people, especially a woman who looked like that. In fact, Brantley was fairly certain the guy had swiped a thumb over the picture as though he could touch her that way.

Feeling dirtier than when he'd gotten out of the truck, Brantley returned to find Reese pacing the parking lot, the phone to his ear.

"Yeah. He's back now. Thanks, JJ. Let me know."

"What's up?" he asked when he approached.

"She's gonna see what she can find on any rentals, but it's after five, so she figures it'll be a long shot on getting answers from apartments or condos, but she said she'd do what she could and pick it back up in the mornin'."

Fuck.

Brantley hadn't wanted another day to slip by without finding Kate. The little girl had been missing for roughly fifty-three hours now and every minute that passed was one too many. He couldn't imagine how Travis, Kylie, and Gage were faring, but he had to think that if they didn't get her soon, Travis was going to break the leash they were keeping him on.

"I take it you had no luck?"

"No. Woman at the front desk didn't recognize her, and Rick, the sleazy security guy at the casino, was more interested in ogling the image. Said he would've definitely remembered her if he'd had the pleasure of her presence."

"Real sly one, huh?"

"Oh, yeah." Brantley motioned toward the truck. "Wanna head over to Diamondhead?"

"Yep. Maybe we could hit up the Dairy Queen, grab some dinner."

"Dairy Queen?"

"You got a problem with that?"

Smiling, Brantley shook his head. Nope, no problem.

REESE WAS EXHAUSTED.

Sure, it had been a long day that involved a whole hell of a lot of walking, but it was more than that. Probably had more to do with his mental state than anything.

Not that there was anything wrong with it. He was feeling fine and dandy. Or as much as any man who'd recently discovered he had the hots for another man could. And no, he wasn't fretting over the idea that he was attracted to Brantley. In fact, it made sense. The guy was … well, he was a lot of things, but intense came to mind first.

Spending the entire day watching him work, chatting it up with people in an effort to get information out of them was like watching an artist. He had a way with people, that was for sure. Beneath all those hard layers was a man who was comfortable with himself and those around him. Almost as though he didn't have a care in the world.

So, yes, Reese admired him, liked him, even.

Which wasn't the problem.

No, his issue was with the fact Brantley had promised they would take things slow, but turtle-crawl wasn't exactly what Reese had envisioned when he'd made the statement. The orgasm he'd had simply from Brantley touching him felt like a lifetime ago, but his cock remembered it like only a few minutes had passed and the damn thing was interested in a serious replay.

Needless to say, he was rock fucking hard and Brantley ... well, Brantley was doing what he did best when they were in a hotel room. He was passed out, having hit the pillow only a couple of minutes ago. When Reese had asked him about it this morning, Brantley had copped to having insomnia at home. But while on the job—how he'd referred to this trip—he knew he had to catch z's when he could. So he was. How the guy did it, he would never know, but he envied him the ability. Seemed all the cool tricks Reese had learned in the military had evaded him, slowly slipping away the longer he was a civilian.

Which was the reason he was staring at the flickering television screen, wishing like hell there was something on that could bore him to sleep. Problem with that was he wasn't paying much attention to the TV. No, he was currently wondering how inappropriate it would be to take his cock in his fist and jerk the fucker until there was a modicum of relief.

He rolled his head to the side, glanced over at the bathroom door.

Or he could take a shower, get himself off in there. Probably not quite as rude as rubbing one out only a few feet away from where Brantley was sleeping soundly.

Except, the thought of getting up didn't appeal.

Cutting his eyes back to the television, Reese groaned.

"What's the problem?" Brantley mumbled.

Fuck. "Nothin'. Go back to sleep."

"Hard to when you're makin' racket over there."

"I groaned one time," he said defensively.

"But you've been huffin' for the past ten minutes."

"You haven't been asleep for ten minutes, only—" Reese glanced at the clock, grunted again.

Fine, so Brantley had been passed out for thirty, which meant Reese had been suffering for much longer than he'd thought.

"All you have to do is ask," Brantley said.

"Ask what?" he spit out before he realized what Brantley was referring to. "Never mind. Don't answer that."

A soft chuckle sounded from the other bed.

"You find this amusin', do you?"

Brantley rolled to his back, drawing Reese's attention. The light flickering from the television cast him in shadows, highlighting his chest and the defined muscles of his abdomen. The sheet currently covering his lower half obstructed the view of more, but he could see enough to be intrigued.

Not helping.

At.

Fucking.

All.

But Reese would soon learn that torture was something Brantley excelled at.

He watched as Brantley slid one hand beneath the sheet and his imagination filled in the rest, right up until it wasn't necessary. When Brantley flipped the sheet away, Reese got an eyeful of his cock. Christ Almighty. He was long and ridiculously thick, the head swollen and darkened from the blood flow.

"What're you doin'?" he asked, the words coming out on a strangled moan.

"What you wanna do," he said easily, his head turning so his attention was on Reese.

"Brantley…"

"Just watch. That's all you hafta do."

And watch he did. His gaze was locked on the fist that slowly wrapped around Brantley's erection, stroking upward at an absurdly slow pace before reversing. If he didn't know better, he would think the man was dragging this out on purpose.

Oh, wait. He definitely was.

The fucker.

"Watch me, Reese," Brantley rasped. "Keep your eyes open."

They were fucking open, all right. Hell, Reese wasn't sure he could look away if he wanted to.

He was enraptured, checking out Brantley as he stroked himself slowly, surely, teasing the head of his cock, every now and again his torso rolling as pleasure assaulted him. It was the most satisfyingly erotic show he'd ever watched. If Brantley Walker wanted to make some serious money, he should probably consider porn.

But what made it so satisfying was seeing the way Brantley watched him while he jacked himself off. His eyes remained fixed on Reese, as though he was the fantasy that made this all possible.

Minutes ticked by, the only sound Brantley's choppy breaths as he inched closer and closer to release. That and Reese's own labored breaths ramped up by watching this sexy man touch himself.

"Let me see," Brantley whispered.

The words brought his eyes into focus, his attention shifting to Brantley's face. It was then he saw Brantley's gaze had traveled south, watching...

Oh, fuck.

Reese hadn't even realized he'd been stroking himself, his hand hidden beneath the sheet as he worked his cock in a rhythm that matched Brantley's.

Peering back at Brantley, he met his gaze, saw the desire there. It was enough to lower his inhibitions, have him kicking the sheet away, the cool air caressing his cock like a lover. Enough to have his breath hitching.

"Let me touch you, Reese."

The shocking request had his hand stilling, his mind whirling.

"I'll only touch unless you tell me otherwise."

The promise was sincere, and Reese knew he couldn't ignore the fact he wanted Brantley's hand on him.

"Okay," he whispered, nodding his head. "Yes."

Unhurried, with his hand still gripping himself firmly, Brantley rolled to a sitting position, got to his feet. Reese watched with rapt attention as he cleared the scant two feet between the beds. He noticed the flex and pull of Brantley's muscles as he kneeled on the mattress, his legs parting so that he was straddling Reese's thighs.

He was fairly certain he stopped breathing altogether when Brantley took him in hand, his long, strong fingers curling around his cock.

Reese's hips lurched upward, his legs restrained by the man sitting astride him. He was aware of Brantley in every way. The crisp hairs on his legs brushing his own, the warm, calloused palm gliding intimately over him. He was still captivated by the sight of Brantley stroking himself in tandem, one cock in each of his skilled hands.

Seconds felt like an eternity, minutes like infinity as Brantley gave him a hand job that rivaled all. It was all he could do to keep his eyes open, his brain foggy from lust and the intense urge to come. He held off for as long as he could, though he wasn't sure how he managed. When he came, it was with a brittle cry that sounded overly loud in the room.

He never closed his eyes, though, didn't let the exquisite rush overwhelm him. After all, Brantley wasn't finished, he was still jerking his cock, his movements now hurried, as though he was chasing his own release.

"Fuck. I'm gonna come," Brantley warned.

Reese wanted to tell him to come all over him, but the words remained locked in his throat as he watched Brantley's dick jerk and twitch in his fist, cum spurting forth, covering the man's rippling abs.

It was almost enough to have him coming again.

Chapter Sixteen

THE SHRILL SOUND OF A CELL PHONE was what brought Brantley into consciousness. He blindly reached out for the nightstand only to end up smacking a hard, warm body beside him.

"Shit," he grumbled, rolling the other way and reaching over to grab the phone before it went to voicemail. "Hello?"

"I'm sorry to wake you," JJ said, her voice rushed, "but I think I've found her, Brantley."

His mind came online a second after his body clearly registered her meaning. He was sitting upright, eyes opening as he took in the darkened room.

"Where?" he demanded, throwing his legs over the side of the bed and getting to his feet.

"I've got an address, and as soon as you give me the go-ahead, I'll call the local police."

Brantley was processing her words even as he dragged on his jeans. He was vaguely aware that Reese was behind him doing the same thing.

"Okay. How far is it from me?"

"Based on your GPS signal, it looks to be about ten minutes to your north. It's a small house rented by a Marie Aronda two weeks ago. Juliet's middle name is Marie, so I figured it was a safe bet. I've been up for a couple of hours, working to hack the local traffic cameras, but unfortunately there aren't that many in the area, so I haven't been able to confirm she's in the vicinity."

"Doesn't matter," he assured her. "We're headin' that way now. I need you to call Travis for me, JJ. Actually, no. I need you to go to his house. Right now."

"Of course. I'm at my house, so only a couple minutes away."

"Perfect. I'll call you when we get there, let you know what we find."

He disconnected the call, tugged on his T-shirt, boots, then stuffed the rest of his shit back in his bag. Reese did the same without a single question, clearly reading the situation without the need for details. Two minutes later, they were in the Tahoe, the address plugged into the navigation.

Until that point, Brantley hadn't even noticed the time. It was a few minutes after seven and the sun was already rising in the sky, brightening the almost-fall morning. But it wasn't the warm air that had him sweating. No, that was thanks to the adrenaline rush, the thrill of the chase that had been drilled into him by the Navy. It didn't matter that the little girl they were going in to get was family, either. At the moment, she was the package he was sent in to retrieve, and come hell or high water, he was going to retrieve it successfully.

"What's your plan?" Reese asked, his voice low and even, eyes scanning the streets as Brantley raced to their destination. "Think we should wait for the police?"

As much as he wanted to say yes, Brantley wasn't sure that was possible. Policy and procedure had never really been his thing. It was one of the reasons he could never be a cop. The only thing that mattered to him was Kate. Juliet had already sealed her fate by taking the little girl. What happened to her after they got to safety wasn't his concern.

"I know your mind's racin', Brantley. I can practically hear it. And while I'm on board with runnin' in without a plan and saving Kate, we have to consider a couple of things."

"Such as?" he bit out, hating that he already knew what Reese was going to say.

"For one, Juliet Prince needs to be brought to justice. If we rush in there and steal Kate away, the police aren't gonna have anything to go on."

True.

"And two, if Juliet did take Kate but stashed her elsewhere and we go off the reservation, we're only puttin' that little girl in danger."

True again.

"So, what do you wanna do?" Brantley snapped. "Waltz up to the door like a couple of Jehovah's Witnesses? Knock and see if she'll answer?"

"Actually, I was thinkin' more along the lines of you sneak around the house, see if you can get eyes inside. I'll watch the front in case Juliet tries to run for it. Once you give me the go-ahead, I'll call the police and we'll sit on the house until they get here. Small town. Can't imagine it'll take the cops long to roll up."

Sounded incredibly anticlimactic.

It also sounded like the best option to keep Kate safe.

"Fine," he agreed.

"Really? It was that easy to convince you?"

Brantley grinned at his sarcasm. "Provided it doesn't go sideways, we'll do it your way."

"Thank you."

"But I want you to call JJ the minute I give the signal."

"Will do."

Brantley pulled the Tahoe to the curb a couple of houses down from the address JJ had given them. He scanned the surroundings, checked out the house where they believed Juliet was holed up, hopefully with Kate. There was a nondescript silver Kia parked in front of a single-car garage that was separate from the house.

There was nothing to show that there was possibly a child inside, but Brantley hadn't really expected there to be.

He took a deep breath, exhaled slowly, then popped the center console. After pulling out his Sig, he checked the weapon, then tucked it into the waistband of his jeans at his back, letting his T-shirt fall down to conceal it.

Before reaching for the door handle, he glanced at Reese, who simply nodded as though he understood the severity of the situation and was ready to do whatever was necessary to get the little girl back.

If any of the neighbors were watching, they would most definitely see a suspicious man lurking, but Brantley couldn't very well blend into his surroundings out here. However, he could act normal, as though he had as much right to be hanging around as those who lived here.

When he was convinced no one was outside, he slipped easily beyond the hedges that separated the target house from its neighbor. Once he was shielded from the street, he moved with stealth, his back to the siding as he reached the first window. He quickly peeked in, noticing there were no blinds, but there were curtains blocking his view. He shifted, finding the opening between the panels, and looked inside. It appeared to be the kitchen, which was empty save for the white cabinets and a wooden rolling cart that worked as a makeshift island.

At the next window, Brantley was unable to see in at all. He continued his trek around the house until he made his way to the front, on the opposite side from where he'd started. Except for taking a peek in the windows facing the street, there was only one more and he prayed like hell he located Kate. Otherwise his next step would be to knock on the door and announce his presence.

Hugging the wall, he scanned the street in front of the house, the yard at the back. From his vantage point, no one was watching him, so he stepped forward, peeked into the window. It was then his breath halted in his lungs.

Between the gap in the curtain panels, he saw a small white bed with a metal headboard and footboard. Curled in a ball on top of a stripped-down mattress was a little girl, her face obscured by her position, but he saw enough to know whoever that child was, their situation was dire. It was the little wrist handcuffed to the headboard that made his blood burn as fury raced through him.

Thankfully, he'd been trained by the Navy to deal with situations such as this one, so he didn't lose his cool. Rather, Brantley pulled his phone from his pocket, keyed in a quick message to Reese, then tucked it away. For now, he would stay right where he was and wait for the cavalry to arrive.

But if they didn't hurry their asses up, he was going in regardless.

REESE JUMPED WHEN HIS PHONE BUZZED IN his hand. He'd been staring out the window, scanning the neighborhood to ensure no one approached the house and that no one tried to leave while Brantley did his thing.

His heart kicked again when he read the message.

Two breaths later, he was on the phone with the 911 operator, relaying the information, referencing the Amber Alert.

"Sir, I'm gonna need more information before—"

"Ma'am, with all due respect, I've got a Navy SEAL currently positioned outside that house, and if your officers don't get here ASAP, I've got the feelin' he's not gonna wait around for this woman to do harm to that kid. So, it'd be in everyone's best interest if you'd send someone. Now."

There was hesitation on the other end of the line before the woman confirmed there was a patrol car en route to their position and that they should absolutely not approach the house on their own.

He assured the woman he understood, but also that he couldn't make any promises, then he disconnected the call and prayed they wouldn't consider this a prank.

His next call was to JJ, who answered on the first ring.

"Where are you?" she demanded by way of greeting.

"Sitting on the house," he said, his voice a rushed whisper, though he wasn't even sure why. No one was around to hear him. Clearing his throat and ensuring his voice was steady, he asked her the same question.

"I'm at Travis's."

"Is he with you?"

"Actually, no." She choked on a laugh. "I'm standin' on the front porch, Reese. I was all gung-ho to get here, then wondered what the hell I was gonna say to them if y'all didn't call."

Though he was tempted to give her shit for not trusting them, he considered the levity of the situation, decided against it.

"Knock on his door, JJ," he demanded, "and put me on speaker."

He heard a muted rapping of knuckles on wood as well as her labored breathing. Evidently she was anxious. That or she'd run from wherever she'd come from.

"Hi," she greeted, clearly talking to whoever answered the door. "My name's JJ … err … Jessie James." She exhaled heavily. "I'm a friend of Brantley and Reese."

"Put me on speaker," Reese insisted, repositioning the rearview mirror so he could scope the street behind him.

"Okay, okay." There was a rustle, followed by, "All right. You're on speaker."

"Who is this?" the male voice questioned.

"It's Reese, Travis." Before he could launch into details about what was going on, he saw a police cruiser turn down the street. "JJ, I want you to give him a heads-up of what's goin' on while I talk to these nice policemen."

With the phone to his ear, Reese got out of the car and waved the officers down. He waited patiently for the men to exit their vehicle, not wanting to appear aggressive in any way. These guys had enough to deal with. The last thing they needed was a six-foot-five-inch man coming at them.

"Hi," he greeted, keeping his tone pleasant. "My name's Reese Tavoularis. I called 911."

Both men sized him up quickly before searching their immediate surroundings. "You said you've located a kidnapped child?"

"Yes, sir. Taken by the woman who's rentin' that house." He nodded over his right shoulder, in the direction of the house Brantley was currently staked out at. "My ... friend ... he's over there. Based on his observation, there's a small girl, who we believe to be the one we're looking for, handcuffed to a bed."

He was pretty sure the handcuffed to a bed was what had them straightening. Probably didn't matter to them if it was Kate or not, that was enough of a concern for them to be paying the homeowner a visit.

"Do you own this house?" the one closest to him asked.

"If I did, would I be standin' out here waitin' for you?" he huffed, then realized they didn't deserve his frustration. "No, I don't. From what we can tell, it's being rented by Marie Aronda. She's a person of interest in a kidnapping case."

"You're not from here, huh?"

Reese smirked. "Texas."

"You said your friend's over there?"

"Yeah. Brantley Walker. Navy SEAL. He believes that's his niece inside," he said, figuring the same last names would sustain that little lie.

The guy nodded while the other officer said, "Sir, we're gonna need you to stay here."

"Of course." Reese had no problem staying back. Last thing he wanted to do was get in the way and he suspected Brantley was already keeping an eye on the back door in the event Juliet Prince opted to rabbit.

When the officer strolled toward the house, Reese turned his attention back to the call.

"Reese Tavoularis, you better tell me somethin' right now," Travis bellowed.

There wasn't much to tell, but he relayed the details, knowing that Travis had already heard what he'd told the police. He could imagine the fury on Travis's face at the thought of his daughter shackled to a bed frame. He only hoped Kylie wasn't listening in. He didn't want Kate's mother terrified about what was going on. She'd already been through enough.

He watched, feeling oddly helpless as the police officers knocked on the door, the banging getting louder and more insistent when no one answered.

"Just go in," he muttered. "Kick in the fucking door and go in."

"Reese, talk to me," Travis pleaded, pain echoing in every word.

"They're knockin'. No answer."

"Where's Brantley?"

"No idea," he admitted, but immediately recanted. "Wait. Hold on. Brantley's at the side of the house. He just… Well, he's strollin' to the front door, demanding the cops go inside. Lots of hand movements, some shoutin'. They've got guns trained on him."

Son of a bitch.

Because the last thing they needed was for Brantley to get arrested, Reese headed their way at a jog.

"Take a look for yourself," Brantley was growling, motioning toward the side of the house, both hands up so they could see he didn't have a weapon.

In his hand.

One of the cops started down the steps, gun aimed at Brantley as he moved around behind him, toward the side of the house. The other called for Brantley to remain where he was, then lifted a Taser, the red dots aligning with Brantley's chest.

This was the problem with situations like this. The police had procedures to follow, protocols that were meant to protect people as well as themselves. In this case, Reese figured asking for forgiveness was a better idea than seeking permission.

Based on the gleam in Brantley's eyes, he felt the same way.

Just as Reese made it over, the officer who'd gone to check it out came running back around, motioning for his partner to go inside. The man turned, used his foot to kick back against the door, shattering the jamb and gaining them access.

"I'm goin' in with you!" Brantley demanded. "That's my cousin in there!"

"I thought she was your niece?" the cop shouted back.

"She's related," Brantley countered. "All that fucking matters."

Reese heard voices on the phone, realized Travis was shouting at him.

"Hold on, Trav," he said, trying to keep his voice steady as he ignored the officer's instruction for him to stay outside before radioing in the situation.

The officers went to clear the house, and of course, Brantley disappeared down a hallway. Reese followed, hesitated. He sent up a silent prayer that...

"Kate?" There was so much emotion in Brantley's voice, it was a surprise the word came out at all.

From the hallway, Reese heard, "Uncle Brantley! I wanna go home. Please let me go home!"

Tears slammed into Reese's eyes at the sound of Kate's tormented voice.

"Travis," Reese said on a ragged breath, "we've got Kate. Trav, we've got her."

A shattered sob sounded through the phone and Reese felt a father's pain, his relief, and his desperate need to be with his daughter.

Reese stepped through the door, saw Brantley working the handcuffs with what he assumed was a lock pick.

"Uncle Reese," Kate cried out, tears streaming down her dirty face. "I wanna go home!"

"You're goin' home, darlin'," he assured her. "Here." Taking the phone from his ear, he tapped the button to put the call on speaker. "Your daddies are on the phone. Talk to them, Kate."

"Kate!" Gage shouted.

"Daddy," she sobbed. "I wanna go home."

"You are, sugar," Travis told her. "You're comin' home right now."

Kate peered up at Reese, so much hope in her eyes even as tears tracked down her grimy face.

He couldn't speak, emotion clogging his throat, but he managed a nod to assure her it was true.

Chapter Seventeen

TWO HOURS LATER, AFTER SOME INTENSE PHONE calls, the private jet was carrying Brantley, Reese, and Kate back to Texas.

It hadn't been easy to get out of Mississippi, what with all the red tape and the Feds wanting to chat about what had happened, but evidently, Travis Walker knew some mighty powerful people and a few well-placed phone calls had ripped right through all the unnecessary bullshit, allowing them to leave Mississippi with the little girl.

They had allowed the EMTs to check her over, relieved to know she hadn't been physically injured and, despite some dehydration, she was in good shape. With the help of a kind female EMT, Kate had been able to get cleaned up and they'd given her clean clothes to change into. It was with the blessing of the EMTs that they'd opted to seek medical attention once they got her back home where she would feel safe.

Now, as the jet soared through the air, Brantley stood at the open door to the bedroom, peeking in at Kate, who was passed out on the bed, her tiny body curled beneath the blankets, her arm wrapped securely around a stuffed dog one of the police officers had given her. If he had to guess, she hadn't slept much since she was taken, and now that she was with family, she was able to relax.

It pained him to think about what she'd been through, more so that Juliet Prince had vanished without a trace. The police were scouring the area looking for the woman, but as of the time of their departure, there had been no signs of her. The FBI would be handling the matter, likely spurred by Travis's insistence.

She would be found, Brantley was certain of that. Even if it meant he had to be the one to chase her down. No way was that woman getting away with what she'd done. No one even knew how long Kate had been left alone in that house, secured to that bed. Kate had gone missing on Tuesday, found on Friday. It was possible she'd been in that condition for forty-eight hours. All alone. Had there been a fire…

Shaking his head, Brantley dislodged the thought. She was safe now, and in roughly thirty minutes, she would be in her parents' arms. He knew Travis, Kylie, and Gage would be waiting at the airport. Were probably there already, fidgeting and pacing, desperate to see their baby girl again.

"She still asleep?"

Turning away from the door, he nodded to Reese. "Yeah."

After sticking his head in the room to see for himself, Reese came to stand in front of him.

"You did good," he said softly.

Brantley smiled. "I'm pretty sure it was a team effort."

"Yeah, maybe."

Unable to help himself, his gaze shifted to Reese's mouth. He was about to lean forward when Reese lifted a hand, cupping Brantley's jaw in a gesture that surprised him. Not that he wasn't familiar with a man's gentle touch, but Reese had yet to do anything of the kind.

He found himself leaning in, accepting the comfort because he needed it. Brantley hadn't expected to be quite so overwhelmed when he found Kate, but there had been something different about this mission. Sure, he'd gone in to extract K and R victims before. Kidnap and ransom was a way of life in some countries and Americans abroad were easy targets. And while the US government did not negotiate with terrorists, that did not mean they turned a blind eye. More than once, Brantley's SEAL team had been sent in under the radar.

But with Kate … he wondered who would've gone to extremes to find her. The police would've done their jobs, yes. The overworked detective assigned to the case would've added it to his workload, followed every lead, probably even lost sleep over it. He would not have been able to locate her the way they had. With help from Reese and JJ, they'd been able to find her quickly. How many others were there out there? Cold cases that were now frigid because people hadn't been located. Hell, in Texas alone, he figured there were more than enough.

"What's on your mind?" Reese asked.

"Just glad we're takin' her home," he said because it was the truth.

"Now what happens?"

Staring into those golden eyes, Brantley knew what Reese was referring to. This thing between them … it might've been slow going, but it was going, nonetheless.

"I think that's up to you, isn't it?"

Reese's eyes bounced over his face before lowering to his mouth. When he leaned in, Brantley gripped the front of his shirt, pulled him in so they were chest to chest. Their lips brushed, lingered, and when Reese sought entry with his tongue, Brantley opened for him. They'd had plenty to distract them for the past few days, but he knew that was about to come to an end.

The question was, could Reese handle Brantley turning his full attention on him? Or was it better that they remained as they were, letting things progress slowly, easily?

"We'll be touching down shortly," came the voice through the speakers mounted within the aircraft. "Please take your seats and we'll get this little girl home where she belongs."

Pulling back from Reese, Brantley smiled. "To be continued."

"Most definitely." Reese released his hold, stepped back. "I'll get Kate so we can seat belt her in."

Kate was still half asleep when the plane finally touched down. Rather than jar her awake while they taxied to their final destination, Brantley remained where he was, watching her from across the aisle where he and Reese were sitting.

The relief he felt at seeing her there, knowing she was safe, was more than he'd expected. It was perhaps the first real mission he'd tackled where the outcome was personal. Kate was family. No, she didn't know him all that well, being that he'd only spent the past five months getting to know her, but that didn't change a thing. Walkers took care of their own, no matter what.

"She's goin' home," Reese said softly.

"Where she belongs," Brantley commented. Exactly where she belonged.

The door to the aircraft opened, stairs extending to allow people on and off. Feeling a surge of emotion filling his chest, Brantley remained in his seat. The silence only lasted for a few more seconds. Feet pounded up the stairs, into the cabin, toward them.

Kylie appeared first, her eyes wide as they darted around until they landed on Kate. She burst into tears, a mother's sobs waking the child.

"Mommy!" Kate was instantly alert in only that way kids could do. She threw her arms around her mother and held on for dear life.

Brantley got to his feet, stepped out of the way as Travis and Gage descended, wrapping mother and daughter up together as they held on to one another. This was what satisfaction felt like, he realized. It wasn't only to be had by fulfilling the goals of the government. It was this. Bringing a little girl home to her family.

While the family hugged it out, Brantley was tempted to slip out of the plane, hop in his truck, and head home. He needed to decompress, to come down from the high he'd experienced in the last twelve hours. As it was, he felt a headache coming on, knew it was going to be brutal when it hit. He seriously doubted any of them cared that he was there. They had everything they needed right now.

But he didn't sneak out; instead, he stood to the side, letting his gaze slide to Reese, watching the other man.

"Come on, baby," Kylie crooned, lifting her daughter into her arms. "Let's get you home." She turned to look at Brantley, then Reese. "Thank you. I can't—"

When tears filled her eyes, Brantley felt her gratitude. "We're glad we could do it."

A curt nod was all she could get out before Kylie buried her face in Kate's hair and strolled toward the door, Gage going with her to help them down the stairs.

That left Travis, who turned to face them. He still had tears in his eyes, which was shocking to see. For his entire life, Brantley had known Travis as the larger-than-life presence in the Walker family. Like his father, Travis was one of the ones they all gravitated toward, looked up to.

Travis thrust out a hand and Brantley reciprocated, taking it in his and returning the firm grip. That lasted all of a second before Travis yanked him forward, smacking him on the back then gripping his neck firmly and holding him there for a hug.

"Thank you."

Overcome with emotion, Brantley simply nodded. "You're welcome."

"And you," Travis said, pulling back and shifting his attention to Reese.

"It was all Brantley," Reese said, getting the same back-slapping, neck-squeezing hug Brantley had received.

"Lies," Brantley teased, hoping to lighten the mood. "I think JJ's the one who deserves most of the credit."

"Trust me," Travis told him, stepping back and swiping a hand over his face, "I am forever in her debt."

"Go on now," Brantley urged. "Get Kate home. I'm sure her brothers and sister miss her."

Travis nodded, his eyes darting between them once more before he strolled out.

Grabbing his bag, Brantley did the same, Reese pulling up the rear.

After dumping his bag in the back seat, Brantley rubbed his temples, hoping to thwart the headache for at least another hour. Give him time to get home and into a dark room before the onslaught.

"Headache?" Reese asked him over the bed of the truck.

"It's on the way," he said, forcing a smile. "Thanks for your help."

As though he knew he was being let off the hook for all that had happened these past few days, Reese gave a half smirk before turning to get in his truck.

And while Brantley drove back to Coyote Ridge, he was almost grateful for the headache. After all, it was a distraction he needed. One that would effectively keep him from thinking about Reese Tavoularis.

REESE SUSPECTED WHERE HE WOULD END UP, but rather than go right to Brantley's and insert himself in the man's life, he headed for his apartment. After a quick shower, he put together a turkey sandwich, scarfed it down, and then snagged his keys and phone.

While he probably should've called Brantley, asked if he minded company, he didn't bother. He'd felt the distance Brantley had purposely inserted between them before they landed back in Texas. He knew the man was doing it for his benefit, but the truth was, Reese didn't want distance. Not the way Brantley thought he did, anyway.

Sure, he needed time to mull this over, to figure out where they were headed next. If anywhere. But he didn't have to be secluded to do that. Many men, and probably women, too, looked at running as a way to work through their issues. Reese didn't. He was of the mind big issues needed to be tackled head on. And since this was likely one of the biggest of his life, heading away from Brantley wasn't going to help much.

When he arrived at Brantley's, he found he wasn't the only one who'd thought to stop in for a visit. Besides Brantley's Chevy, there was one truck, a Ford Mustang, and a small SUV parked in front of the house. He knew the SUV belonged to JJ, the Mustang to Cyrus. The truck wasn't familiar, but he didn't let the idea of a stranger stop him from marching up to the house.

The front door was open, and he could hear voices coming from inside. He started to lift his hand to knock, then thought better of it. Something darkly possessive had gripped him, and he figured if Cyrus was allowed to be there, then so was he.

He allowed the screen to slap shut behind him, hopefully announcing his presence. The chattering voices stopped, and when he stepped into the kitchen, all eyes shifted to him.

JJ raced over, throwing her arms around his neck. Surprised, Reese managed not to tip over as he caught her weight, his arms moving around so he could give her a friendly pat.

"I'm so glad y'all are back and Kate's safe," she said when she pulled back, beaming up at him. "Y'all did it."

He returned the smile. "We did it, JJ. You helped more than I did."

The blush on her cheeks said she wasn't familiar with praise, but she accepted it with a muttered, "Thanks."

Reese looked past her to Cyrus, who was sitting on one of the barstools at the island, beside him a man who resembled Brantley with his dark hair, blue-gray eyes, stubbled jaw, as well as his facial features.

"I'm not sure if you've met Trey," JJ said, motioning him farther into the space. "Trey's one of Brantley's brothers. Trey, meet Reese Tavoularis."

Trey was on his feet, shaking Reese's hand and smiling. "Nice to meet you."

Reese nodded, shook the proffered hand. "Where's Brantley?"

JJ responded with, "I think he's got a headache."

"He does," Reese confirmed. "And I hate to break up the party, but his headaches fuck him up."

"I'll take care of him," Cyrus offered.

It would've been easy for Reese to back away, avoid the conversation, and say something along the lines of, Good. I just wanted to make sure someone was takin' care of him.

Only, that wasn't what Reese wanted, nor was it what he said. He addressed Cyrus head on, meeting the other man's eyes when he replied with, "No. I've got this."

Dark brown eyes were pinned on his, holding steady as he said, "So it's like that?"

Recalling Brantley had said this was a game for Cyrus, Reese ignored the idea the man was simply fucking with him. There might not be powerful feelings between the two men, but there had been intimacy. And as far as Reese was concerned, that was over now.

"It's like that," he confirmed.

He could feel JJ's and Trey's eyes on them, knew they were wondering what was coming next. But Reese wasn't here to fight with Cyrus, nor was he there to clarify what his relationship with Brantley was. He would leave that to Brantley when he was feeling up to having the conversation.

"I agree," JJ said. "I think we should head out, let Brantley get some rest." She peered up at him. "You'll tell him to call me when he's back on his feet?"

"Of course."

Trey cleared his throat, stepped up to Reese, and offered a mischievous smirk. "Nice to meet you, Reese."

"Likewise."

Trey peered over at Cyrus. "Come on, man. Whaddya say we grab a beer?"

Cyrus was still staring intently, but there was a glitter in his eyes. Amusement, maybe? Reese didn't know, but it was cut off when Trey distracted him by placing a firm hand on Cyrus's shoulder.

"Come on."

Reese waited until the screen door shut behind them, then followed, closing and locking the front door before heading back to the kitchen. He grabbed another energy drink and two bottles of water before flipping off the lights in the kitchen and making his way to Brantley's bedroom.

The bedside lamp was on, as was the bathroom light, the space brighter than he'd expected. He found Brantley on the bed, fully dressed with a pillow over his head.

He deposited the drinks on the nightstand, trying to be as quiet as possible. He went to the bathroom, retrieved a washcloth, wet it with cold water, grabbed the bottle of pills from the cabinet, and shut off the light on his way out. After taking out one pill, he set it aside, clicked off the lamp so the room was finally dark, only the dim light from the hallway bleeding in through the slight crack in the door.

"Did you take anything?" he whispered, lightly squeezing Brantley's shoulder as he removed the pillow from his face.

"Uh-uh," Brantley groaned.

"Well, I need you to."

Reese cracked open one of the water bottles, then placed the pill near Brantley's lips. When the man opened his mouth, he set it on his tongue, then helped him take a drink to swallow it down. When Brantley dropped back to the pillow, Reese moved to the end of the bed, tugged Brantley's boots off his feet. He worked diligently to undress him. When he was down to skin, he managed to pull the blankets from beneath him and use them to cover him completely.

When Brantley moaned softly, Reese slid the energy drink can beneath his neck, adjusted the pillow, then draped the washcloth over his face but not before he saw Brantley's face scrunch, his pain evident.

After kicking off his Adidas, Reese crawled into the bed, this time beneath the blankets with Brantley, then moved over, propping himself up so he could lightly massage Brantley's temples. He remained like that, in the darkened room, listening to Brantley's deep, even breaths, hoping to ease his pain a little, giving the medicine time to do the rest.

He was content, he realized. More so than he had been in a long damn time. It was strange, sure. This wasn't where he'd ever imagined himself being. Attracted to a man, wanting to care for him, eager to spend time with him.

Then again, he hadn't known Brantley Walker. Now that he did, Reese knew this wasn't going to end here. They were going to explore this, see if it went anywhere. If it did, great. If it didn't … well, he would chalk it up to experience and move on with the knowledge that he hadn't held back.

TRAVIS STOOD IN THE DOORWAY OF KATE'S room, watching over Kylie and Kate, both sleeping soundly in the twin bed they'd bought their daughter this past summer. He knew there were things that needed to be done, calls to return, people to update, but he couldn't bring himself to leave.

Kade, Avery, Haden, and Maddox were with Travis's parents, spending the rest of the day and the night with them so they were free to take care of Kate.

They'd already scheduled an appointment with her pediatrician for the following morning so she could be looked over. At the moment, they were going by what the EMTs had told Brantley and Reese, reassured that she hadn't been injured during the ordeal. But they would get her in for their own peace of mind, then look into counseling because they all knew there was no way Kate hadn't endured some emotional trauma thanks to the bitch who'd snatched their little girl and stolen her away.

When a firm hand landed on his shoulder, Travis peered over at Gage. He put his arm around Gage's shoulders, pulled him in close, and held him there while they both watched over Kylie and Kate.

"We should probably get some sleep, too," Gage whispered.

Yeah, they should. The past three days had taken their toll, and the lack of sleep would eventually catch up to them. As it was, Travis was fighting the exhaustion because the idea of letting Kate out of his sight was one he couldn't wrap his mind around. He knew he couldn't hover indefinitely, but right now, he didn't have to make excuses.

"Was that Jeff who stopped by?" he asked, purposely changing the subject.

"Yeah. He's keepin' tabs on the investigation into Juliet's whereabouts."

Travis nodded. He knew Juliet Prince was on the run, hiding out from the authorities. At the moment, he didn't have the energy to worry about her. She would be found, eventually, even if it meant Travis had to utilize his many contacts to dig her out of her hidey hole. Of that he was certain.

For right now, though, Travis was going to spend some time thanking God that their baby girl was back with them.

He would worry about ensuring Juliet Prince got what was coming to her at a later date.

Chapter Eighteen

BRANTLEY WOKE IN A DARKENED ROOM, HIS brain coming online a little faster than it usually did after one of his headaches. He was instantly aware of the washcloth covering his face, the hard press of something under his neck, but mostly that the headache had shifted from blazing pain to a dull throb. Not completely gone but manageable.

When he pulled the cloth from his eyes, he saw the flickering light, recognized it as the television.

"You're awake."

Turning his head, he peered up at Reese, who was propped up against the headboard, staring down at him with a wealth of concern in his eyes.

"What time is it?"

"Dinnertime," Reese said with a grunt.

Brantley smiled, couldn't help it. "How long was I out?"

"Five hours."

That might've been a new record for him. Usually it took a solid eight before he felt human again. He wanted to think that was possibly a turning point, but he didn't have the brain power to think too hard or long on it.

No, his thoughts were already drifting elsewhere. Namely, to the man beside him, the one who'd clearly come over to take care of him. Again.

"What's for dinner?" he asked, speaking low, not wanting to anger the lingering headache into returning.

"No idea and it's all I can think about," Reese muttered.

Brantley shifted, propping himself up on the pillow after dragging the energy drink from beneath his back. He set it on the nightstand, then turned so he could look at Reese.

"I could give you somethin' else to think about," he said softly, not moving too quickly, not wanting to send the man bolting from the bed.

Reese's eyes glittered both from the flicker of the television and from the heat he could see in them.

"Is that right?" The words were whispered in a low rasp, but Brantley heard the dare in them.

Their eyes remained locked for long seconds, the heat churning, anticipation building. They'd been working to this moment, and yes, Brantley had promised to go slow. He would continue for as long as it was necessary, but he needed Reese to know this was what he wanted. He was what he wanted.

When Reese shifted, sitting up, Brantley thought for a second he was going to disappear on him. Instead, he watched as Reese tugged his T-shirt over his head, tossing it over the side of the bed. More movement resulted in Reese dragging his shorts down his legs. Those were added to the pile on the floor before Reese turned back to him.

Lost to the heat coursing through him, Brantley moved as Reese did, sliding to his back while the big man moved over him. He hissed in a breath when he felt the warmth of the man's skin against his own. Then he was staring up at Reese, those golden eyes imploring him as though Brantley could make everything all right.

Reaching up, he cupped Reese's face, let his thumb brush over his cheek.

"All in," Reese whispered. "That's what I am, Brantley. With you … I want to be all in."

Dark thunder sounded in his ears when Reese leaned down, kissing him softly at first before his tongue slid into Brantley's mouth. He welcomed the intrusion, his hands getting with the program as he roamed them along the smooth contour of Reese's back. He could feel the muscles flex and shift as Reese settled himself over him, his thighs urging Brantley's open.

He curled his arms around Reese, his fingers sliding over the tense muscles in Reese's shoulders as he held on tightly, pulling him down until they were chest to chest, hip to hip.

Reese moaned softly, the sound sending an electric current along Brantley's spine. He expected them to remain like that, to give in to the mind-numbing ecstasy of simply touching, but he soon learned Reese had something else on his mind.

A hand snaked between their bodies and then Reese was fisting his cock, stroking slowly, firmly. A flash fire ignited in his veins, the man's touch fanning the flames until they encompassed him. It was the first time Reese had touched him aside from the time he'd given in to Brantley's demands on the plane. But that had been nothing like this. Hell, he wasn't sure anything compared to this.

Brantley swallowed Reese's moan as the man hesitantly teased. He could feel the tension growing, Reese's uncertainty becoming a living, breathing thing between them.

"Don't stop," he urged. "Just like that, Reese."

As though the encouragement had been needed, Reese's grip firmed, the stroking continued. Euphoria sparked his nerve endings as he succumbed to the exquisite torture.

"I'm not ready to come," he warned Reese, nipping his lower lip.

The hand on his cock stilled but didn't release. He considered that a good sign.

Allowing his lips to trail down to Reese's jaw, his neck, he licked and nipped before returning to his mouth.

"I want to feel you in my mouth," he told him. "Let me taste you, Reese. Let me—"

Reese slammed his mouth over his, then surprised him when he rolled to his back, dragging Brantley with him. He moved, not wanting to break the connection as they traded places, Reese beneath him, Brantley straddling his thighs.

In an effort to take his mind off of it, Brantley took Reese's hands, positioned his arms so that his hands were by his head. Damn, he looked good like that. So fucking beautiful beneath him.

He leaned over Reese, let his breath fan his mouth. "Don't move. Please don't move."

Reese stared back at him, his face flushed, chest heaving. "Not goin' anywhere."

He only hoped Reese kept that promise because Brantley wasn't sure what he'd do if Reese bolted on him now.

Forcing the thought from his brain, he let his hands slide down Reese's arms, his fingers gliding lightly over his chest as Brantley sat up, staring down at him. He admired him as he let his fingertips roam, watching Reese's face for signs of what he enjoyed.

Reese was watching him, his eyes hooded but locked on Brantley's face. Every now and then his chest would heave, a signal he was affected by what Brantley was doing. Inching back, Brantley let his cock slide against Reese's, the friction dragging a moan from both of them. He continued to focus on Reese's chest, dragging his fingers over Reese's nipples. As the small discs hardened, he gave them each a flick, then leaned down and licked one then the other.

"Fuck … yes," Reese moaned.

Brantley drew one nipple between his teeth, nipped lightly, then moved to the other before gliding his lips back up to Reese's neck, spending a few minutes licking and laving before venturing south, back over his pecs, lower. Brantley took his time, getting intimately familiar with the man's body using his hands, his lips, his tongue. Slowly, leisurely, he laved every inch, continuing downward. He trailed his tongue along the grooves of Reese's abdomen, those sexy abs flexing as he went.

Instead of continuing his trek south, he reversed his path, heading up to his chest once more. He let Reese's soft groans and the gentle rocking of his hips spur him on. Gave himself the opportunity to observe the sexy man who was currently at his mercy.

For the first time, Reese wasn't coiled tight. His body was relaxed, as though he was getting used to being with him. It was an aphrodisiac. Knowing that he would be Reese's first. It was a high like no other.

And while Reese might've thought it was all about him in that moment, Brantley was being selfish in his own right. He'd been waiting for this moment since the first time he laid eyes on the man.

And he damn sure didn't intend to rush.

HEAT.

So much fucking heat.

It blasted him from all angles, coursing through his veins, tickling his scalp, awakening every nerve ending in his entire body.

Reese fought to breathe through the onslaught, his brain managing the remedial functions of his body while Brantley assaulted him with sensations he'd never felt before. The whiskered jaw that abraded his skin, the warm lips that teased his flesh, the greedy teeth that nipped at him … he was aware of every touch, every lick, every bite.

And he wanted more.

But he also wanted to participate. It was a turning point, one he knew he would not be coming back from. This road was untraveled, but he suspected it would see a lot of traffic in the coming days. He wasn't sure he would've trusted anyone else— man or woman—to take care of him like this, to ease him into a sea of chaos.

Unable to stop himself, he reached for Brantley, sliding his fingers into his short hair. It was softer than he expected, the shaved sides brushing his palms, igniting new sensations. Brantley's lips moved over him, his tongue snaking out to tease one of his nipples again. He grunted as flames licked at him, threatened to engulf the room.

"Oh, fuck," he growled when Brantley bit him lightly, then licked away the sting.

No one had ever done that before. The women he'd been with … it was rare they would pay attention to his nipples, but he found the pleasure was intense.

"More," he urged, cupping the back of Brantley's head, guiding him back to where he wanted him.

Brantley laved and sucked, nipped and teased, and Reese was intimately aware of everything from the deep, rough groans to the scrape of calloused palms over his hypersensitive flesh to the scent that was uniquely Brantley, both intoxicating and soothing.

Thrusting his chest forward, he tried to get to the mouth that was tormenting him in the best possible ways.

"You like that?"

"So fucking much," he growled.

Brantley shifted his attention to Reese's other nipple again, nipped firmly, sucked deeply.

Pleasure blazed through his veins, made his cock throb, eager for attention.

Then those lips were trailing downward, Brantley's tongue licking along his abdomen once more, dipping into his navel, making Reese's hips lurch off the bed in an attempt to get the man where he needed him. But Brantley simply tongued him more, the scruff on his chin brushing over the sensitive head of his cock, making him see stars.

"Fuck … Brantley … Christ."

He felt Brantley's smile against his skin as he moved lower, his entire body repositioning toward the end of the bed.

When warm breath fanned his cock, Reese lifted his head, watched raptly as Brantley met his gaze before his tongue made one long sweep along his shaft.

Reese's hands fisted in the comforter, gripping firmly as though it would keep him in him place. As it was, there was a powerful tension coiling within him, threatening to snap. When it did, he got the feeling he was going to shatter in a billion pieces.

"Mmm," Brantley moaned, his tongue curling around Reese's cock. His head turned and he used his lips to glide down the rigid length.

Reese couldn't look away. The sight of this man licking his cock kept him rooted in place, the pleasure of his lips secondary to the erotic vision it made. It reminded him of the scene he'd stumbled on when he'd found Ethan and Beau getting down and dirty at the mechanic shop. At the time, that had been a sight he'd been sure he wasn't meant to enjoy, but this… Fucking hell. Reese was never going to forget this moment.

"Suck me," he urged, reaching forward and palming Brantley's head. "Let me feel your mouth on me."

Those blue-gray eyes darkened, as though Reese's words were an aphrodisiac, spurring him forward.

Brantley opened his mouth, his eyes locked with Reese's. His tongue came out to swipe over the head briefly before he leaned down, closing his lips over him.

"Son of a bitch," he groaned, his back arching. "Oh, fuck, yes."

His head slammed into the pillow, eyes closing as a tumultuous storm erupted. His breaths were sawing, his heart rate reaching dangerously high levels.

That sweet fucking mouth glided down, taking his cock deep, all the way to the root. Reese was groaning in earnest now, unable to stop himself. It felt so good … amazing … so fucking amazing.

"Don't stop," he pleaded, gripping Brantley's head firmly as he guided him back down each time Brantley retreated. "Don't ever stop."

Brantley's soft chuckle vibrated through his shaft and into his balls, making his breath catch.

His body coiled into a hot ball of sensation, but he fought the urge to come. He wasn't ready. Not yet. Not until…

"I wanna be inside you," he blurted, the words surprising him as much as they did Brantley.

Brantley lifted his head, remained there, watching him.

"Please tell me you want that, too," Reese said, a sense of trepidation rolling through him. He hadn't considered the logistics, wasn't sure what Brantley had expected out of all this.

Brantley moved over him, a slow, leisurely crawl that rendered Reese motionless, desperate for a response.

But rather than speak, Brantley reached over, opened a drawer in the nightstand, retrieved condoms and lube. The sight of the latex and the little black squirt bottle made it all the more real for Reese, but he didn't try to flee. His cock was throbbing with its own heartbeat, anticipation making him light-headed.

Then Brantley was sitting back on his ankles, his full attention on Reese's cock again. Only this time, he didn't use his mouth to torment, he teased with light grazes of his fingers while he ripped open the condom with his teeth.

Reese inhaled sharply when Brantley rolled the condom over him, his eyes blazing with hunger even as his smirk grew more mischievous.

When Brantley leaned forward again, it was to kiss him, and Reese welcomed the distraction. He felt trapped within his own body, not sure what was about to happen but somehow committed to the outcome.

Brantley's fingers fumbled with his hand, opening his palm before depositing the bottle of lube in it, closing Reese's fingers over it.

"Be generous," Brantley growled. "And you're gonna have to work for it."

"How?" His voice was thin, a little shaky.

"Use your fingers."

Reese nodded, then managed to sit up when Brantley moved off of him, repositioning so that his head was at the bottom of the bed. Instantly, Reese was on his knees behind him, staring at Brantley's ass, his hands itching to touch but, at the same time, his palms sweating, his nerves rioting.

While he was nervous and more than a little anxious, he wasn't going to fuck this up. The last thing he wanted was for Brantley to regret this. The guy's trust in him was humbling, and it made Reese eager to give him the same pleasure he'd offered so easily.

Setting the lube on the comforter, Reese leaned forward, planting his hands on each side of Brantley's back. He let his body cover him, his cock brushing against Brantley's ass.

A soft inhale was how Brantley responded when Reese kissed his shoulder.

"I don't wanna fuck this up," he whispered, giving voice to his thoughts.

Brantley turned his head, peered back at him. "You can't."

"Oh, I can," he said with a chuckle. "I'm sure it'll be better for me than you."

"Doubtful." There was a sincerity in Brantley's tone that surprised him. "I've wanted this since the day I met you."

"I thought you wanted to fuck me," he replied, running his mouth over Brantley's shoulders, kissing and licking while he took pleasure in grinding his cock against Brantley's ass.

"That's a given," Brantley groaned, his elbows buckling, his chest dropping to the mattress. "But I want to feel you inside me just as much."

Reese's cock jerked at the thought, a reminder of what was about to happen.

His own desperate need intensified, spurring him to get on with it. He trailed his lips down Brantley's spine, then sat back on his calves, fumbling around for the bottle of lube. He'd rarely had the pleasure of anal sex with any of the women he'd been with, but he wasn't clueless as to how this worked.

He squirted a generous amount of lube in his palm, dragged two fingers through it, coating them thoroughly, and set forth to prepare them both.

Chapter Nineteen

BRANTLEY WAS REELING, WHICH WAS SAYING SOMETHING.
He damn sure wasn't a virgin, had both given and taken over the years. While he preferred to be the top, there was a unique pleasure in getting fucked. Especially by the right man. He got the feeling Reese was going to be the man who made him crave it.

Why he thought so, he didn't know. However, he did know that this encounter … it was more than sex. He'd figured that out quickly, felt it in the connection they shared. It was the reason he'd succumbed to the idea so easily. He couldn't remember the last time he'd been fucked, didn't really care when or by whom because it no longer mattered. No one else mattered. No one but Reese.

A hot hand landed on his lower back, sending his thoughts scattering. He felt Reese's thumb slide down the crack of his ass, brushing against his hole briefly, teasingly. It disappeared, but the hand remained, firmly parting his ass cheeks. Brantley helped Reese along, widening his knees, bowing his back, his chest flat against the mattress, giving him the access he was requesting.

There was more teasing before a single finger dipped inside him, pushing in slow and deep.

"Oh, fuck yes," he groaned, eyes closing, body relaxing as the pleasure took over. That single finger buried deep inside him made his cock throb eagerly.

He heard Reese inhale sharply as he began fingering him more firmly, his strokes becoming deeper, faster.

"Two fingers," Brantley urged.

Another finger was added, and Brantley relaxed against the intrusion, letting the pleasure consume him.

"God, yes." His hips began rocking, taking Reese's fingers deeper, his lungs working overtime.

He had been riding this edge of anticipation for what felt like an eternity. In reality, it had only been weeks, but his body was eager to feel this man. His cock throbbed, hot and aching with the need that boiled in him. He knew it wouldn't take much for Reese to send him over. Hell, even his fingers would do the trick, but he wanted to feel Reese buried deep inside him.

"Harder, Reese," he growled. "Work me open. Stretch me for your cock."

"Christ," Reese mumbled. "Keep talkin' like that and I'll come before I'm inside you."

A shiver raced down his spine, the same as it had earlier when Reese had blurted his desire to fuck him. He'd been shocked, not expecting they'd be going this far this quickly. Brantley had resigned himself to easing toward intercourse, figuring hand jobs and blow jobs would be on the menu for a while.

He grunted, rocking back against the intruding fingers, letting the pleasure wash away the unnecessary thoughts. It didn't matter where he'd thought they would be. This was where they were and that was all he cared about.

Brantley reached between his legs, gripped his cock to keep the damn thing from getting antsy. His own touch took some of the edge off, but not enough. He wasn't going to last long if Reese continued fingering his asshole. Every now and then he would brush his prostate, likely not even realizing what he was doing. If the man wasn't careful, he was going to blow Brantley's head off his shoulders.

"Reese…" Brantley grunted as he slammed back against the hand working him open. "Fuck me. I need you … to fuck me."

A deep groan sounded, and the fingers disappeared, immediately replaced by the wide head of Reese's cock. And the man's cock was enormous, definitely in proportion to his body. When Brantley had first seen it, he'd imagined this moment, worried that the man would split him in half. He knew he wouldn't, but he wasn't naive enough to think it would be a cakewalk.

Forcing himself to relax, he stroked his cock, attempting to distract himself from the burning stretch as Reese pushed inside him.

"More," he pleaded. "Give me all of you, Reese."

Another grunt. "Don't … wanna … hurt…"

Brantley took the opportunity to drive his hips back, forcing Reese's cock in to the hilt.

The quick surge of pain blinded him momentarily, but it faded quickly. Probably helped that Reese's hands were now gripping his hips as he retreated slowly.

"Fucking heaven," Reese gritted out, pushing in again.

Shallow strokes of Reese's cock washed away the initial pain, his cock stretching Brantley's ass perfectly. His lungs were working overtime as he gave himself over to the man, accepting the pleasure Reese offered in return for the pleasure he gave.

Reaching back, Brantley gripped Reese's thigh, held on firmly, silently encouraging him to continue.

"More?" Reese asked.

"Everything," he confirmed. "Fuck. Me."

And he did.

Brantley was transported to another plane when Reese began driving into him, fucking him hard and fast. Every time Reese's hips slammed into him, Brantley's cock drove into his own fist, the layering sensations sending him straight to the precipice.

Reese's hands tightened on his hips, his fingertips digging in. It was necessary because those punishing thrusts were rocking them both, the bed shaking beneath their combined weight.

"Oh, fuck … Brantley … I'm gonna come. Fuck … I'm gonna come inside you."

Yep. That fucking did it.

Brantley shouted as his release barreled through him. He came in his hand, his asshole clenching tightly around the cock lodged inside him. He felt a swell of pride when Reese shouted his name as he slammed his hips forward one final time. He could feel the thick intrusion pulsing inside him, a shiver racing down his spine.

And just like that, it was over. When Reese pulled out, Brantley fell to his side, his lungs still working double time. His attention darted to the man who was currently climbing out of his bed, making a beeline for the bathroom. For a brief moment, an unfamiliar emotion churned within him. Fear. Fear that Reese was going to regret what they'd just done, that they would never make it back from—

Reese returned, crawling up onto the bed and covering Brantley as though it was the only place he wanted to be. Soft, warm lips found his and Brantley kissed him back, willing him to feel his contentment.

He had no idea what the future held for either of them, but he knew one thing…

They would definitely be doing a whole hell of a lot more of that.

"I CAN'T BELIEVE YOU LET ME FALL asleep without feeding me," Reese grumbled the following morning.

Despite the exhaustion still pulling at him after an eventful few days, he managed to get out of bed, making a beeline for the kitchen. He had the forethought to drag on shorts on his way, otherwise he could've been frying bacon up and taking an unnecessary risk.

"You want bacon and eggs? Or an omelet?" he offered, glancing at Brantley, wondering why the man hadn't spoken yet.

A smile tugged at his mouth, causing him to turn away because he didn't want to interrupt Brantley's ogling. The man had a hip propped against the island, beefy arms crossed over his chest, and his eyes glued to Reese's backside.

It took a moment, as though the words finally registered before Brantley answered with, "I thought it was my turn to cook."

"Well, you did treat me to a steak dinner," he said, then realized—again—how that sounded.

"I did, huh? And here I was thinkin' it was the other way around."

Reese hissed in a shocked breath when Brantley's warm body pressed up against his back, big arms wrapping around him, palms sliding upward over his chest.

This was the part that confused him most. The big alpha male had no qualms about showing his softer side. And if Reese was being honest, it was one of the things that attracted him to Brantley. There was something about a strong, powerful man who could so easily let down his guard when he wanted.

Covering Brantley's hands with his own, Reese leaned back into him, pressing those calloused palms to his chest, letting that delicious scrape of his palms send shards of electricity down his spine. Another thing he found confusing was how much he wanted Brantley to touch him. Just like this.

Warm lips grazed his shoulder. "That breakfast's not gonna cook itself."

"Maybe if you stop molesting me, I could get to work."

"Mmm. But this has become my favorite pastime. Touchin' you…" His hands squeezed Reese's pecs. "Tastin' you…" His tongue slid up Reese's neck. "Wantin' you…"

"Yeah, well…" Reese moaned. "It's Saturday, so I'm sure you'll have plenty of time to do more of it later."

Before he was ready, Brantley released him, heading for the coffeepot. "An omelet sounds perfect." He peered back at Reese over his shoulder. "Provided you don't strip out the best part of the egg."

"Provided you don't get used to me spoilin' you," he teased, heading for the refrigerator to retrieve the eggs. "May I ask how it is that you have a fully stocked refrigerator but no couch?"

"If I told you, I'd have to kill you."

Chuckling, Reese carried what he needed back to the island, set up his ingredients to prepare them. "I assume you have a personal shopper?"

"My mother," he admitted, and Reese didn't detect an ounce of shame.

"Really?"

"Yep. In my defense, I've assured her time and time again I'm quite capable of doing my own shoppin'."

"And she knows just what to buy?"

Brantley nodded his head toward the fridge. "There's a list. I jot down things I think about. She gets what's on the list, along with whatever she feels is a healthy option."

"You really are spoiled, huh?"

That sexy smirk was Brantley's only response.

With precision and efficiency, Reese set to work making omelets, dishing them up, scarfing them down with Brantley sitting across from him on a barstool. The conversation remained light, neither of them discussing what had happened the past few days, including what had transpired between them last night.

Reese was grateful for the reprieve as he had yet to wrap his head around it all. He had absolutely no regrets, but that didn't mean he didn't need time to process it, to figure out what it all meant and how they would move forward. He'd never considered himself relationship material, hence the reason he hadn't had a real one in years.

"I'm gonna hit the shower."

Reese nodded, Brantley's firm statement drawing him out of his thoughts.

"Wanna join me?"

Looking up, he studied Brantley's face momentarily. His first thought was to tell Brantley he needed to head home, take care of something or other. But the truth was, he wasn't quite ready to go. Not yet.

"That look tells me you're thinkin' about me naked in the shower," Brantley said with a teasing grin.

Reaching for his orange juice, Reese gulped it down. "I should probably—"

"Shower with me, Reese."

Swallowing, he met Brantley's intense gaze, saw the hunger brewing there.

And when Brantley reached out and took the glass from his hand, setting it on the counter before gripping his wrist, Reese was once again grateful. This time because Brantley wasn't giving him time to retreat.

He found himself following the man down the hallway, through the darkened bedroom with the bed they'd put to good use last night, into the bathroom. He was aware of the shower being turned on, Brantley discarding his own shorts, disappearing into the glass enclosure. Reese stared at the open door, beyond to the man whose golden skin was being sluiced by water.

His cock enjoyed the sight immensely, and then Reese was ditching his own shorts, padding across the tiled floor, joining Brantley.

"Slow, Reese," Brantley whispered, his wet hands finding Reese's face, cupping it gently as their eyes met. "I'm not pushin' you."

No, he wasn't.

Reese leaned in, taking Brantley's mouth with his own, shoving away everything that plagued his mind, letting the sensations take over. As his hands raked over smooth, warm skin, he sank into the kiss, gave it the attention it deserved.

He was aware of how hard he was, not only his cock but every fiber of his being. He'd never felt this kind of attraction, this level of desire for anyone. It was as though he'd been waiting for Brantley to come into his life, to awaken him.

His back met the wall and then Brantley was crushed up against him, his hand sliding around Reese's neck, squeezing gently, holding him there as though it was the only thing that mattered. And right then, it was. For Reese, anyway.

A soft grunt escaped him when Brantley's fist curled around his cock, stroking, teasing. Reese's mouth broke from Brantley's, his head falling back as pleasure consumed him.

"You like that?" Brantley whispered. "You like me touching you?"

"God, yes."

Another grunt followed by a groan when he felt the smooth flesh of Brantley's cock pressing against his own. Then Brantley was stroking them together, both hands working them as one.

Reese couldn't deny himself the pleasure of watching, so he looked down between their bodies. The eroticism of the act had his breaths coming faster, his heartbeat speeding up. Brantley's groans intensified the moment, and Reese realized how fucking hot it was to hear those deep growls of pleasure.

"Come for me, Reese," Brantley crooned. "Let go."

The hands gripped him more firmly and Reese's legs weakened, the wall at his back the only thing keeping him upright as the tingling at the base of his spine ignited into an electric storm that blasted through him. He did as Brantley requested, letting go, a dark, rumbling growl announcing his orgasm.

An aftershock came on its heels when Brantley tilted his head back and came.

Chapter Twenty

On Sunday, Brantley spent the morning at the gun range, given access to the underground range because Roger had remembered him coming in with Reese. He'd considered telling Reese of his plans but decided against it, figuring the guy needed some time alone with his thoughts. Since they'd spent the majority of the past few days together, Brantley figured it was the least he could do.

Not that he intended to give Reese too much alone time. He knew from experience being alone for long periods wasn't good for his mental health. He got the feeling he and Reese had that in common, which was why he ended up driving by Reese's apartment on his way to Curtis and Lorrie's for Sunday dinner. The invite had come via Travis and he hadn't been able to say no. He'd actually been relieved because checking up on Kate had been on his to-do list, but he hadn't wanted to bother the reunited family at home.

Brantley rapped his knuckles on Reese's door, waited for the man to answer. Like last time, the door across the way opened and a man stuck his head out, his curious gaze swinging along the corridor before he slipped back inside. Brantley wondered if all neighbors in apartment buildings were that nosy or if Reese had simply gotten lucky.

The door swung open, Reese's frowning face greeting him. "Hey. I didn't… I hadn't heard from you."

Brantley was tempted to lean in for a kiss but could sense the hesitation in Reese, so instead, he simply smiled before shouldering his way inside. "You know the phone works both ways, right?"

The door closed behind him, darkening the space significantly. He noticed there was a pillow and blanket on the couch, as though Reese had been camped out there for the day.

"What's up?"

"We're goin' to dinner," he told the man, not leaving it open for discussion.

Of course, Reese hadn't heard it that way, his immediate response a rebuttal.

"Get dressed," Brantley demanded, ignoring the protest. "Curtis and Lorrie are expectin' us."

Reese stared back at him, but some of the argument drained out, visible by the way his shoulders relaxed.

"Six o'clock on the dot," he reminded Reese. "If we're late, I'm sure there'll be hell to pay."

"Brantley…"

"Travis invited us," he tossed in, planting his hands on his hips and staring at the handsome man. "Just get dressed."

With a sigh that made Brantley grin, Reese pivoted around and stormed across the room. That was when he realized Reese lived in a studio apartment. One big room with a separate bathroom. There was no bed, only the couch. There was a small kitchenette that didn't look big enough to make a sandwich in. Didn't stop Brantley from snooping. He strolled to the refrigerator, opened it. Half gallon of milk, half-empty jar of mayo, small bottle of mustard, and a few slices of processed cheese were all that occupied the interior. He flipped open what passed for a freezer but found only two empty plastic ice trays.

He wondered if this meant Reese was rarely home or if the guy preferred to eat out.

"How long have you lived here?" he shouted, opening the cabinet doors for a peek.

He found a couple of plastic plates, one glass, two red Solo cups, and a handful of plastic utensils still wrapped in plastic from whatever fast-food joint he'd picked them up at.

"A few years," came the muffled response.

Interesting.

Well, Brantley figured the interesting part was that the actual apartment was in great shape. The counters were some form of manmade rock, the sink stainless, the refrigerator as well. The cabinets didn't look bottom-of-the-line cheap. The floor was engineered hardwood in a grayish color, designed to look rustic, the walls a light gray, trim bright white. And the blinds covering the single window at the front of the space were two-inch faux wood slats.

All in all, it was a nice space, with the exception of the furniture, which appeared to be older than Reese.

It was actually similar in layout to the design Brantley had for the loft in the barn. He'd originally intended to move into that space rather than the house but decided against it when his sisters and brothers started dropping by. Last thing he needed was for them to give him shit because he didn't make his bed every day and the damn thing was the focal point of the space. So rather than experience loft living, he'd decided on fixing up the house. There was still plenty of work to be done, but for now it worked for him.

Reese appeared wearing jeans and a T-shirt, his feet bare. He wandered over to the TV stand, pulled out a drawer, and retrieved a pair of socks. He flopped on the couch, tugged them on along with his boots before getting to his feet. The man seemed put out by the idea of having dinner with the Walkers, but Brantley didn't much care. He wanted to spend some time with the guy, and he figured this was the best way to do that. No temptation for either of them.

"You ready?"

"I'll follow you?"

"You'll get in the truck," he countered, not waiting for Reese to argue.

He heard some mumbling and smiled.

An hour later, they were in the middle of Grand Central Station at the height of rush hour.

Or at least Brantley figured that was very much like what he was experiencing. There were so many people crowded into Lorrie and Curtis's two-story farmhouse, taking up all available seating, some spilling out on the back porch, others standing on the front. A lot of talking, laughter, and hugs, everyone expressing their sincere gratitude to have Kate back in their clutches.

When they'd first come in, they'd been greeted as family was. Smiles, handshakes, hugs. Before dinner was served and food and drink consumed, Curtis had said a prayer, all heads bowed, amens to follow. Brantley had never been much into prayers, but even he had bowed his head out of respect and, yes, a deep gratitude that they'd been able to bring Kate home where she belonged.

As for the little girl … one wouldn't even know anything had happened based on the way she was running around, giggling with her cousins. Brantley had accepted her neck-squeezing hug when she'd greeted them upon their arrival, calling out to Uncle Brantley and Uncle Reese with delight. He found it amusing that all the kids seemed to refer to them as uncle, though that wasn't the case. Then again, it didn't really matter, it was merely a way of acknowledging them as family.

His gaze swung to Reese, who was currently talking to Zane and Kaleb, laughing at something that was said. He'd been silent on the drive over, clearly not eager to come, but now that he was here, it was as though he was exactly where he belonged. And Brantley suspected the rest of Curtis Walker's family agreed.

It made him want to introduce Reese to his own parents. He knew Iris and Frank would like him. And if he knew the small town as well as he thought he did, they likely knew more about Reese than Brantley did. Considering the man was a vital part of Travis's world, running things for Walker Demolition, he seemed to be very well known in this circle.

At that moment, Reese's gaze swung his way. They locked eyes for a second and Brantley could practically see the man's thoughts. He had figured Reese would spend a tremendous amount of time picking apart what they'd done the other night. And he had vowed to give him the space necessary to do so, hoping against hope that Reese would embrace this thing between them. After all, Reese had told him he was all in. Only, he'd said that in the heat of the moment, before the inevitable had happened. Now that they'd crossed that line from friends to lovers, he doubted it was that simple. Not for Reese anyway.

"Hey, you got a minute?"

He was dragged out of his thoughts when Travis appeared in front of him.

"Of course."

"You mind gettin' Reese, meetin' me out front?"

He studied Travis's face for a second as though he could read his thoughts. When it didn't work, he offered a nod, then sauntered over to Reese.

"Well, there's the big, bad SEAL who saved my niece," Zane said. "Glad you could make it. Your seat at the table's been empty the past few Sundays."

"He does have his own family," Kaleb inserted. "Probably gets tired of seein' your ugly mug, wants to spend it with people he actually likes."

Brantley chuckled. "Been a little busy."

"Savin' the world," Zane noted, his face turning serious. "We honestly can't thank you enough, man."

"I do what I can." Embarrassed by the praise, he glanced over at Reese. "Travis would like to talk to us."

Reese nodded, excused himself, and fell into step with Brantley as they made their way through the throng to the front door.

As he gripped the knob, he resigned himself for more thanks, not realizing what was about to come at him was going to change the entire course of his life.

WHEN BRANTLEY SAID TRAVIS WANTED TO TALK to them, Reese expected the man to offer his thanks again, so he was a little surprised to find Travis standing outside with another man, one he didn't recognize. Before the front door could close behind him, someone tugged on it and then Curtis appeared, following close behind.

"What's goin' on?" Brantley asked, glancing between Travis and the other man.

"Brantley, you know Gerard Greenwood, the governor of our great state."

It wasn't a question, Reese realized.

Brantley nodded. "Good to see you again, sir."

"Governor," Travis said, "this is Reese Tavoularis. He's currently the man who's runnin' Walker Demolition for me and my brothers."

"Nice to meet you," the governor said, offering his hand.

Reese shook it as was the polite thing to do. "Nice to meet you, too."

"The pleasure's all mine, I assure you."

The governor glanced at Curtis, then stepped over to him, smiling as he did. They engaged in one of those hugs men who'd known each other a long time did. A couple of slaps on the back, although gentler because of their age, before they stepped away from one another.

Evidently, the governor of the great state of Texas was good friends with Curtis Walker. Didn't surprise Reese in the least.

Governor Greenwood turned his attention to Brantley. "Dante told me what you did, how you tracked down Travis's daughter and brought her home safely."

"I merely played a part in it," Brantley said, his tone lacking any warmth.

Reese figured his lack of interest in seeing the governor had something to do with Dante. He had yet to learn what Brantley's problem with Dante was, but evidently it extended to the man's father.

"I heard that, too." Governor Greenwood glanced between all the faces, then met Brantley's stare again. "I honestly didn't mean to interrupt the Sunday festivities, but I felt this was a discussion I couldn't afford to hold off on."

Reese looked at Travis, noticed the way the man's expression was masked completely.

"What can we help you with, Governor?" Brantley asked, the chill in his voice not subtle.

The man exhaled slowly, then relaxed, making his way over to the porch rail, staring out into the night.

"When Dante told me what was going on with Travis's daughter … it brought back a lot of memories. Ones I'd thought I'd made my peace with. Turns out, they'd simply been hiding beneath the everyday hustle of life." Governor Greenwood glanced over at Brantley, who had stepped up to the rail beside him. "I'm sure you remember my daughter, Corinne."

"Of course."

"Perhaps you even remember Cori's best friend, Lauren."

"I'm sorry, no."

"Yeah, well, Dante is quite a bit older than his sister, so it's understandable that his friends didn't know Cori's. Anyway. Lauren lived across the street from us when Cori was growing up. From the time they were old enough to talk, they were inseparable. That was the case through elementary, middle school, and into high school."

Reese had a feeling he knew where this story was going and he wasn't sure he was ready to hear it, but he listened intently.

"They were in the tenth grade when Lauren went missing. She simply vanished one day on her way home from school. Cori had stayed home that day sick, so Lauren was walking by herself, something that no one worried about. After all, this is Coyote Ridge. Bad things don't happen here." Governor Greenwood hung his head. "Until they did."

Yep. The worst-case scenario, as Reese had expected.

"Despite efforts by her friends, family, and the police, Lauren was never found. They had a couple of leads early on, but nothing ever came of it. After a while, the police stopped looking as is the way with many missing person cases. The trail goes cold, the file gets tucked away in a drawer because they have to devote their resources elsewhere."

"You'd like us to find her?" Brantley asked, his tone hesitant as though he knew he couldn't promise anything.

Governor Greenwood turned around, leaned against the railing. "Of course I would. Her and all the other people who've gone missing. It's what everyone who's experienced that sort of loss wants, right? Someone to open that cold case, to delve in and find the child, sister, brother, mother, friend they lost."

"Governor Greenwood—"

The man held up his hand, halting Brantley. "It's not feasible, I get it. However, I can tell you, those people won't ever be found if someone's not actively looking for them. Someone who doesn't have to follow the rigorous rules and regulations put on them by an overtaxed law enforcement agency. You did it, right? Kate was your single focus and you worked diligently to bring her home."

"Sir—"

Governor Greenwood glanced at Reese, then back to Brantley. "Don't get me wrong, I know they won't all have a happy ending. Unfortunately. However, I do believe I owe it to the residents of this great state to give them a chance at finding their loved ones."

Confused, Reese continued to stare at the man, trying to understand what he was requesting of Brantley. Based on the way Travis and Curtis remained silent, they knew where this was headed. The only two out of the loop were him and Brantley.

"What I'd like is for you to lead a special task force dedicated to locating missing people. Past, present, future. You would report directly to me, and from a legal standpoint, I can offer you and your team immunity and means, although, when it comes to your actions, you'd be answering to me, of course."

Reese knew there wasn't a halfway when it came to immunity and means. The governor was stating he would ensure there were no legal repercussions for their actions used in obtaining a desired result. In this case, locating a missing person.

"What about funding?" Brantley asked, as though he was seriously considering this.

"You'll have a budget funded by the state."

Brantley chuckled. "With all due respect, Governor——"

"As a silent member of your task force," Travis inserted, "I can provide additional financial resources."

"So you want us to come to you when we need money?" Brantley laughed.

Travis's expression remained firm. "No. You'll have an account. Manage it as you will."

Brantley glanced over at Reese for the first time. "What do you think about this?"

"Me?" Reese looked at Travis. "I already have a job."

"If it's any consolation, I've been meanin' to fire you."

Reese smiled, hearing the teasing note in Travis's voice. At least he hoped the guy was joking.

"There you have it," Brantley told him. "You're free for the taking. What do you say?"

"Y'all are serious?" Reese wasn't sure he understood. "A rogue task force funded by the state and cushioned by a millionaire?"

"Millionaire." Travis snorted. "You hear that, Pop? He left off a few zeros."

Reese wasn't even going to touch that one.

"You wouldn't be rogue," Governor Greenwood clarified. "More like … off the books."

Because there was a difference.

"What do you say, boys?" Curtis asked, his question directed at the two of them.

"We get to put together our own team?" Brantley asked Governor Greenwood.

"Absolutely."

"Meaning I don't have to include Dante?"

Reese was now more curious about Dante. He'd been introduced the one time at the barn because the guy had been helping JJ, but they hadn't had a chance to talk. However, it was clear there was some animosity on Brantley's part, and he was eager to get the story.

Later.

"Like I said," Governor Greenwood said, "your team, your decision. I assume you'll utilize whatever resources necessary to accomplish your task."

"No politics? No hoop-jumping?" Brantley asked.

"None."

"You came up with this idea on your own?" Reese asked, curious as to what had prompted such a plan.

"Actually, no." Governor Greenwood's gaze darted to Curtis. "As much as I'd like to lay claim to it, I received a phone call. Several, actually. We all know the Walkers have a tremendous amount of pull. Needless to say, the seed was planted, and I've spent a lot of time thinking about it. It makes sense on many fronts."

"And the fact that we have yet to bring Kate's kidnapper to justice holds no bearing?" Brantley inquired.

"None. As far as I'm concerned, you've accomplished your task, bringing the child home safely and identifying the person who took her. The FBI and local law enforcement will now take over, ensuring she's held accountable for her actions."

From the corner of his eye, Reese noticed Travis's eyebrow quirked. Didn't look as though the man agreed with the governor on that one.

Brantley looked back at Reese again. "He seems to have all the answers."

"That he does," Reese concurred.

"What do you say?" Brantley's eyes narrowed as they locked onto his. "You wanna be my partner?"

He heard the double entendre, and when he answered with, "Yes," Reese wasn't sure if he was answering one or both.

Not that it mattered.

Looked as though he would have plenty of time to sort it all out.

All In

Alongside the man who seemed to be single-handedly changing his entire world.

Chapter Twenty-One

AFTER AGREEING THEY WOULD MEET UP IN the coming week to discuss logistics of the new endeavor, Governor Greenwood made his exit and Brantley followed suit, saying his goodbyes to the family and waiting for Reese to do the same.

"Off the books, huh?" Reese muttered from the passenger seat of his truck as they pulled out of Curtis's driveway.

"Pretty common in military practice."

"Maybe, but in case you haven't noticed, we're not in the military anymore."

No, they weren't. And yes, Brantley was very aware of the fact. Perhaps that was part of the reason he'd been on board with the idea as soon as it had come out of Governor Greenwood's mouth. He instantly thought about the progress the police department had made in Kate's case and knew it would've taken a tremendous amount of time for them to bring Kate home. The officers who put in the work would be the first to admit their hands were often tied, undermining their ability to accomplish their task. Those legal hurdles didn't usually work in the best interest of the victim. Sometimes not even when it came to getting justice for the crime.

"Did you know your cousin's a billionaire?"

Reese's shift in topic surprised him, but the question made him smile. "I long ago stopped making assumptions about Travis. The man's resourceful and he plays by his own rules. I imagine he's doubled his money through investments numerous times. God only knows what all he's got his finger in."

"And you think this is a good idea? Us being … partners?"

Now there was the uncertainty he'd sensed. "I can't think of a better person I'd want to go into business with."

"Look, Brantley … about what happened…"

Grinning, he cut his gaze to Reese's. "I know you want me to interrupt here, to tell you that I'll back off, give you space to wrap your head around it, let you close yourself off until you decide if what happened meant somethin'. I'm not gonna do that, Reese. Because it did. To both of us. You can stop questionin' that."

Like he expected, there was no response.

"But you need to remember one thing."

"What's that?"

Brantley pulled into the parking space in front of Reese's apartment, put the truck in park, and looked over at him. "Even though I let you fuck me … I'm still the alpha in this relationship."

It took a moment for those words to sink in, but Reese finally barked a laugh.

"Oh, you think I'm kiddin'?" he said, trying to keep a straight face. "I'm not."

He unbuckled his seat belt, leaned over the console, and hooked his hand around Reese's neck, tugging him closer.

"I want you. Probably more than I should. And you want me. Pretend otherwise if you'd like, but I'm gonna be here to remind you every single day. And I'll keep on remindin' you until you realize it's the truth."

"Doesn't change the fact I'm confused," Reese grumbled.

"No, probably not. But you told me you were all in, Reese. I'm gonna hold you to that. I'm not in any hurry, have no agenda. I want to spend time with you. Yes, a good majority of that time, I hope like hell we're both naked. The rest of the time … well, we might as well give this task force thing a shot. We've already proven we're good together." He leaned in closer, let his breath fan Reese's mouth. "Both in the bedroom and out."

A soft moan was the response that had him closing the distance, pressing his lips to Reese's. As though he'd been waiting for Brantley to make the move, Reese's arms came around him, rough and urgent as the kiss went nuclear.

Daring to push for more, Brantley slid his hand down Reese's stomach, his fingers quickly finding the button on Reese's jeans, tugging it free from the mooring. He continued to plunder Reese's mouth with his tongue while he slipped his hand in as far as it would go, but the positioning proved too difficult.

Rather than stop, he merely pulled back. "Lean your seat back."

Reese's eyes darted to their surroundings before he unhooked his seat belt, then reached down on the door side and pushed the button to recline the chair. In the process, Reese lifted his hips, allowing Brantley to push his jeans down enough to free his rigid cock.

"You miss this, don't you? Me touchin' you like this."

"Brantley…"

"I fuckin' love when you say my name," he whispered, watching Reese's face as he jerked the man's cock. He gave no quarter, working him toward release, wanting Reese to remember what he was capable of doing to him.

He damn sure wasn't going to let Reese push him away. Not when they'd already crossed the line. There was nothing and no one stopping them from moving forward, and Brantley damn sure wasn't of the mind to let what this was between them slip by. He'd waited his whole fucking life to feel like this. There was no teen lust disguising itself as something more. This was real, it was potent. Did he love Reese? Hell, he didn't know the man enough to safely answer that question. But he was more than willing to let things play out until he knew for sure.

"Fuck … Brantley … you're gonna make me come."

"That's the plan."

A few grunts escaped Reese as his stomach muscles tensed beautifully. Brantley turned his attention to the cock in his hand, watching his hand move over the velvety length, the tip glistening more with every passing second.

"Brantley … oh, fuck…"

It wasn't comfortable, but Brantley leaned over as far as he could, propping his torso on the center console as he took Reese's cock in his mouth. He sucked him in deep just as the man exploded with a roar.

He drank him down, then gently lapped at him before returning to his seat.

"Son of a bitch," Reese growled softly, working to fix his jeans and sit his seat back up.

"Don't worry, I'm not gonna ask you to return the favor." He knew Reese wasn't ready for that yet. He would be, of that he had no doubt. But again, he saw no reason to rush this.

They had plenty of time.

⁓ℓℓ⁓

"COME INSIDE WITH ME," REESE WHISPERED, TURNING to Brantley after he'd righted his clothes.

"Probably best if I head home."

"Come inside," he repeated, reaching over and curling his hand around the back of Brantley's neck. "Don't make me do this out here."

Brantley pulled back, his eyes searching. Brantley evidently heard the uncertainty in his tone. He hadn't meant to show that particular emotion, but it had slipped out, nonetheless.

"Okay."

Releasing Brantley, Reese grabbed his house keys from the cupholder where he'd stashed them earlier. He got out of the truck, shut the door, all while his stomach churned with nerves. And while it was a bit disconcerting, it wasn't necessarily a bad feeling.

Once inside, he took a deep breath, locked the door behind them. Before he could lose his nerve, he reached for Brantley's hand, tugged him toward the couch.

"I don't have a bed," he said as though it wasn't obvious. "But I figure this'll work just fine."

"Work for what?"

Fearful he was going to lose his nerve, Reese reached for Brantley, pulled him close until their mouths met. He kissed him, not caring that Brantley would likely sense his anxiety. In fact, he was hoping he would, because right then, Reese could've used the man's steadying hand. Brantley always seemed to know what he needed.

Warm hands came up to cup his face, Brantley slowing the kiss but not pulling away. Their lips brushed, tongues mingling and drifting apart only to come back together until Reese's mind stopped spinning.

When he felt as though he wasn't going to topple over, Reese reached for the button on Brantley's jeans, intending to remove them. His movements were halted when Brantley wrapped a firm hand around his wrist.

"I've never done this before," he whispered.

"And you're not gonna do it right now, either."

Pulling back, Reese felt shame wash over him. Was Brantley seriously rejecting his advances?

Before he could retreat, Brantley's arm snapped out, his hand curling around his neck, keeping him rooted in place. Those stormy blue eyes peered into his, had Reese's breath locking in his throat.

"That's not how this works, Reese. It's not tit for tat."

"But I thought…"

"You thought what? That I want to feel that sexy mouth wrapped around my dick?" Brantley's eyes were hooded, the words spoken low. "More than anything. But not like this."

"But I want to."

"If I thought that was true, I'd be naked right now."

"I was gettin' to that part," Reese said defensively.

Brantley's thumb dragged along his jaw. "We're in no hurry."

As they stood there, nearly nose to nose, Reese realized his heart had slowed, his pulse no longer frantic. And the anxiety had waned.

"I just want to return the favor," he said, desperate to explain.

"If you thought what I did was a favor"—Brantley's smile turned mischievous—"you've got a lot to learn about me, Reese. For one, I do what I do because I want to. Not because I expect anything in return. And when it comes to you … there's a whole hell of a lot I want to do to you."

"I'm gonna fuck this up," he said, accepting it as truth.

"You won't. You can't," he declared, clearly sensing Reese's need to argue. "But I will tell you what I want right now."

Reese cocked an eyebrow, waited.

"I'd like you to come home with me. Sleep in my bed tonight." He briefly glanced at the couch. "As much as I'd say we can stay here, there's no way both of us'll fit on that couch."

No, they wouldn't.

"That seems the opposite of slow," Reese retorted.

Brantley grinned. "I'll put a pillow between us if it makes you feel better."

Reese laughed, all the tension that had wound him tight a minute ago gone.

Twenty minutes later, they'd arrived at Brantley's. Reese had followed in his truck, parked behind Brantley, and headed inside like it was his normal routine.

"You really should consider gettin' a couch," he told him when Brantley had gone to the kitchen for drinks.

"Why?"

"That's where normal people hang out, watch TV. Talk."

"What if I don't want normal? Ever think of that?"

He smiled.

"Plus, if I had a couch, what would be my excuse to get you in my bed?"

"Doubt you'd need excuses."

"Indulge me, Reese."

Brantley motioned for him to come along, so he followed the man down the hall to the master bedroom. It didn't take long before Brantley was buck naked and in the bed, the sheet pulled up over his hips, the pillows propping him up. He grabbed the remote, turned on the TV, then tossed it to Reese's side of the bed.

With Brantley's eyes on him, Reese managed to strip down to his boxer briefs. He considered sleeping in them but then felt like that was a chickenshit move, so he shoved them down his legs and joined Brantley in the bed.

And while he appreciated the gesture, was grateful that Brantley understood how hard this was for him, he had no intentions of watching television. Just because he was anxious about doing certain things, that didn't mean he hadn't come to enjoy what they'd done up to this point.

"What're you doin'?" Brantley rasped, his eyes following Reese as Reese crawled over him, straddling his thighs.

"Exploring," he said, shifting until Brantley was laid out flat beneath him. "You don't mind, do you?"

Brantley's hand curved over his cheek. "I'm at your mercy, Reese. For as long as you want me."

There was a warmth that filled his chest. It was another foreign feeling stirred by this man. Brantley had awakened something inside him, made him want, ache, need. But most importantly, he'd made Reese feel in a way he hadn't before.

"Just touchin'," Reese said softly, smiling as he laid himself out over Brantley. "That's all I'm gonna do."

"Touch away," Brantley said with a chuckle.

That chuckle died quickly, replaced by a sexy moan.

There were quite a few more that followed.

∽ℓℓ⁀

"A TASK FORCE?" GAGE ASKED WHEN HE stepped into the office.

Travis looked up from his computer screen, then reached for the glass of scotch he'd set on his desk. "You knew I would, given the first opportunity."

Gage smiled, one of many Travis had seen in the past twenty-four hours, ever since Kate had been safely returned to them. "Of course I did. It's what you do. I knew all that research you were doin' wasn't for naught."

"You know me better than most," he admitted to his husband.

"No," Gage said firmly, "I know you better than anyone."

True. He did. Because they both worked and lived together, Gage knew every detail of his life and Travis wanted it that way. In return, he knew all of Gage's secrets, too. And they shared as much as they could with Kylie, never wanting her to feel as though she wasn't the center of their world. Truth was, that was exactly how it worked in their world. Kylie was the very heartbeat of their existence. Travis's, Gage's, the kids'. Keeping her happy was all that mattered.

"The question is," Gage said, "can you be a silent member of the team?"

Travis considered this as he leaned back in his chair, stared up at his husband. "Yes. And you know me, I wouldn't say that if it wasn't true."

"No, you wouldn't." Gage took a long pull on his beer. "You trust Brantley."

"And Reese," Travis added. "The two of them together…"

"Are they?" Gage asked, smiling. "Together?"

"From what I've ascertained, yes. It's a tentative relationship at the moment."

"The way ours was in the beginning?"

"If you mean by you pretendin' you didn't want me and me pursuin' you ruthlessly, then yes. That's very much the way theirs appears to be. From the outside lookin' in, anyway."

Gage chuckled. "You did pursue me ruthlessly."

"And you eventually caved." Travis set his drink on the desk. "Are you glad you did? Knowin' what you know now?"

Gage's eyes softened. "More so every single day."

"Even after the past few days?"

Gage's eyebrows lowered.

Travis sighed, figuring he had to get this off his chest sooner or later. "I can't help but think if I'd gone after Kate, we could've gotten her back sooner."

A soft sigh escaped the man standing before him. "You wanna know the truth?"

"Always."

Gage's eyes locked with his. "You did exactly what we needed you to do, Travis. Yes, you could've hit the streets, bullied your way through to finding where Kate was. You're more capable than anyone I've ever met."

Travis continued to stare up at him.

"But that wasn't what we needed from you. Although the bull in the china shop routine is sexy on you, it wouldn't have worked the way we needed it to. And it's easy to speculate about what might've happened if, but that doesn't matter anymore. You trusted Brantley and Reese because you knew what they were capable of even when the rest of us didn't. Just because you can go off the reservation, take matters into your own hands, doesn't mean you should."

Travis had needed to hear that. He hadn't realized how much until right then. "Thank you. For sayin' that."

"It's the truth." Gage stepped around the desk, propped himself on the top. "And based on all that emotion I can see brewin' in your eyes, you could use a distraction right about now."

He smirked, pushing his chair back. "You know me too well. What did you have in mind?"

Gage set down his beer bottle, moving to stand directly in front of Travis. "I figured I'd let you decide. After all, it is one of the things you do best."

Travis grinned. "In that case, how about you use that sweet fucking mouth on me, baby. Show me one of the things you do best."

For the next few minutes, Gage proved how exquisite his mouth was, then they both went upstairs together so they could show Kylie what they could do when they put their heads together.

Chapter Twenty-Two

Five days later

"ALL RIGHT, BRANTLEY, OUT WITH IT. WHY am I here?" JJ asked the instant he stepped into the barn.

Hell, she hadn't even given him time to close the door behind him.

With a slow exhale, Brantley allowed the door to shut, lock, before he turned his attention to the woman who looked as though he'd dragged her right out of her bed. Her dark hair was piled haphazardly on her head, held in place with a clip. She was sans makeup and the T-shirt she wore looked as though it had seen better days.

"Take a seat," he suggested, motioning toward the black leather couch she had purchased last week with the intention of slipping it into his house. Luckily, he'd caught the movers before they could deliver it, had them reroute it out here. He didn't want a couch. On principle, dammit.

"First of all, I wanted to thank you for all you did in helpin' bring Kate home. I can honestly say, without you, we wouldn't've accomplished the task as quickly as we did. Maybe not at all."

"No thanks necessary," she said, staring back at him with that skepticism he was used to seeing on her face. "But you didn't need to bring me here. A text message would've sufficed."

"Agree. But that's not why we've asked you here."

She glanced over at Reese, narrowed her eyes. "You were holdin' out on me, Tavoularis."

"I figured Brantley could do the honors," he countered with a shrug.

Brantley planted his hands on his hips, glanced at the impatient woman now staring back at him.

"I've got a proposition for you, Miss James. And if you don't want in, feel free to say no. But Reese and I talked, and before we did anything else, we wanted to approach you first."

"Cryptic much?" JJ's green eyes shot back and forth between them. "Get on with it."

"Fine." He smiled. "Reese and I were approached by Governor Greenwood with the request to start an off-the-books task force responsible for handling missing persons cases. It's a full-time gig. And yes, before you ask, there's a salary." He pulled an envelope out of his pocket, held it up.

"A task force?" JJ's eyes widened. "Did you sell out, Brantley?"

He should've known she'd jump to that conclusion. "I didn't sell out. Like I said, this is off the books. I am the team leader. If you decide to join us, you'll report directly to me. There's no red tape, no political bullshit. We accomplish our goal how we see fit."

Her gaze dropped to the computer monitors sitting in front of her. "Within the law, I presume?"

"The plan is to work within the law, yes. Whenever possible. But the governor has granted us immunity in regard to how we go about doing it. That's not to say we're gonna go rogue, but we will use whatever means we have to get the job done."

"Meaning I can hack the NSA?"

Brantley canted his head to the side, lifted an eyebrow.

"Okay, fine," she huffed. "I won't hack the NSA."

"You'll have all the state databases at your disposal," Reese noted. "Should help tremendously in tracking people down."

"Nicely put, Reese. You mean I won't have to illegally obtain my information?"

He chuckled. "Let's hope."

"Who else'll be joinin' our little team?" JJ asked, watching him.

"Haven't decided yet," he said truthfully.

"Cyrus?"

He could feel Reese's gaze heat as it moved over him. "We've discussed it. Right now, we're takin' it slow. Figured we'd see how the three of us do for a bit."

"I assume we're workin' cases in Texas only."

"Correct. We'll delve into cold cases when there's not a current one that draws our focus."

"And you think the three of us can cover this?"

"No," he admitted. "I don't. I think we'll accomplish what we can. As things progress, we'll decide how we want to expand."

"There won't be set hours?"

"Correct."

"And you'll expect us to travel?"

"Yes, when it's necessary."

"And I'll be able to use your fancy setup?"

"Yes. We'll convert the barn to our official office."

"Are you and Reese a couple?"

Brantley damn near fell for it but managed to cut himself off with a cough, which got him a laugh from JJ.

"Can't blame a girl for tryin'."

"So? What do you say? You in?"

"Damn straight I am," she declared with a bright smile.

Brantley passed over the envelope that held all the information regarding salary, benefits, and whatnot. JJ took it quickly but didn't open it, instead sliding it into the pocket of her jeans.

"When do we start?"

"We'll have all the access we need by Monday," he explained. "Until then, I figure we'll work on gettin' this place set up."

"More shoppin'!" JJ announced.

Reese strolled forward, held out his hand to JJ. "Welcome on board."

"Thanks for havin' me," she said with an easy smile. "I mean it. This is definitely a good thing."

Brantley agreed wholeheartedly.

When JJ turned to him, thrust out her hand, Brantley took it, shook firmly, then pulled her toward him. He reached in his back pocket, retrieved the other gift he had for her, then placed it in her palm.

"What's this?" She turned it in her hand. "Holy shit. Is this…" Her eyes shot up to his face. "It's a badge? A real one?"

"It's official," he told her. "Keep it on you at all times."

"I'm gonna sleep in it, are you kiddin' me?"

He was relieved to see her excitement. Brantley had no illusions that this would be easy, but in the end, he knew it would be worth it.

And right now, having two of the most important people in his life working alongside him … he was definitely eager to see how it all played out.

Stay Tuned

I hope you enjoyed the first installment of the Off the Books Task Force. There's definitely more to come for Brantley and Reese. Each book in this series is a full-length novel involving new case and the continuation of the relationship for these two men. And I promise not to keep you waiting long for each installment.

If you enjoyed *All In*, please consider leaving a review.

ACKNOWLEDGMENTS

First and foremost, I have to thank my wonderfully patient husband who puts up with me every single day. If it wasn't for him and his belief that I could (and can) do this, I wouldn't be writing this today. He has been my backbone, my rock, the very reason I continue to believe in myself. I love you for that, babe.

I also have to thank my street team–Naughty (and nice) Girls–Your unwavering support is something I will never take for granted.

I can't forget my copyeditor, Amy at Blue Otter Editing. Thank goodness I've got you to catch all my punctuation, grammar, and tense errors.

Nicole Nation 2.0 for the constant support and love. You've been there for me from almost the beginning. This group of ladies has kept me going for so long, I'm not sure I'd know what to do without them.

And, of course, YOU, the reader. Your emails, messages, posts, comments, tweets… they mean more to me than you can imagine. I thrive on hearing from you, knowing that my characters and my stories have touched you in some way keeps me going. I've been known to shed a tear or two when reading an email because you simply bring so much joy to my life with your support. I thank you for that.

Continue for a sample of the next book
in the Brantley Walker saga

Without a Trace
BRANTLEY WALKER: Off the Books, 2

Chapter One

Saturday, October 3, 2020

"So how exactly are we s'posed to refer to you?" Trey asked, his words tipped with amusement. "Officer Walker? Special Agent Walker? Task Force Leader Walker?" He chuckled. "Naw. That last one's too much for the tongue."

Brantley Walker cocked an eyebrow, waiting for his brother to finish.

"How 'bout Governor's Pet?"

"You done?"

Trey tapped a finger on his stubbled chin as though considering it, then grinned wide. "Yeah. I'm done."

"Mama, you wanna know why I don't stop in more often?" Brantley turned to look at the woman flitting about the kitchen. "Him."

Iris smiled. "Your brother's harmless."

Brantley snorted. "Maybe. Doesn't mean he's not annoying."

Trey moved into the kitchen, smacking Brantley on the back of the head when he passed. "You say that like it's a bad thing. And you know I don't live here, right?"

Brantley cocked his head to the side. "Yet you're *always* here."

"Munchkin alert!" someone shouted from the living room.

Brantley turned on his barstool to see his nephew racing into the room. Without warning, the little boy donning his favorite cowboy boots and his daddy's trucker cap—which was several sizes too big for his head—launched himself in Brantley's direction.

Chuckling, he caught Eric, his sister Tori's boy, swung him up, and planted his butt on the bar. "What's up, kid?"

"Nothin'," Eric said, his grin revealing the fact he'd lost both his front teeth.

"Now why don't I believe that?"

"'Cause Mama said to play it cool," he whispered loudly.

"Play what cool?"

"She wants to know where Reese is."

That must've been the trigger word, because both his mother and Trey turned to look at him expectantly.

"Who's Reese?" Brantley asked his nephew, feigning ignorance.

The little boy shrugged, clearly just the messenger. "Maybe he's the chocolate and peanut butter guy."

Leave it to a six-year-old to think that.

"Like Reese's Pieces," Trey noted.

"Eww, no." Eric wrinkled his nose. "Not those, Uncle Trey. The peanut butter cups."

Great. Reese would forever be thought of as candy in this house.

"Why don't you go tell your mama to mind her own business," Brantley suggested, depositing the kid on the floor before turning his attention to his mother. "Anyone ever tell Tori she's nosy?"

"Mama! Uncle Brantley said to mind your own business!" The giggle that followed made Brantley smile.

Before Trey could launch his own questions, Brantley held up a hand. "Reese is off-limits."

Trey sulked. "For how long?"

"Until I say otherwise."

And he didn't intend that to be for a while. Right now, his relationship with Reese Tavoularis was new. The last thing he wanted to do was jinx himself by flapping his gums. While they weren't technically an item, they were exploring to see where this might lead. And Brantley was determined to enjoy the hell out of the journey.

"What I wanna know is why in heaven's name are you here on a Saturday night?" Frank inquired, joining them in the kitchen. "Shouldn't you be takin' that boy out or somethin'?"

Now his father was going to give him a hard time. Great.

Brantley shot a glare in Trey's direction. This was his doing.

He should've known his brother would run his damn mouth to the entire family. No one else knew about Reese. The only reason Trey did was because he'd swung by the house to check in after Brantley's last mission, when they had successfully located Kate Walker and delivered her back to her frantic parents. Brantley had suffered one of his migraines that night and Reese had apparently sent everyone on their way so he could take care of him. His brother had read into it how he chose to, then spread the word accordingly. Brantley wouldn't be surprised if his mother was gearing up to plan their wedding.

"Tell me this," Trey said, stepping up to the counter and passing over a beer.

Brantley waved him off. He wasn't staying.

Trey offered the beer to their dad, who accepted it easily.

"If you're seein' Reese," Trey asked casually, "does that mean Cyrus is fair game?"

Curious, Brantley studied his brother. "You interested in Cyrus?"

"Hey, it's just a question."

A question that had drawn the attention of everyone in the kitchen, taking the heat off Brantley. Thank God.

"What?" Trey glanced from one face to another. "Just a question. Damn."

Frank chuckled, evidently enjoying making his oldest son squirm.

"For the record," Brantley stated, "Cyrus has always been fair game. I've got no claim to him."

Trey glared his way. Probably pissed that Brantley hadn't simply said so in the first place.

Content he'd done his duty in putting his brother in the hot seat, Brantley got to his feet. "Well, I think I'll be headin' out now."

"No dessert?" Iris asked, her pale blue eyes shifting to him.

Patting his stomach, he grinned. "Watchin' my figure."

"Not gettin' enough exercise?" Trey quipped, the mischievous gleam in his eyes returning.

"Oh, I'm gettin' plenty," he mumbled, passing by his brother to give his mother a hug.

"You goin' to Curtis's house tomorrow night?" Frank asked when Brantley turned to him.

"Not this weekend, no. Got some stuff to deal with on the work front."

His father nodded. "Lorrie called, extended us an invite."

"You goin'?"

"Thought about it. Been a while since I've seen my brother's young'ns."

"There's a lot of 'em. Might bring your earplugs."

Frank chuckled. "All those little ones? That's the best part of goin' over there."

Yeah, Brantley happened to be quite fond of the kiddos himself. All twenty-plus of them.

Not that he wanted to spend every waking hour with them. He valued his sanity far too much for that.

Thirty minutes later, after saying his goodbyes to the rest of the clan, Brantley pulled into his driveway, parking beside JJ's SUV. He should've expected she would be there being that she'd spent a good majority of the past week in the barn, getting it in order, or so she claimed.

Rather than go inside the house, he made his way to the barn in the dark, briefly wondering if he should have a walkway put in. Would detract from the country vibe the property had, but might be better than trekking through the mud when it rained. For JJ, of course. Brantley couldn't give a shit less if he got mud on his boots, but she might.

Once he reached the big red barn, he slid the enormous door back, keyed in his code, then opened the steel security door he'd installed shortly after he acquired the property. Colt Ford's voice spilled out into the night, JJ's favorite country star singing about showing Vegas how the country folk party.

And because JJ'd gone to the efforts of installing it, Brantley instructed Alexa to turn the volume to three. The shift in decibel was instant, drawing JJ's attention from the computer screen.

"Hey. I like that song."

"I'm aware. Not sure the neighbors are fans though."

"Place is sound-proofed. Neighbors can't hear." JJ rolled her eyes. "Even if there were any."

Semantics.

"Whatcha workin' on?" he inquired, walking down the wide aisle created by the scattering of furniture JJ'd had delivered recently.

Using his credit card, JJ had outfitted the once empty space with desks, chairs, rugs, a couch, couple of small tables, and a foosball table. The state had coughed up the money for the electronics, save for what Brantley had prior to agreeing to put together a task force solely responsible for working missing person cases, both old and new, for the great state of Texas.

And while they'd brought in more computers, monitors, and a dedicated server, Brantley had agreed JJ could keep his original equipment, ensuring it wasn't connected to the government-owned stuff. While they had immunity and means when it came to solving their cases, JJ had convinced him there were perhaps a few things the government might not approve of; therefore it was important they kept the prying eyes of Uncle Sam out of their business. Who was he to argue with that?

"I've been goin' through the case files that were sent over," JJ explained, "tryin' to find one for us to work on."

"I thought we agreed we'd focus on Lauren Tyler." That was what they'd agreed on shortly after he'd brought her on board. Their first official case would be that of a teenage girl who'd gone missing from Coyote Ridge nine years earlier. She'd been best friends with the governor's daughter, and since this task force had come together at the behest of the man himself, seemed fitting they would find some closure for Lauren as well as her family and friends.

JJ sat back in her chair, stared up at him.

She looked tired. And a bit out of sorts. Her dark hair was piled haphazardly on her head, face clean of makeup, her green eyes weary. The crease in her forehead gave away her worry and had him curious.

"We are," she said quickly. "Yes. We're definitely gonna prioritize that case. But…"

Brantley raised an eyebrow. "But what?"

She sighed, spinning around in her chair as she motioned toward a glass whiteboard she'd had him and Reese hang on the wall. The thing was roughly five feet by five feet, looking as large as it was because there were very few words scribbled across it.

"That's what I have on Lauren," she said, her tone clipped and anxious. "We know she vanished into thin air back in 2011."

"Okay."

JJ pivoted to face him. "That's the problem. That's *all* we know, Brantley."

"Which is why we've decided to take on the case."

Her green eyes were pleading as they stared up at him. "I don't know how to do this. I don't know how to unearth information on someone who's just *gone*." She gestured toward her desk. "That's why I was lookin' through some of the other files, hopin' to find something that has more for us to go on."

"Chances are, they wouldn't be cold if there'd been more to go on, JJ."

She huffed. "I know."

Brantley leaned his hip on the desk. "Unless we catch a current case, we're startin' with this one. Lauren Tyler's from here. From our hometown. We owe it to her and her family to find her. Bring her home."

"And if we can't?" She sounded desperate.

"We can," he stated firmly. "One way or another, we're gonna get closure for Lauren."

JJ sighed. "You're right. I know you are. I'm just… I guess I'm overwhelmed. I'm used to a definitive end goal."

"Finding her *is* a definitive end goal."

Another sigh, this one reflecting her frustration. "No. I mean … a structured path. Some sorta guideline. Hackin' a system, breakin' through firewalls, creatin' back doors. That's what I'm good at. Findin' clues … not so much."

"Good thing you're not doin' this by yourself then."

JJ rubbed her fingertips on her forehead.

"It's gettin' late," he told her. "You should go home, get some rest. We're not supposed to meet up until tomorrow night."

Another sigh, this one more resigned than anxious. "Fine. I'll go home." She marched to her desk, grabbed her car keys and cell phone. "Where's Reese?"

"He said he'd be over later."

JJ's eyebrows hopped. "Sounds kinky."

Shaking his head, Brantley planted his hand on her back, directing her toward the door. "Nothin' about that sounded kinky."

"Maybe not. But you should see the images I've got in my head right now."

"JJ."

She laughed, stepping out into the night. "Hey. Let me have my fantasies, Walker."

"Only because I can't stop you."

"No, you can't."

After locking the barn, Brantley walked JJ around the house to her SUV, opened her door, waited for her to get inside.

"Go home. Enjoy what's left of your time off. Because once we get started, you'll probably wish you had more of it."

She smiled. "I hope so."

Brantley huffed a laugh. "You would. Go home, JJ."

"I'm leavin'. Have a good night. And make sure you do everything I wouldn't do."

He closed her door, stepped back, then watched JJ do a quick K-turn to head toward the road. When her taillights disappeared into the darkness, Brantley went inside. Before making his way to the bathroom, he shot Reese a quick text, letting him know he was home.

Without waiting for a response, he headed for the shower.

About Nicole Edwards

New York Times and *USA Today* bestselling author Nicole Edwards lives in the suburbs of Austin, Texas with her husband and their youngest of three children. The two older ones have flown the coup, while the youngest is in high school. When Nicole is not writing about sexy alpha males and sassy, independent women, she can often be found with a book in hand or attempting to keep the dogs happy. You can find her hanging out on social media and interacting with her readers - even when she's supposed to be writing.

Want to know what's coming next? Or how about see some fun stuff related to Nicole's books? You can find these, as well as tons of other stuff on Nicole's website. You can also find A Day in the Life blog posts, which are short stories about your favorite characters, as well as exclusive contests by joining Nicole Nation on Nicole's website. To join, simply click ***Log In | Register*** in the menu.

If you're interested in keeping up to date on any new releases and preorders, you can sign up for Nicole's notification newsletter. This only goes out when she's got important information to share.

Want a simple, fast way to get updates on new releases? Sign up for text messaging. If you are in the U.S. simply text NICOLE to 64600 or sign up on her website. She promises not to spam your phone. This is just her way of letting you know what's happening because Nicole knows you're busy, but if you're anything like her, you always have your phone on you.

Connect with Nicole

Website: NicoleEdwardsAuthor.com

Facebook: /Author.Nicole.Edwards

Instagram: NicoleEdwardsAuthor

BY NICOLE EDWARDS

ALLURING INDULGENCE
Kaleb
Zane
Travis
Holidays with the Walker Brothers
Ethan
Braydon
Sawyer
Brendon

THE WALKERS OF COYOTE RIDGE
Curtis
Jared
Hard to Hold
Hard to Handle
Beau
Rex
A Coyote Ridge Christmas
Mack
Kaden & Keegan

BRANTLEY WALKER: OFF THE BOOKS
All In
Without a Trace
Hide & Seek

AUSTIN ARROWS
Rush
Kaufman

CLUB DESTINY
Conviction
Temptation
Addicted
Seduction
Infatuation
Captivated
Devotion
Perception
Entrusted
Adored
Distraction

DEAD HEAT RANCH
Boots Optional
Betting on Grace
Overnight Love

DEVIL'S BEND
Chasing Dreams
Vanishing Dreams

MISPLACED HALOS
Protected in Darkness
Salvation in Darkness
Bound in Darkness

OFFICE INTRIGUE
Office Intrigue
Intrigued Out of the Office
Their Rebellious Submissive
Their Famous Dominant
Their Ruthless Sadist
Their Naughty Student
Their Fairy Princess

PIER 70
Reckless
Fearless
Speechless
Harmless
Clueless

SNIPER 1 SECURITY
Wait for Morning
Never Say Never
Tomorrow's Too Late

SOUTHERN BOY MAFIA/DEVIL'S PLAYGROUND
Beautifully Brutal
Without Regret
Beautifully Loyal
Without Restraint

STANDALONE NOVELS
Unhinged Trilogy
A Million Tiny Pieces
Inked on Paper
Bad Reputation
Bad Business

NAUGHTY HOLIDAY EDITIONS
2015
2016

Printed in Dunstable, United Kingdom